Stevan Treleaven Eldred-Grigg is a novelist, historian and essayist. He was born in Te Tai Poutini West Coast in 1952 and spent his first six years in Blackball. Afterwards he lived for seventeen years in Waitaha Canterbury, mostly in a cul-de-sac in the suburb of Shirley. Canberra was his next home, for three years. Graduating with a PhD in history from the Australian National University, he began his writing career in Whangārei. The rest of his life has been spent mostly in Aotearoa New Zealand, although he has lived and written in Berlin, Mexico City, Shanghai, Beijing and Singapore. His home now is Te Whanganui a Tara Wellington, where he hosts Gallery Hanrad in his mod 1960s flat.

by Stevan Eldred-Grigg

Fiction
Oracles & Miracles & Zombies (with Helen Mae Innes)
Pru Goes Troppo
Bangs
Shanghai Boy
Sheng Xian Qu Ji
Kaput!
Blue Blood
Mum
Gardens of Fire
The Shining City
The Siren Celia
Oracles and Miracles

Autofiction
Green Grey Rain
My History, I Think

Non-Fiction
Phoney Wars (with Hugh Eldred-Grigg)
White Ghosts, Yellow Peril (with Zeng Dazheng)
People, People, People
The Great Wrong War
Diggers, Hatters and Whores
Xin Xilan de Wenxue Lucheng
The Rich: a New Zealand History
New Zealand Working People
Pleasures of the Flesh
A New History of Canterbury
A Southern Gentry

NOT SWINGING, SWOONING

Stevan
Eldred-Grigg

Piwaiwaka
Press

Published by Piwaiwaka Press
Copyright © Stevan Eldred-Grigg 2024

Cover artwork and design: Alexander Kirzhbaum
xeladesign@gmail.com

an autofiction

x

for
nine babies

FOREWORD

This story was written in a tiny green text easily readable only by the severely shortsighted. Narrow rows of words, wee green ballpoint words, were crowded onto white pages packed inside thirteen neat yellow exercise books stacked on top of a lately mown lawn, a closely shorn lawn, grassgreen crewcut, well rolled, next to a green summery suburban vege bed. Green peas, runner beans, baby lettuce. A verdant vege bed. Alive. Well tilled. Straight rows. Clipped, cropped, lopped.

Shiny yellow exercise books.

Budgerigar yellow.

Books stacked on the lawn by a boy. A bookstack seen by a youngish dad soon after the dawning of one of many sunny summer suburban mornings during the Space Age. A golden dawning in a colourful cul-de-sac in a swinging newish city, a mod metropolis, last midcentury. A young sun like an atom bomb in a bright blue sky.

A story written by the boy.

'Chirp, cheep,' sings a caged budgie preening himself in his itsy bitsy silvered plastic mirror.

A white boy who wrote with his left hand and rammed thousands upon thousands upon thousands of those green words inside thousands of thin blue lines, ruled horizontally, sticking out straight as laws to the right of a thin red line ruled vertically and printed midcentury, Government Printing Office. Thin lines lightly spat at white paper by steel nozzles on an assembly line inside a big, light, orderly, glazed factory.

A printworks paying wages well above award. Wages, in other words, among the highest in the world.

Spat with mad rigidity.

Hoicked at white paper, blank leaves, felled forest, pulped pine, pine plantation, carry me back to de ole plantation, de whistle o de steamboat coming round de bend, money, slaves, freeborn, pine tree, pine green, resinous, scented, sappy, rippling, whispering, quivering, living, stabbed, felled, stripped, trucked, chipped, shredded, screaming steel wheels, toothed discs, spinning under a red sun, a white star. Flayed. Mashed. Minced. Stewed in steel vats. Bleached, whitened, drying, dead. Flattened by steel rollers, flattened more, furled, whirled, white cylinders in a big light orderly glazed factory also paying wages well above award. White light. Black toxins. A chemtrail of hot gases, soot, smoke, lead, mercury, furans, cadmium, and dioxins, and nitrogenoxides, and sulphuroxides hexachlorobenzenes polycyclichydrocarbons fuming skywards. A chemcocktail of manganese lead alcohols chlorates chelating agents puked up by concrete pipes so richly as to make a whole long river, black.

Thirteen yellow exercise books, neatly stacked, firmly shut, lacking any bookmark, seen by a youngish white dad.

One suburban summer dawning.

A white youngish dad who moments ago strolled into an up-to-date kitchen to switch on a stainless steel black plastic electric jug. A youngish white dad about to make a youngish white mum her first cup of tea of the day. As he does every day. She will say ta to her husband in a gruff contralto. And drink from the fragrant cup, propped upon two pillows, while poring over The Good Earth by Pearl Buck. Only, this very morning, right now, our white wiry youngish dad looks out a window.

And throws himself at the back door. And thrusts the door open.
And flings himself at the books.

And at the boy.

A boy whose story, in reality, is the following.

Thora Pattern
(Editor)

It's early in the morning on the first day of the first year of the most modern decade in the whole of human history. Get in the groove! I'll be seventeen years old at the end of the decade. Like, crazy! I'm only seven years old now. Seven and standing inside a brand new bedroom looking out at the world on the other side of a brand new window. A picture window. Glass, smooth, clean. A window cleaned with Windolene. A window letting in summer light. Hard and bright.

A window as modern as lasers. Or transplanted bone marrow. Or Sputnik.

Ten, nine, eight, seven, six – two – one – blast off!

We're shooting into the Space Age.

I look at the glass.

I see a lot of things. I see nothing on this side. Well yes, a weak white ghost of the inside sill. You know, a white sill shining in the bright sunlight. A ghost white sill sort of bounced upwards. Up into the glass. Other than that I see nothing else inside. Inside the bedroom where I'm standing. Standing and looking out. I can't see myself. I can't see the cowboy wallpaper. I can't see the two sets of bunks. The bedroom isn't only mine. It's for all four of us younger boys.

Percy Faith's Orchestra is playing A Summer Place.

On our new radio.

Which is plastic. A brand new plastic radio dyed a colour they call festival pink.

I know that's what they call it because I looked it up on my Taubmans colour chart. It's not what they call the radio. Festival pink. Decca is what they call the radio. Festival pink is what they call the colour. I looked it up on my newest chart of colours for the latest range available in Taubmans Vitalised Oil Paints suitable on all outside timber surfaces, cement render, stonework, brick, fibro and wallboards. I collect colour charts. Resene. Dulux. British Paints. I love all the new colours. The colours of modernity.

The world has never been modern ever before, and now it is.

It's New Year's Day.

It's 1960!

It's hard to believe. Already the world is so cool. And it's going to get cooler and cooler. Forever! And everything is going to be a blast. It's progress. Our plastic radio is down the passage. All our doors are open because it's a beautiful day. The radio just said that the temperature's seventy degrees, sunny. And a very light easterly. Which is a breeze off the Pacific. The breeze wafts through our house. Waft is a good word. A breeze from the bayou, murmuring low.

Our brand new house!

Percy Faith is really unhip. His orchestra doesn't swing, it swoons. A Summer Place is on the charts. It's playing every day.

Not cool, man.

I look through the glass. I make out I'm listening to the Jamies. The Jamies singing Summertime. A hit a year or two ago. Summertime, summertime, sum-sum-summertime. No more studying history. No more dull geometry. Sorry, teacher, but zip your lip. I feel so happy that I could flip. We've got two picture windows in our bedroom, us younger boys. Windolene swipes away every speck, leaving only sparkle. Sparkle – and a beaming summer sun. Our sun. A white star blitzing us with X-rays and gamma rays, light rays, radio rays, infrared rays, ultraviolet rays.

While we spin around it in our wide blue sky.

Outside the glass, in long grass, under the summer morning sun, is a section of Olivine Street. We're Eleven Olivine Street. In the suburb of Shirley. In the city of Christchurch. In the province of East Midland, Middle Island, Oceania, World, Milky Way. And it's all brand new. Olivine Street. Or anyway, our end of Olivine Street. Our end is a cul-de-sac. Which is French for a blind street. Ooh la-la! A cul-de-sac with nice new black tarseal. And nice new kerbs of white concrete. And long grass. A whole overgrown paddock of long grass. A wilderness of weeds. Very high weeds. All around the cul-de-sac. And, poking up from the weeds, up from their trembling, tussocky, seedy, green tresses, are walls. Walls, spanking new. I've known the word tresses for ages. Walls poking up in nice new straight lines through the weeds. It's a word in Rumpelstiltskin. And new picture windows. And new roofs.

Gleaming bungalows.

Bungalows is what you call these sorts of houses.

Modern bungalows fitted with every modern convenience.

Kids in shorts are running up and down the street. Kids in Roman sandals, which are leather. Kids in Japanese sandals, which are rubber. You know, jandals. Also lots of kids barefoot since it's hot and the holidays. Kids biffing balls. Kids wriggling hula-hoops. Tapping down our street with rhythm in our shoes, tapping away our blues. Sunfrocked mums stand in the street, too. Stand and gossip, and smoke, and laugh. And a group of dads in shorts and Hawaiian shirts.

Olivine Street.

A cool new cul-de-sac of cool new houses, fourteen beautiful new houses. All the houses are one storey. Some are weatherboard.

Others are brick, like ours. Others are Summerhill stone. And some of the houses are roofed with coloured tiles. And some are roofed with steel, like ours. Steel and woodwork paint full-gloss flaxen green, skyline blue, Bermuda turquoise. Caprice yellow. Flamingo. A cul-de-sac of shiny new modern bungalows in a wilderness of weeds. Tall weeds flowering and going to seed. The seeds are calypso yellow, hazy gold, powder pink. Weeds and seeds gleaming under the sun. Seeds and weeds waving and falling, waving again, in a fresh clean sea-smelling easterly.

I know the easterly must smell fresh but I can't smell it because I'm on the other side of glass wiped Windolene clean.

No speck, only sparkle. And sunlight!

And now on the radio a new song starts playing.

All I Have to do is Dream. The Everly Brothers are hip. I start singing along. Dream, dream, dream. I love singing along. When I want you, all I have to do is dream. I'd like to be a pop singer when I grow up. Can you dig it? When I feel blue, all I have to do is dream. Dream, dream, dream.

That's the song. It's not me.

I'm not dreaming.

I'm happy.

I go outside. It's hard, bright, green, yellow, white. Mum's sitting in the sun on the concrete front steps. The brand new concrete front steps. Sitting with a cigarette and Lorna. The colour of the concrete is dove grey. Lorna's the mum from next door. Mum, our mum, is big. Big and red. Her hair is a dark mess cut anyhow and brushed back. She's wearing a teal green shirt thing. With short sleeves. Her arms are sunburnt, mottled, freckly, flabby. And she's wearing a Cambridge blue skirt. And jandals. The jandals are Royal Navy blue. And she's flicking fag ash into a cracked swirly silver and purple paua shell.

She's flicking ash and she's laughing.

I love hearing her laugh.

She laughs a lot.

'Be buggered if we're going to get the weeds down and the ground dug over and lawn sown before the end of the holidays,' says Mum. 'Let alone all the other bloody work, boxing out paths, putting up fences, and that.'

Lorna laughs sort of goofily.

'Gil's going great guns, isn't he?' she says. 'Getting the weeds down?'

'And then where's the money coming from for lawn seed and boxing and concrete and fences and that?'

'We don't want fences,' says Lorna. 'It's neighbourly not having fences.'

Mum grunts.

Mum hates not having fences.

A silver plane is flying high in the sky over our cul-de-sac. Lorna's eyes are brown and big. Soft eyes. Hurt eyes.

'We've got bang-up houses, Val,' she says. 'All mod cons.'

'I wake up every morning and think I hate this bloody house,' says Mum. 'And after I think I hate it, the second thing I think is, twenty years before we bloody pay it off.'

'Aw,' says Lorna.

Mum looks up at me.

'And as for you, Master Nosey-Parker,' she adds, 'good to see you getting out into the sunshine, not being such a girl sitting inside beak in books all day.'

Mum doesn't know that boys hate being called girls. Other boys know. Dads know, too. Dads were once boys. Our dad's out the back. I walk around the side of the house to take a look. Dad's working. He's bent over a tool. He's getting the weeds down. Mum doesn't get weeds down. She just talks about it. The tool is called a sickle. It looks like the sickle on the flag of the Soviet Union. Dad's got a good grip on its wooden handle. Japanese oak, he says. The blade of the sickle is steel. Sharp, shiny. Dad's slashing. The blade is all streaked with green slashed grass. A green you call grass green. Which is pretty obvious. And the streaks on the sharp shiny steel of the sickle look like the blood of grass.

Getting the weeds down is hard work. It's really hard work. Dad's running with sweat.

Lucky he's fit.

I stand looking at him for a while. Dad knows what he's doing. He grew up on the land seventy miles away from Olivine Street. That's what they say. Griggs. His family. On the land, they say. So he knows about weeds. And wheat. And silage. And hay. Not like Mum. Mum grew up in slums in the city. A city rat. That's what she says. Only she's too fat to be a rat. Mum's more a sow. Anyway, when he swings the sickle he makes every move count. Dad. He holds his hips steady. He tucks his elbows in. He keeps his eye on where he's cutting.

'How long will it take to get all the weeds down, Dad?' I ask.

He shakes sweat out of his black eyebrows. He looks up at me quietly.

'A day or two, I'd say. You want to pace yourself when you're handling a sickle. Otherwise you'll do in your back.'

'Oh,' I say.

He's wearing shorts. The shorts are quite short. They're sage green. Two tanned legs slide out of the shorts. Ochre, that's the colour of the tanned legs. Gold ochre. And fleecy. Fleecy with little black hairs that shine and shimmer in the sun. And he's wearing a thin tartan shirt. The tartan colours are sandalwood and chartreuse and Monterey red.

I watch his muscles moving.

Only you say playing when it's muscles.

I watch the play of his muscles. Gold ochre, yellow ochre. On top of his head the hair is black and shiny. Shiny and black under the sun like tarseal at midday. I always feel funny, sort of, when it's men. You know, when I'm watching.

You know, even when it's Dad.

So I look away.

I look instead at the walls of our bungalow. New red bricks, clean, neat, in straight rows. Mortar, pointed white. Window facings painted a bright butter yellow. And next I look up at our roof. It's like a vast steel tent. Vast means very, very big. I like the word vast. A vast, glossy, gleaming, green steel roof. A wide, sheltering, spreading, full-gloss, galvanised roof. A hip roof, that's what you say.

I bet it's the hippest roof in Olivine Street.

I bet we're the hippest family!

A boy comes mooching up. Quite a handsome boy who's got olive skin and black hair and lives next door. We're the same age. He's gentle and reads a lot. He's the oldest of Lorna's two boys.

'Hi, Paul.'

'Hi, Singer.'

Him and the other kids in our street call me Singer because I'm always singing. Only in reality my name is Stevan Eldred Grigg. I quite like having the nickname Singer. Eldred Singer would be a good name for me when I grow up and become a pop star.

'What are you doing?' I say.

'Nothing,' he says. 'I was just wondering about John.'

'Oh.'

'Where is he?'

'I think he's in the sunroom lying down.'

'Can we go and see? Is he trying to breathe?'

'Yes. He was trying to breathe all last night. And now he's trying to breathe today.'

The walls of the sunroom are mostly window. So it's all rays of light. Rays lasering through glass. White rays. Which make me think about death rays in stories about alien worlds. Anyway, you see a white boy lit up by white rays. A slim boy, wearing British racing green shorts, curled up in a bunk.

A boy who's gasping.

John is the oldest in our family. He's eleven years old. I love John. His hair's black like Dad's. And his eyes are the same as Dad's. Brown eyes, kind eyes, beautiful, beautiful, brown eyes.

'Hi you – wheeze – guys,' he says, looking up.

'Hi,' we say.

'Hey – wheeze – can one of you – wheeze – turn up the – wheeze – radio?'

John's had trouble breathing ever since we came to Olivine Street. At first, Mum and Dad said it was probably hay fever from all the high grass. Mum took him to a doctor. And the doctor said it was asthma. Which is when you can't breathe because you're allergic. And the doctor did lots of tests. He scraped little tiny bits of skin off poor John. And he's allergic to a lot of things, John. Not only grass seed, also house dust. And – all sorts of things.

It's really, really, horrible for poor John.

'How are you, John?' says Paul.

'I want to – wheeze – die,' he says.

Which means it's really bad because usually my big brother's a very brave boy.

It's scary. I can't bear to stay. I say I'll go into the dinette to turn up the radio. So I do. The dinette walls are lemon yellow, glossy. And the ceiling's imperial ivory, glossy. And the floor's glossy, too. It's lino. Dad put it down a week ago. That's what you say about lino. You put it down. And the pattern on the lino is what glossy magazines call contemporary.

A pattern of pick-up-sticks. All colours of pick-up-sticks.

Jaipur pink, iris blue, regale blue, canyon coral.

On top of the festival pink plastic radio is the last newspaper of last year. The Press has the largest circulation in the Middle Island. Which is a lot bigger than the North Island. And more beautiful. Higher mountains and flatter plains and the only fiords. Anyway, it sits tidily. The Press. Dad must have been the last one to read it. Mum never leaves anything sitting tidily.

And we're the only three in the house who read The Press. You know, me and Mum and Dad.

I haven't got around to reading this one yet, so grab it.

The Press Nihil Utile Quod Non Honestum VOL XCVIII No 29091 Christchurch Thursday Dec 31 1959. East Midland: weather clearing. West Midland weather fair. Marlborough weather cloudy and cool. Price 3d. I don't know what they mean, those words in Latin. I do know what the Roman numbers mean. Dad was the one who told me the words are Latin.

Anyway, I sit down on the shiny pick-up-sticks with The Press. I open out its vast, thin, sheets. White, floppy. Drooping. Newspaper pages are like flags on flagpoles without a fresh breeze off the Pacific.

Only they're really interesting.

You know. Newspapers. They have lots of stories.

For example, stories about how modern the world is now.

Like, did you know there's now three thousand million people in the world?

And did you know the last emperor of China is still alive? He's only now been let out of prison. There's a photo of him standing in a glasshouse, holding a watering can. I wonder do they clean the glass with Windolene? Or do they use other brands in China? And next to the ex-emperor is an advert for fly spray. Aero-Blast. Laboratory-tested. More killing power in Aero-Blast.

Also there's a story about our new decade. Peace, Prosperity, Man On Moon In Sixties?

And of course there's the court news.

The court news sometimes is the most interesting section in The Press. It's scary too. Though not this time, luckily. It's only a man who broke a window at the Nannette Cake Kitchen. And another man who stole a case of gin from a lady. No indecent assault on a male. Which is what you see some days. Which I don't know what it means. Only whatever it means, it's scary.

When it's time for lunch Mum and Lorna fling some sandwiches together and we eat them outside. Tomato and egg, cucumber and chives, and slippery slices of cold ham with beetroot chutney. And John comes outside for a while and tries to eat a sandwich. But he starts coughing. And he starts choking.

We all look at him, worried.

And he goes back inside.

After lunch most of us kids grab our togs. We jump in the car with Mum. We drive to North Beach. It's hot. We play in the sandhills. Cowboys and Indians. Other kids say cowboys and itchy bums. Which I think is rude because Indian tribes were only fighting for their rights. A posse of us Apaches, sweaty from being on the warpath, run down the sandhills and pelt straight into the sea. Splish, splash! We hurtle into the warm green waves. We jump over the waves. We duck under the waves.

And after a while, by myself, I run out of the sea and up into the sandhills where we've left our towels.

And my book.

It's about ships. I got it for Christmas. Mum bought it because she knows I love ships. Ships are huge. Ships are heavy. Ships are hollow. Steel bows slip through the sea like the needle prow of a rocket in space. It's got good photos. The ships book. One photo is of a new vessel, white and streamlined, called the Savannah. It's American. And it cost nearly fifty million dollars. And it's the first ever nuclear-powered cargo ship. The first ever in the whole history of the whole world.

All power all over the world soon will be nuclear power.

Which will be great because everybody will be able to have as much power as they want, really cheap. All the poor backward countries will be able to turn into rich modern countries like us.

Which is good, because it'll be fair to everybody.

I read for hours.

And then it's time for tea on the sand. Cold new potatoes with mint. And more sliced ham. And lettuce salad with lots of dressing. And pickled onions. And after, poached peaches in pineapple jelly. Which I have with lots of whipped cream. Which is fabulous. Although the cream's a bit off, in reality. It's the heat, says Mum. And the sky slowly goes mandarin and umber and pink. And we drive back to Olivine Street. And we brush our teeth. And we go to bed. Mum and Dad stay up. They listen to the radio. Which they do every night. They listen to the radio till it's time for their supper. Which is a cup of tea and a plate of biscuits. Afghans. Which I know because I eye them up in the dinette on my way to the toilet for a wizz.

Mum laughs when she sees me looking at the big brown crunchy Afghans.

'Watch you keep your mitts off those,' she says.

I have my wizz. I flush the toilet. After, Mum says I can have one biscuit but not to tell the other kids. So I do. Afghans are great. Chocolate. And a nice chewy walnut on top. And then I go back down the passage and into the bedroom where the other three boys are asleep. And I climb into my bunk. And it's hot. So I pull back the sheet and blankets.

And I close my eyes.

And I sleep.

And that's the end of the first day of the first year of the most modern decade in the whole of human history.

FORD ZEPHYR, FORD ZODIAC

And happy days follow one another, one by one. Dad gets the weeds down. And he starts digging the ground over. And because the tresses of weed seeds have been cleared away, well it's great because John gets his breath back. Or he sort of gets his breath back. He still has a bit of trouble breathing.

'I'm all – wheeze – right,' he says. 'Look!'

And he leaps up and starts doing star jumps.

You know, jumping, throwing his hands high and kicking his feet out. Not a jump that looks a lot like a star, in reality. Not like a white star, or a yellow star, or a red star, or a black star. Anyway, it's what they make you do in the army. Star jumps. Dad was in the army. In the war. Of course most dads were in the army in the war. Or the air force. Or the navy. Or locked up behind wire because they wouldn't go to war. And most granddads were too. You know, in the army or locked up behind wire, in the other war.

I think perhaps I'm a Jew.

Do you think that?

You know, wonder whether in a war you were packed into a cattle car with a whole lot of other worried Jews? On the way to a death camp. Auschwitz. Bergen-Belsen. Only luckily you got out? Zyklon-B. The gas they did it with, to the Jews. Also, do you know about Doctor Mengeles? He was the one who did the experiments on Jews. Without anaesthetics. Anyway, back to John. After he's done sixteen wheezy star jumps he smiles at us. He smiles at us because he's brave, like I said. He doesn't want us to worry. And I sort of aren't worried because if the asthma gets really bad they'll give John modern medicine.

Nowadays any citizen young or old may seek treatment in any one of our nation's many up-to-date hospitals.

And it's free!

The state gives it to you. They give you free drugs. Or if you need an operation you go free to theatre, which is all clean and gleaming. Swipe away every speck, leaving only sparkle. And they put you under. You get a mask. They pump in a gas. And of course the gas isn't Zyklon-B. The gas is an anaesthetic.

You breathe it in deeply.

And they cut.

A blade, sharp. And you feel nothing. And they fix you. And they sew you up. A dancing steel needle. And you get meals on trays. And you get better quickly. I've never stayed in a hospital. I'm healthy and happy. All I have to do is dream, dream, dream. I hope he gets all better from the asthma. John. I hope he can keep breathing. John's our hero. We call him King of the Kids. He's kind. He's clever. We love following him round. We love it when he organises games for us. We play a lot of games. We play cards when it's wet outside. We play board games when it's wet outside. We play schools a lot when it's wet outside and sometimes we play schools when it's sunny.

Which it is, mostly.

Sunny.

East Midland's a sunny province. It's dry.

Dad says it's semi-arid. Which when you ask him about it he says means so dry it's halfway to desert. Which is very interesting. Also a bit scary. I don't quite know why. Only it is.

A bit scary.

SOS!

Anyway, when we're at home together playing school our headmaster always is John. Our infant mistress always is Sissy. She's strict. Our school librarian always is me. I'm not strict. I make cards for each book in our school library. And I sit the little kids down and tell them a story. Which I like, a lot. The little kids like me telling them a story too. A story about a family who live in a house of glass.

A story about how you mustn't throw stones.

Also, we play outside every day.

We play startlingly many outside games. We play with the other kids in our cul-de-sac. We've got forty kids in the cul-de-sac. We're a gang of forty. An up-to-date, with-it, digging-it, swinging gang of cool city kids! We play pussy-in-the-corner. We play street cricket. We play bar-the-door. We make go-carts and pretend to be speedway aces like Stirling Moss. You know, ace speedsters helmeted and strapped inside chromed, rubbered, steel racing cars burning up petrol and tarseal for the Lady Wigram Trophy. We hold a weekend go-cart tournament and call it the Lady Griggram Trophy.

I'm so lucky to live in a modern suburb, in a modern world.

And –

Charles Bloy on trial for indecent assault on a male. Stuart Overton on trial for indecent assault on a male. A man with a suppressed name on trial for indecent assault on a male. A suppressed name means they won't tell you who he is. Odds are it's a man with money, says Mum. It'll be some purseproud bloody snob, she says. Mum, like me, always lingers on the court news because she finds it extraordinarily interesting. Kevin Whitehead on trial for indecent assault on a male and attempted suicide by swallowing an overdose of sleeping pills.

Anyway, other things in the newspaper are also very interesting. Soviet Scientist in Christchurch on Way to Antarctica.

Swastikas Painted on Wall at University.
Car Overturns in Collision.

And now it's the start of the new school year. And me and two of the other kids walk past three houses and come to Voss Street. A little street of bungalows. After, if we walk left along Voss Street we'll end up on Quinns Road. Which is narrow and winding. And it's got a creek and willows. Which is good for playing. Quinns Road in olden days was a pack track beaten out by hooves and boots trekking the east bank of the creek.

So it's quite cool.

Only we don't walk left, today. We walk right.

And quickly end up on Marshland Road. Which isn't cool. It's cooler than cool. Marshland Road is an arterial road. Which is what you say when you want to talk about a highway going from the middle of a city right out to beyond its suburbs. All the way out to far away. Marshland Road is really wide. And really long. And really straight. It's dead straight. And it's got two rows of tall steel lamps. At night they glow like napalm bombs. As the arterial lasers its way northwards, shiny black tarseal mile after black shiny tarseal mile, to the Main Trunk. After, it joins up with State Highway One. Vauxhall Velox. Triumph. Vauxhall Victor. Ford Zodiac, Ford Zephyr. Travel the Caltex Way.

Quinns Road School is a quarter of a mile down Marshland Road. It's in a green park. A wide, big, green park. Grounds is what you call the green park. It's lawn, mostly. Other than a row of dark young shrubs growing along each side of the grounds. The four rows look like shrub walls guarding the school. Only they're low, the shrub walls.

I'm taller than the tallest of those shrub walls.

I'm only average tall for my age.

Anyway, so there's four shrub walls to the school. And there's two gates to the school. A west gate. An east gate. And other than those two gates to the school, and those four shrub walls to the school, there's only lawn. Also some red and pink geraniums in front of the school blocks. And the caretaker keeps the lawn close mown right down to the ground.

Is that why they're called grounds?

We go through the east gateway and walk along dove grey concrete paths inside the sunny green grounds. My teacher's in front, wearing a light pink cardigan. Mrs van Dalsum. A blush pink cardy. She's nice. Now we come to a classroom block. A long block. And we see other classroom blocks. Red brick and glass like our bungalow. Also strips of weatherboard painted lime green and gloss.

Altogether there's three classroom blocks.

Infants Block. Primers Block. Standards Block.

I'm in the Standards.

In the groove!

Three of us go to Quinns Road School. Me, in Standard One. Sissy, who's in Standard Three. And Noel, who's in the Primers. Noel's alright. Only he hangs around with me when we're in the grounds. Which sometimes is a bit boring. We can't hang around with Sissy because boys and girls have to stay on opposite sides of the grounds. Noel has fair hair and does jigsaw puzzles and is quite a quiet boy.

And what me and Noel mostly do is wander around the grounds wondering about one or two whys.

'Why do teachers get a staffroom to sit inside all comfortable with cups of tea while us kids have to stay outside in the grounds?' I say one day when dark clouds in the sky start spitting. 'It's not fair.'

'I don't know why,' he says. 'I know it's not fair.'

'And why do we have to call them Mr and Mrs and Miss and

they just call us Stevan or Noel?'

'I don't know why.'

'We're supposed to live in a democracy.'

He says he knows. And then we start talking about ships. And after, it stops spitting. So we sit down and read war comics. Only there's something about Noel. Something that worries me. I mean, you look at him, and you see this neat, quiet boy with fair hair, brushed smooth, and you think he looks nice but –

One day we were at our Aunty Bella's. Which is in Woolston. Aunty Bella's got four kids. Anyway, here's the story. Mum and us kids are over there with Aunty Bella and her kids, our cousins, for the day. Mum and Aunty Bella are sisters, two out of seven sisters. Which is quite a crowd of sisters, isn't it?

And they've got a budgie in a cage.

A budgie's a sort of parrot. A little parrot. You can call them parakeets. Millions and millions of parakeets used to fly in flocks through the sky here in East Midland. You know, in olden days. Bright green, and bright red, and bright yellow. And now there aren't any.

Nowadays it's starlings and sparrows.

Which are brown or grey.

Which sounds pretty boring, doesn't it?

Only when you look closely at a sparrow, even a very mousy little hen sparrow, you see she's not grey. She's not even brown, in reality. She's cinnamon, and she's mocha, she's cocoa, she's coffee, she's ochre, umber, fire, flaxseed, tussock, gold, indigo – she's even violet! So many things are like that, aren't they? Things in the world. We think we're looking. Only we're not, really. We're not looking at what's there in reality.

Anyway, let's forget about our wee hen sparrow.

Let's get back to cheepy chirpy budgie.

So, a budgie is a parakeet that mucks around inside a cage saying chirp, cheep. A steel cage. Stainless steel. Shiny. A parakeet who sits on a pink, or purple, little plastic swing, cheep, chirp. Or who pecks at a plastic box of seeds, chirp, cheep. Or who looks at itself in a round plastic and glass and silver mirror inside its stainless steel cage and doesn't go cheep and doesn't go chirp.

And that's life for a budgie, and I bet budgies think that their life's pretty boring.

I bet they wish they could fly away.

So, we're in Woolston. Mum and Aunty Bella are in the dinette singing and smoking and joking. I'm in the lounge, beak in books. Aunty Bella has quite a lot of books. My beak's in a book about dinosaurs. After, a book about war tanks. German troops gaped with awe at the new Soviet T-34 protected by its strong armour sculpted into a perfect shape and armed with its fearsome long-barrelled seventy-six millimetre gun. And next I mooch outside to see if anything interesting might be happening. Kids are playing cricket in the frontyard.

I mooch out to the backyard.

I mooch past the woodshed. A woodshed painted highway yellow. I look inside and see two boys. And one's Noel. And the other one's Ross. Who comes next in our family after Noel.

Noel's holding a hatchet that's got a worn wooden handle and a sharp red blade.

You know, a hatchet for cutting kindling.

Only he's not cutting kindling.

The budgie's lying on top of a wooden block. A wooden block you use for cutting kindling. A hunk of tree trunk. Blue gum, I think. The bark on the sides is ochre, and pale violet. And stringy. The budgie's lime green and cobalt blue. On top of the block, where you count rings to know how many years the tree lived before we killed it, blood has spurted out. The hatchet blade is red like the green on the shiny steel of Dad's sickle. You know, the green that looked like grass blood.

'We're looking for eggs inside its bum,' says Noel.

'Noel's looking,' says Ross.

And you can see he's not happy, Ross.

I don't say anything. The budgie has been folded out like two wings. Meat wings. And inside, where innards should stay tucked up snug, everything's burst. You can even see seeds spilling out of the budgie's wee crop. Green seeds sticky with red blood.

It's so sad I can't breathe, hardly.

No, that's not it.

I mean, yes, it's so sad it does make me nearly stop breathing. Only also I don't. Stop breathing. I make out I'm looking at a thing not on my side of the glass. Glass kept specklessly clean with new pink Windolene. The meat wings aren't inside. No, they're outside. Also the bill, bile, liver, lung. It's not reality. It's on the other side of the glass. You can look at it without knowing that the whole world is sort of cold, and hot, and hard, and strong, and oblong, and brittle, and hollow, and dry, and killing you.

You can look at it because it's not true. It's only a story.

A too sad to be true story.

So that's quite good. It means that instead of spewing, or dying, you just make your eyes see things another way. And that's enough. Glass comes sliding between you and the thing. The thing that stops you from breathing. A slice of hard sliding glass. You can slide it up or down like you do inside our Ford when you want to open or close a window. And then you're breathing. You're breathing safely. I wish it wasn't so old. You know, our Ford. It's from before the last war. Musty suede. Tobacco ash. A sweet reek of squashed and molten old liquorice allsorts, black and orange, black and lime, black and red.

Also, of course, the stink of petrol.

BP. Shell. Europa. Atlantic. Travel the Caltex Way. Now with more lead octane!

So anyway, it's only a story. Red meat wings, and yellow budgie feathers, and red budgie blood on a blue gum block, aren't reality. And that makes you feel sort of – you know, you feel – well, you don't feel anything in reality.

So that's good.

Of course in the end he gets found out. Noel. Aunty Bella finds out. And when she finds out she bursts into tears.

'That's cruel,' is what she says.

Noel's bottom lip sort of trembles for a tick or two but he doesn't say anything.

And that's the only stink she makes, Aunty Bella. Aunty Bella never blows her jets. She's kind. She looks a lot like Mum. Only skinny. She smokes more even than Mum. Also, when Mum looks at you what you see is two peering green eyes, little green eyes, peering past you at someone more extraordinary. Aunty Bella looks at you, not past you. Her little green eyes meet yours.

And you see that she knows.

I don't know what she knows. I only know that she knows.

Anyway, Uncle Charley comes home with Dad. They've been at the pub. Mum and Aunty Bella call it the rubbedy dub. Dad says it's rhyming slang. Mum and Dad get busy in the kitchen frying eggs and chips. It's for our tea. I go back to the lounge to beak more books. Aunty Bella and Uncle Charley come into the lounge to stack discs on the turntable of the radiogram.

'Everly Brothers on top,' says Aunty Bella.

'Why not someone with a voice?' asks Uncle Charley.

'Voices don't matter any more,' answers Aunty Bella. 'It's a new sort of music.'

'Huh! Can you call it music? Three chords on electric guitars and a lot of falsetto caterwauling.'

They're both smiling. And then Aunty Bella sort of moves a bit closer to Uncle Charley. She whispers something. I can't quite hear. But I hear what she whispers next.

'Darkie's kids look lost.'

'You reckon? They've got a roof and get fed.'

'I'd rather they got fed a bit less if it meant they were a bit less lost.'

After they leave the lounge I go and take a look at the cover of the disc on top of the stack. It's smooth and sleek. Mum's nickname in her family is Darkie. The colour of the disc cover is tropical turquoise. It's because her hair's dark. Also you see a photo of the Everly Brothers. A dark mess. I love the Everly Brothers. Their songs are startlingly cool. I wish they were my brothers. I wish they'd sing to me. Or one of them, at least.

One Everly Brother.

You know, sing to me only.

And the weeks go by. Week after week after week. Why do weeks go by? And why do they go only one way? You know, away from yesterday. And towards tomorrow. Why not the other way? Or do weeks go anywhere in reality? Do we only think they do? Very interesting. Anyway, it's winter now. And our new bungalow is cold. Which it isn't supposed to be. Is it? It's modern, so shouldn't it be sunny? Well it isn't. It's cold. A cold house where we clonk around on bare floorboards. Which is what Mum says. We've got no floor coverings anywhere other than the kitchen and dinette. The shiny pick-up-sticks lino. Canyon coral, iris blue, regale blue. Floor coverings is what you say. Jaipur pink. We can't get more floor coverings till we've saved up.

'It'll take us years,' says Mum. 'We'll have to buy things a bit at a time.'

'We'll manage, darling,' says Dad. 'We'll get on top of it.'

'Hmf,' says Mum.

Our land and bungalow cost us nearly four thousand pounds. We borrowed most of it from the State Advances. We got no help from Dad's family. Mum says. She says his family's bloody busting with money. Purse proud on the sheep's bloody back, she says. Dad says they're not. They're only well-to-do, he says. Mum says they've got the shekels but money sticks to money and they watch not to lob any bobs our way. Only she's not being fair because Dad's family gave us hundreds and hundreds of pounds to buy our other house before Olivine Street. Anyway, we've got two mortgages. That's the word. Mortgages aren't free, you have to pay them off. And you have to pay back more than you borrow.

Which doesn't seem fair. Dad says in olden days the church called it usury. I had to ask him to spell it.

Anyway, our land is one sixth of an acre. Our bungalow is twelve hundred square feet.

And why is it so cold?

We go to bed at night and our bedrooms are freezing. We wake up in the morning and water is streaming down the inside of the windows. You call it condensation. It's our breathing. Our breath on the glass. You can't wipe it away with Windolene. Windolene will clean specks. And streaks. It won't wipe away breathing. And we haven't got any curtains on our windows. And we haven't got any blinds on our windows. We haven't got any curtains or any blinds anywhere in the new bungalow.

We can't afford blinds, or curtains, yet.

So you get dressed, shivering.

You go into the vestibule, which is cold. You go down the passage, which is cold. You get into the kitchen, which isn't quite so cold. A pot of porridge steams, plops, on top of the electric stove. I want to go home, the radio is singing. I feel so lonesome, I want to go home. It's a new song by Lonnie Donegan.

'Can I have golden syrup as well as butter on my porridge, Mum?' I say.

'Tt, eyes bigger than your belly,' she says.

But she spoons out a big dollop of golden syrup and drops it on top of the melting butter.

'Ta, Mum.'

'And shut the passage door,' she says. 'The draught's cutting through to my bones.'

'Alright, Mum.'

The whole house is sort of empty.

'All I hear all bloody day is the kids clonking round on these bare bloody boards,' Mum says to Dad.

'We'll get carpets down by next winter,' says Dad.

'Yeah but what about this winter?' says Mum. 'It gets on my nerves, that endless bloody clonk, clonk, clonk.'

'We're well off when you stand back and look at the whole thing,' says Dad. 'And worse things happen at sea.'

'We're not at bloody sea, we're landlubbers and we're landlocked,' says Mum.

'I love you, darling,' says Dad, which is something he says every day.

'It's that second mortgage kills us,' says Mum.

Anyway, there's a whole lot of swinging going on. Brazil has moved its capital to a hip new city. Brasilia. Brasil is how they spell Brazil. Brazilians speak Portuguese. A lot of adults think they speak Spanish. Adults are often wrong rather than right. It's a bit worrying. Well, back to Brasilia. They bulldozed many square miles of jungle wet with rain to build it.

Also it's our planet's most modern city.

I love the word city.

Wouldn't it be great if all the wet jungle, and all the dark bush, and tussocks, and flax, and creeks, and swamps, got bulldozed away? And turned into city after city after city? They've planned Brasilia so if you fly over it and look down what you see is a jet airliner. Which is the pattern of the streets and parks and avenues. A jet airliner miles long. A city laid out like a vast, silvery plane, only not flying, lying flat on the newly bulldozed rusty red ground.

I'd love to fly over Brasilia.

Also the old empires are ending. The Press says that within half a century every country everywhere in the world on our side of the iron curtain will be both independent and a democracy. A lot are already. Independent. And a democracy. You know, countries like us. The iron curtain is a sort of wall of wire and guns between the Communist nations and the nations of the free world.

'A lot of good things to be said about one-party red states,' says Uncle Charley.

'You don't reckon the party in those places runs a racket?' asks Dad.

'Well that's what they might say in The Press.'

Dad and Uncle Charley are having a smoke and a jug of beer in the backyard. It's a cold sunny day. The sky is smoky yellow. You call it smog. And they're grinning. Uncle Charley and Dad. They see eye to eye. Which is a saying. And Dad takes a long quiet sip of his beer. I like the way weak winter sun strikes the brown beer and shoots rays of wishywashy rainbow light onto the flat grey concrete of our back steps. Beer's really bitter. I won't drink it when I grow up.

'And the leader writers on that paper,' says Dad, 'they're intelligent educated men even when they're wrong.'

'They're intelligent educated men with blind spots.'

Dad and Uncle Charley are on striped canvas deck chairs in a long triangle of cold smoggy sunlight. The canvas stripes are lime green, orange, poppy red, and black. Dad's wearing a holey old bottle green jersey. A gardening jersey. Uncle Charley's jersey is chartreuse. They've been digging over a vege garden. Well, you should say vegetable garden. Me and a few other kids were helping. I love being near the two dads. It's great when they talk like this. It's important. It's startlingly interesting. I wish there was some way they could talk like this every day.

And me listening.

'I know if I was stuck inside Russia I'd be doing my darnedest to get out,' says Dad.

'I'd make the best of it, give it a go,' says Uncle Charley.

Only they're nearly always busy. Dads. Also I don't know what it means, leader writer. Do you? Anyway, Belgium has given independence to Congo. France has given independence to the Mali Federation. So that's swinging. Only there's a lot of wars in the world. A war in Indochina where they're fighting France. A war in Algeria, where they're also fighting France. Cameroon, too.

'Only the lonely,' sings Roy Orbison. 'Only the lonely can hear me cry.'

Although we haven't got any heating in the bedrooms, at least we've got four. Four bedrooms, I mean. Also, there's two picture windows in the bedroom for us four youngest boys. I think you know already. Getting back to my story, I sit in our two-windowed bedroom a lot. Sitting alone. I like it. Sitting on my bunk. Which is a bottom bunk. Sitting with a library book about railways. And now and again I look up from my book at our cowboy wallpaper. Our cowboy wallpaper is beaut. When we lived in that other house we had cowboy wallpaper and us boys loved it so much we asked if we could have cowboy wallpaper in our new house.

So we did.

Cowboys in a desert with lots of cactus poking up all spikily.

And other spiky plants. Spiky green plants a bit like cabbage trees. Harlech green. And if you peer at the spiky plants, you see slivers of citrus yellow and negro black. Slivers is a very good word. One or two of the wallpaper cowboys are on bucking broncos. Others are taking a siesta after a hard day's riding.

All my nights I hope, I pray, a dream lover will come and stay.

One cowboy's sitting by a campfire with his another cowboy. The two of them are best friends, probably. And they're wearing shoes, trousers, and hats, of cinnamon and tango. And neckerchiefs of grass green and oriental red.

The two cowboys look handsome and they look young.

I wish I was a cowboy.

Our planet is good. Our solar system is good. Our galaxy is in the groove. Our universe is a vast, fascinating, very massive, mystery. Also, the August holidays are coming. And can you guess where some of us kids are going for the August holidays? You'll really dig it when I tell you. We're going to spend the whole two weeks of the holidays in – well, where do you think?

Blackball!

I told you you'd dig it.

PIG TROTTERS

'I asked my love to take a walk, just a little walk,' we sing along to a black plastic disc spinning over a plastic black turntable. 'Only say that you'll be mine, in no other's arms entwined.'

The disc spins on a rubber mat. A maroon mat. Round, ribby.

'Down beside where the waters stray. On the banks of the grey green Grey.'

We're singing with Aunty Ikey. And it's raining. We're cosy. A red hot coal fire is roaring. Black, black, black is the colour of my true love's hair. We're onto the next song on the disc. His lips are something wondrous fair. We're not in a modern cul-de-sac. The purest eyes and the bravest hands. We're not somewhere new, or four-square, or dry. I love the ground whereon he stands. We're somewhere wet. And old. And green. And grey. We're in West Midland. It's bush, and it's rain, and it's more rain, and it's rust, and suddenly it's sunshine, and it's Blackball! Bush. Black beech. Charcoal grey clouds. Rain, rain, shower, sun, steady downpour, rain, rain, rain, running into creeks, swamps, raupo, toetoe, cabbage tree, flax.

'Oh, what a beautiful city,' we're now singing. 'There's three gates – '

'This is a Negro spiritual,' says Aunty Ikey.

Which is sad. Negro slaves used to sing on the cotton plantations in olden days. Carry me back to de ole plantation, de whistle o de steamboat coming round de bend. We're lucky we're not slaves.

We're very lucky. Twelve gates in the city. Alleluya! Only we're not so much lucky as cabbage looking, says Aunty Ikey. We're still slaves, she says. Wage slaves. Five dollars a day is white man's pay, says Aunty Ikey. Two dollars a day is white woman's pay. One dollar a day is black man's pay. Oh, what a beautiful city!

'And always taking his cut, Aunty Ikey adds, 'is Mr Kike.'

Aunty Ikey loves singing. Mum loves singing, too.

Also, Aunty Bella.

Aunty Ikey's the youngest. Aunty Bella's the oldest. All three of them sing a lot. All three of them talk a lot. All three of them have got quick wits. Also, they know nothing about many things. And they know a lot about a few things. And some of those few things are very boring, such as who's getting engaged, and who's trying a new ointment for her piles. And some of the other few things are startlingly interesting.

'The disc's by a folk singer called Joan Baez,' adds Aunty Ikey. 'She's a red Indian.'

Which is startlingly interesting indeed, don't you think?

'Which tribe?' I ask. 'Sioux? Seminole?'

'South of the border down Mexico way.'

After, we keep on singing. All us kids. And Aunty Ikey. And an old lady from down the road. There's three gates in the east, we sing. An old lady who lives in a little wooden cottage painted chrome yellow and mustard, with a red roof all rusty, There's three gates in the west, we sing. She's got silvery whiskers, the old lady. That makes twelve gates in the city, we sing. Alleluya! And she's a bit smelly. It's a song about dying. Well, she's a poor harmless old granny. The city means dying. Or being dead. It's good she can get out for a singalong.

Metaphor, you call it.

Saying that the city means being dead.

Mrs van Dalsum explained to me about metaphor. At school.

She was marking a story. She was wearing a flowery cotton frock that day. Pink and yellow and blue and white so she looked like a granny's garden. My story was about a ship. A ship sinking on a still cold night under white starlight.

Anyway, it's always very, very interesting to think about being dead, isn't it?

And whether you're alive anyway, in reality.

I think about it a lot.

Black is the colour of my true love's hair, we sing. His eyes so brown they make you stare, the handsomest face and the strongest hands. I love the ground whereon he stands. I love that man, and well he knows, I love the ground whereon he goes. We sing, us kids. And Aunty Ikey. And the white-whiskered, whiffy, old granny.

I go for a walk all by myself. I'm wearing gumboots. Which is great. So I step into the puddles. Splish splash, there's a party going on. The rain's teeming. I love it. And it's not making me wet. It's not making me wet even though it's teeming. Rain here comes down straight. East Midland rain doesn't. East Midland rain, which there's not enough of, comes down sideways. Which is because it blows in on a southerly. Here there's no wind to blow rain sideways.

Or mostly.

A whirlwind blew roofs off Westport once.

Anyway, I've got on an old parka. It's really baggy and big. Two of me could fit inside it. Aunty Ikey says. And it's got lots of holes, the parka. Only little holes, so that's all right. It's the parka Uncle Arthur wears when he's out shooting deer and goats. And the parka is stiff and crinkly, and oily and wrinkly, and black as Blackball coal. Cool! I step into more puddles. Splash, splish. And soon I'm standing at the spot you call the Crossing. Which is where Stafford Street meets two other streets and Main Road.

I love the Crossing.

I stand right in its middle, which I can do because there's no cars. It's only a tiny little town, Blackball. Not a vast city like Christchurch. So you can stand in the middle of the Crossing. And nothing's moving, hardly. Only the rain. And a wood pigeon up in that budding rowan. And a damp grey cat that's just poked its nose out from that flax.

And in that other flax I think a weka's up to something.

Yes, it's a weka.

I watch the weka till a dog barks in a yard and the weka runs away, sort of lurching his head forward the way they do. After that, I look one way down South Town Belt. And then I look the other way down South Town Belt. And then I spin forty-five degrees on the spot. It's geometry. Which I know because John taught it to me. And it's in the summertime song. Geometry. You know, the song by the Jamies. Summertime, sum-sum-summertime. Only it isn't, of course. Summer.

It's winter, in reality.

I look down Stafford Street.

Which is a narrow strip of wet shingle. A sopping shingle strip with, on both sides, swirls of spiny blackberry. Dying blackberry leaves, emerald green and dark purple. And tufts of stiff wiwi on both sides of the sopping strip. Waxy green tufts of wiwi spiked with seed clumps, lime green, tangerine, parrot red. And tall black power poles, trunks of felled trees, poking out of the wiwi and blackberry. And black wires sagging. And soft pads of green yellow moss.

Also, two rows of old wooden miner's cottages.

I look at the nearest two cottages, and think about the families who lived inside in olden days.

And then I look at the next nearest ones.

And so on.

After looking all the way down Stafford Street, I look up. Up, up. Craning my head, cricking my neck, up so high there's only rain, and grey clouds, and black clouds. And I see –

I make out I see –

A peak!

A snowy peak. The top of a snowy peak. A snowy peak so steep it could scrape the steel flank of a Sputnik. Of course I can't see it in reality. It's only a story. The Tale of The Seen Yet Unseen Peak. The snowy peak really is there, that's reality. Only you can't see it right now. It's hidden by heavy wet clouds. Anyway, back to the story. A snowy peak. A cold bright sky. A cold blue sky. Sky blue, like a newly opened pot of Taubmans Vitalised. A golden sun glowing over the peak.

Which of course is a winter sun, so it's glowing low.

Or perhaps it's an atom bomb?

You know, perhaps we've begun a world war? A war which will be over in only a few days. Once the bombs start dropping. Anyway, that day's not today, probably. Governments nowadays are too mod to drop atom bombs. Other than test bombs, of course. At Bikini. And in Algeria. And in South Australia.

A boy at school says he saw one of those bombs.

'Dad was working on the power station at Port Augusta,' he says. 'They make electricity by burning brown coal.'

And he says the bomb test was on a weekend. The dad and the boy drove to the nearest point you could get to where they were testing the bomb. A lot of people drove to that point, says the boy. The boy says his dad held him up high so he could get a really good look at the glow. And after watching the glow they heard the boom. And they saw the mushroom cloud.

'What colour was the mushroom cloud?' I ask the boy.

'It was red and brown and rust and cocoa,' says the boy from Port Augusta. 'After, it was iron grey. And dun yellow. And buff. Prussian blue, too. And gunship grey. And stars and stripes blue.

And butcher's apron blue. And steel blue. And socialist red. And butcher's apron red. And rising sun red. And stars and stripes red. And black. And white. A lot of white. A lot of black.'

You see his words inside your head, don't you? I see them inside my head. I see the words.

'Black and white and blue?' I ask the boy. 'And white and red and dead?'

'You can dig it,' says the boy from Port Augusta, who's pretty hip. 'And after that, only a black thing, sort of hanging there in a dry sky, a big black toadstool thing doing the twist in the blue desert sky.'

'Slowly?' I ask the boy. 'A big black toadstool thing doing the twist slowly?'

'Slow like crazy slow,' answers the boy. 'Baby, baby, doing the twist.'

'Cool, man,' I say. 'I'd love to see a nuke do the twist.'

Anyway, it turns out there's no atom bomb today. The rain's teeming. So, on I go. I step into more puddles. Splish splash. Blackball is where we used to live when I was a little boy. We came here yesterday. Alan and me and Noel and Ross. John had to stay behind in Olivine Street because he's got a job. It's a job delivering goods for a Four Square. Anyway, when we came yesterday we came on the afternoon railcar, which is beautiful and modern and streamlined and made in Italy. Mamma mia! Mambo italiano! And it's painted railway red with white racing stripes. And soft shiny brass.

And we went da-dack da-dack.

And here we are!

And I go around the block. I step into puddle after puddle after puddle. Splish splash. A party going on. After, I go back to Aunty

Ikey's and see a man standing on her veranda. A strong dark man. He's smoking a roll-your-own. He's screwing up his eyes. He's looking out at the lovely rainy sky. A big handsome man wearing old footy shorts. And an old footy jersey. A big, tall, strong, dark, handsome man whose hair is black. Black and brylcreemed. Black is the colour of my true love's hair. His eyes so brown they make you stare. Brown eyes, beautiful, beautiful, brown eyes. And his false teeth are Persil white. White like a painted paling fence in a cool new suburb. A new fence white with gleaming full-gloss.

His real teeth rotted away. The handsome man's teeth. They rotted away before he was twenty.

Aunty Ikey says.

She's still got most of her own teeth, Aunty Ikey. Mum, too. And Aunty Bella. And the reason why I can see the tips of the handsome man's teeth is because his big lower lip hangs open while he rolls his own.

And he's Uncle Arthur.

And the shorts are ripped a bit down one side.

He's what you call a hewer on the front shift. Uncle Arthur. Which means he's one of the men who goes down the mineshaft and cuts out the coal. Which is hard work. Which is why he's big and strong. The mine's idle today. And he sees me walking up the path, which is all mossy. And he doesn't say anything. He waits. And I step up onto the veranda. And he holds out one of his big brown hands. Which feels sort of exciting. And sort of scary.

And he cups the back of my head.

And I love feeling his hand.

And it's really scary.

A dog. A black, big, dog.

A red worm.

Milk.

And I go inside. And through the kitchen doorway I see Aunty Ikey hoisting rows of white singlets and white petticoats and white underpants high over the coal range to dry. And I feel good. I love seeing Aunty Ikey. She isn't a hewer in a mine isn't Aunty Ikey. Mums can't be miners. Aunty Ikey stays at home like mums do. She cooks. And she does the washing. And she looks after our cousins. And she sweeps. And she shops. And she jokes. And she scrubs. And she sings, and she sews, and she dances, and she knits.

And she listens to the hit songs on the radio.

'Lipstick on your collar told a tale on you,' sings Aunty Ikey.

And now it's tomorrow. And now it's the tomorrow after tomorrow. And now it's the day after that day. And all of a sudden ten days have gone by. And we've only got two days left out of our stay. And there hasn't been any rain for a week. It's been frosty and sunny. Which I don't like. I don't want it to be hard and bright. I want it to soak. And be soggy. Also, this morning it's only us men at home. Alan and me and Noel and Ross and Uncle Arthur. Which is what he says, Uncle Arthur. It's all us men.

Although he's the only man, in reality.

We're boys. Aren't we?

Aunty Ikey has gone shopping. She's taken taken our girl cousins, who are Wendy and Heather. They caught the bus to Greymouth. Which is what they think is a city in West Midland. And the mine is still idle. Which is why Uncle Arthur's looking after us boys. The radio's on. Well, it's always on. Paul Anka's singing Lonely Boy. Uncle Arthur says we're going to burn gorse in the section next door. Which sounds exciting. I'm a sad and lonely boy. I'm lonely and blue. Uncle Arthur says we've had a good dry week so the fire will take good. Which I don't know exactly what that means but I can guess.

And we all go out onto the veranda and start tugging on our

muddy rubbery gumboots.

And now Bobby Darrin's singing Dream Lover.

'Right, men, let's get cracking with that gorse.'

A man from over the road has started burning already. And his two boys. A man from round the corner, too, with other boys. The man from over the road is whistling. His boys are holding wet sacks. The wet sacks will be in case the fire gets away. All my nights I hope, I pray, a dream lover will come and stay. I see tiny licks of fire, orange red fire. And then I see little leaps of fire. Orange red fire flying. And in the sky, smoke. White, dove grey. The fire's waving a white and dove grey tablecloth up at the sky. A tablecloth washed by Aunty Ikey. Washed by her, then hoisted up to dry. I go to sleep. I dream my dreams, can't do nothing else, or so it seems. A gorse bush now starts snapping and crackling and flicking orange sparks at a rusty old shed.

The smell of gorse burning is – I don't know words for the smell – only I know I love it – I love the smell of gorse burning.

All my nights I hope, I pray, a dream lover will come and stay.

Also, I don't know why.

Why I love the smell of gorse burning. And it's sort of worrying me that we're burning gorse. What did gorse do to us? What did it do wrong? Gorse is green and springy. Gorse grows quick and strong. Its flowers are lemon yellow. And smell good. Bees love gorse blossom. Only it's a weed, gorse. You have to kill weeds. You have to work hard to kill weeds. And you have to keep working hard because weeds come back. It's not like the weeds at Olivine Street. We got those weeds down, like I said already. Well, Dad did. He got them down because you can get weeds down in East Midland.

You can't in West Midland.

West Midland weeds – us boys and men work like navvies, whatever navvies are, most likely Negro slaves or massacred Indians. Anyway, we work like navvies over those weeds. We torch.

We hack. We poison. Only they come back quick. Weeds in West Midland. Very quick. Come back, and come back, and keep coming back, and keep coming back.

And you don't need X-ray eyes to see it's sort of crazy.

Weeds don't care about us trying to kill them, I don't think. Not as weeks go by and years go by. Weeds come back. Green weeds. Yellow weeds. Red weeds. Reedy weeds. Weedy weeds. Sap, spider, web, twig, root, grub, worm, mushroom, moss, rush, sedge, midge, sandfly, leaf, fern, fire, lizard, life, light. We say we're killing weeds. Only we're not. We're not doing anything, in reality. We're killing time, not weeds. Above us, a cold, windless, cloudless blue sky.

A sky blue sky. Taubmans Vitalised Oil Paints.

And an atomic explosion glowing in the sky.

The Platters start singing. Smoke gets in your eyes. I love this song. Smoke's getting in our eyes now. Smoke from burning bush after burning bush. We're blundering around, men and boys, gripping phosphorous matches and wet sacks. We're saving the rusty old shed. We're tripping over gorse stumps. We're bumping into gorse trunks. Prickly gorse, scratchy gorse, stabby gorse, blossoming gorse, scented gorse.

They asked me if my love was true. They said someday you'll see you're blind.

And the gorse stumps, the gorse trunks, they hold fast, they hug the ground, tug the ground, tough, stubborn, stubby.

We burn the gorse for ages and ages.

After, when it's time for lunch, we go back to the house to eat. We stand on the veranda and jump around taking off our gumboots. Roy Orbison's singing. Only the Lonely. And through the doorway and the open window I can smell our lunch stewing away stinkily on top of the coal range. Arthur calls lunch, dinner. Which is wrong. You don't call it dinner when you eat in the middle of the day.

Not unless it's Sunday, which I don't know why.

Anyway, it's pig trotters, our lunch.

Pig trotters boiled with onions and swede. Which I've never eaten before. I've eaten lots and lots of swede and onion but never pig trotters. I didn't know you could eat pig trotters. And I don't want to know. Only the lonely know the way I'm feeling. Only the lonely know this feeling ain't right. And now he's just spooned two trotters and a few slices of swede into a bowl. Uncle Arthur. And he's handed it to Alan. And now he's spooned two more trotters and some more slices of swede into another bowl and he's handed it to me. And I don't know what to do.

Help! Save me!

SOS!

A pig trotter looks quite a lot like a boys' foot. Or a man's foot. A white man or boy. Only the lonely know why I cry. Trotter skin looks exactly like the skin on a white man's foot, or a white boy's foot. Pink, pasty. Uncle Arthur's skin doesn't look pink and pasty. Uncle Arthur's skin looks sort of brass, even though he's very fair for a Maori. And the Everly Brothers are singing.

When will I be loved?

I pick up my spoon to stir the trotters and swedes. Swedes and trotters swirl in a yellow swill. And each trotter has got two toes. Which look like a boy's toes. Or a man's toes. Only trotter toenails are long. Not short. Not like on a man or boy. Long and pointy. You know, pointy like some ladies let their nails grow. Also, toe claws on pig trotters are red like a lady's toenails. Red with nail polish. A bright, slippery, scarlet.

Only, ugh, I don't think it's nail polish.

Ugh! Ugh, ugh, ugh, ugh!

I want to spew.

Uncle Arthur sits down with his own steaming swill. Only he has to get up again because a man comes to the back door to see about a dog. So the two of them talk. And while they're talking I whisper to the other boys.

'Anyone want one of my trotters?'

'Yeah, me,' says Alan, sticking a fork into it, lifting it out.

'Anyone want my other trotter?' I say, thinking it'll be great if I can get rid of it too.

'Yeah, me,' says Alan again, sticking his fork into it and lifting it out and grinning. And the big brown freckles on his big round face are already greasy from eating pig trotters.

'Can I have your onions and swede for a fair swap?' I say.

'You're mad,' says Alan. 'Help yourself.'

Alan likes meat. I like swede. So that's alright. Uncle Arthur doesn't notice anything about me giving away the trotters because he talks for quite a long while with the man. When he gets back to the table us boys' bowls are empty. Well, except for bones. So he has to eat his own pig trotters in a hurry. After, he lets out a big belch. Which is rude, but at least it's not a fart. And he stands up and says it's time to get back to the burning.

'Boy, you stay and help with the dishes,' he says, looking my way. 'Yous others get stuck into the gorse.'

So the other boys go out. And I stay.

And I know he's going to do it.

He does it every day.

He's been doing it for years now. A big dark dog in black moleskin. A dog up on its hind legs. A dog unbuttoning its black moleskin flies. Unbuttoning with its forepaws. Lonnie Donegan is singing. I Want to go Home. Big, thick flies. On the black dog. Worms are red. And they're big. And they're thick. They're wet. They're sticky.

Which makes me feel excited because – because it's exciting! It's exciting that he wants to do it to me. You know, a strong handsome man like Uncle Arthur. Glossy black hair, eyes so brown they make you stare. He must like me more than he likes the other boys. Which feels great. Only it makes me feel sick, too. It makes me want to spew even more than I feel like spewing when I see pig trotters in my soup bowl. And – and –

Help – help – help! Help!

SOS! SOS!

Can't breathe, can't breathe – black, black – white stars – can't breathe – need to be sick. Black, black. White stars. Black is the colour of my true love's hair. I want to go home. Beautiful, beautiful, brown eyes. I want to go home. I feel so lonesome. I want to go home. I'm a sad and lonely boy. I'm lonely and blue. Only say that you'll be mine, in no other's arms entwined. Only the lonely know this feeling ain't right.

When will I be loved?

I hate Arthur.

I love Arthur! The handsomest face and the strongest hands. Oh, what a beautiful city. Whippoorwill. Mockingbird Hill. Tra la la, tweedle dee dee dee. Cool, cool, cool of the evening. The loveliest night of the year. Days grow short. Dark clouds. Shadows deepen. Leaves wither. Precious days. The bitterberry tree. Each lonely night. The darkest night.

'Do we really have to do the dishes?' I say afterwards, sort of complaining.

'Nah! Your aunty will do them. Heck, you're lucky, eh?'

And he leans down and gives me a wink.

'You're a nice looking kid, Noel.'

Only I'm not Noel. Am I?

I can't breathe.

SOS!

Wendy and me are lying on her bed reading comics in her and Heather's bedroom. Wendy's bedspread is chartreuse candlewick. Heather's is royal blue candlewick. She's probably with Aunty Ikey. Heather. Wendy's comic is a Mickey Mouse. Mine is a Donald Duck. Donald's swinging. Mickey's square! I like lying on the bed with Wendy. Donald and his nephews are living in a lighthouse. They're keeping the light bright and feeding fish to sea lions. Only here come the Beagle Boys! We've always liked each other, me and Wendy. She's only a few months older than me so she's sort of my twin. Her head when we were little was big and round and orange like a pumpkin. Round and orange and freckly. Now she's skinny, like Aunty Ikey.

Also, lithe and clever and laughing, like Aunty Ikey.

Lithe is an extremely good word.

Also they've both got red hair. Only of course it isn't really red. It's orange. Red is what people say. I don't know why. Aunty Ikey's orange hair is a shortish tangle. Wendy's is shoved back, pinned down, with two big tortoiseshell combs. Only the combs aren't really shell from tortoises. Good. They're plastic.

Quite a lot of words are like that, aren't they?

You know Why do we say red when we mean orange? Why do we say tortoiseshell when we mean plastic? Why do we say blackberry when really we should say purpleberry?

And it's not metaphor.

Is it?

Shazam! Wendy and me can hear the radio playing. Duane Eddy and the Rebels.

'Finished my Mickey,' says Wendy. 'Want to swap?'

'You can have my Donald when I've finished it,' I say, 'but I don't want your unhep Mickey Mouse.'

'Alright. I've got an Uncle Scrooge under the bed.'

'Boss.'

Shazam stops playing. The radio tells us how Lifebuoy soap gives you bath-to-bath BO protection. After, more music. And it's Chubby Checker. Fabulous. He's nice, and young. And he'd be quite handsome but he's a bit fat. He's a Negro. His grandmums and granddads were slaves in the cotton plantations. Or their mums and dads, probably.

And he's singing –

The twist!

I jump up. I jump off the bed.

Wendy jumps up, too. She jumps off, too.

'Yeah!' I say to Chubby Checker. 'Rock it, daddy-o!'

The twist is so in it makes everything else out. The twist is so far in it's far out. No dance has ever been so swinging. Well, not since the charleston. Which was the twist of the Twenties. Which were like the Sixties. Hip. The opposite of other years. Which were grey. Grey with the war, and the slump, and that. Also, years and years of embarrassingly uncool songs. And clothes were startlingly cheesy. Anyway, what's so swinging about the twist is it's a dance where you don't touch the person you're dancing with. You just stand on the spot. And you sort of jerk from side to side.

Your knees go one way. Your elbows go the other way.

You don't even need another person to do it with.

You can twist all by yourself.

Which our mums and dads seem to think is weird. Dads and mums don't understand the Sixties. They can't, they're too old to swing. Also, they're too young to have jazzed to sax in the Twenties. Mums and dads seem to think that there's only two bits to history. They think one bit is the slump years and the war years. And they think the other bit is the sunny years after the war. After the war, they say. Before the war, they also say.

I think it's going to be like that for us. Only it'll be the twist. When we're old like our mums and dads we'll look back, too.

'Before the twist,' we'll say.

'After the twist.'

Wendy and me stand on the lino. You know, worn old blue and buff lino. And we get in the groove. Cool, man! Dig it! Come on, baby! Yeah! Wendy and me do the twist. Wendy and me sing the twist. Go on baby, just do the twist. Baby, baby, do the twist. We know how to twist. We know how to rock. And we get the stitch, and laugh a lot.

And soon we're puffing, and panting, and hot.

'Now let's play dress ups,' says Wendy.

'Alright, swinging.'

And we do.

I take off my jersey. Which is Richmond blue and quite scratchy. Mum knitted it. And I take off my shirt. Which is just some old grey flannel shirt. And I take off my shorts. Which are grey flannel, too. We don't take off our singlets and underpants. Once we did take them off and had a good look at each other and it wasn't very interesting.

Also, of course, I've often seen a bare-bummed Sissy.

I hand my clothes to Wendy.

She hands me hers. A jungle green cardigan. A chocolate and coffee frock. So I start putting on the frock. A frock printed with big coffee and chocolate coloured squares. A chequerboard. An ordinary warm woollen frock like the woollen warm frocks most girls and mums wear on cold days. You know, a frock that on top looks a bit like a boy's flannel shirt. And stops being a flannel shirt when it gets down to its wide woollen belt. A belt made from the same wool as the frock. Only it's been stiffened, somehow. And then below the belt the woollen cloth sort of flies out. Goes out everywhere sort of puffy.

Which is really quite interesting.

How does it do it – fly out – the wool below the belt?

I learn how when I put on the frock. I learn that there's a petticoat thing. A nylon petticoat thing. A white nylon petticoat thing that someone's sewn in underneath the wool. Aunty Ikey sewed it in, I bet. Yes, I bet the woollen cloth was woven by a mill then sold to shops. And one day, Aunty Ikey takes the bus to Greymouth. She wants a length of warm wool to make a new frock for Wendy. She doesn't want to take out a mortgage to pay for it. She finds the woollen cloth with the big chocolate and coffee squares. She fingers it. She rubs it. She tugs it. She holds it up to the long fluorescent lights glowing overhead.

And she looks at the price card. And she closes her eyes.

She does some sums in her head.

She opens her eyes.

'Not too dear, good enough wool,' she says to the shop assistant, who happens to be the sister-in-law of a couple two houses down Stafford Street. 'Corker colours, too.'

And she brings a yard back home with her in the bus. A yard of chocolate and coffee coloured squares, wrapped up in brown paper, tied with green string. As soon as she gets home she has to cut straight into her jobs. It's next morning before she finds an hour or so for the coffee and chocolate woollen frock. She gets my cousins off to school. She gives a lick and promise to the housework. She makes herself a brew. And she gets out her paper patterns. She slips pins between her lips. She holds the pins steady with her tongue. She takes pins out, one at a time. After pinning, she gets thread and needle. She bastes loosely.

Pinheads wink in tidy rows like tiny white stars. Aunty Ikey gets her steel shears.

She cuts the cloth out.

She's sewing.

And now, today, a finished frock flying out with a white nylon petticoat thing. Loop, after little loop, after little little loop, of nylon in white tight nets. White little nets looped together like the webs of three cubic acres of spiders in Lilliput. A million, million, little spiders. And, on top of the white webs, a warm woollen chequerboard. Coffee. Chocolate. Chequerboard squares all the same size, perfect rectangles. Which is more geometry.

Or are the squares not a chequerboard? Are the squares a chessboard?

Help!

Chess is for big boys. Am I a white pawn?

Anyway, wearing the chocolate and coffee frock makes me feel sort of good. It's funny in a frock. It's sort of airy. The flying-out puffiness is really interesting. It's against gravity. Also, I feel bad. It's wrong. I'm a boy.

Aren't I?

I want to cry.

Which I don't know why.

Only it must be sort of easy being a girl. It's hard being a boy. To be a boy you have to work. You have to work to look like a boy. And walk like a boy. Talk like a boy. Throw like a boy. Think like a boy. You even have to work to dream like a boy. And you have to keep doing it always. Otherwise they'll find you out. Other boys. So you always have to keep up your guard. If you don't, they'll say you're a girl.

Sugar and spice and all things nice.

Snips, snails, puppy tails.

Worm milk.

'Give me back my shorts,' I say to Wendy. 'Swapping clothes is boring.'

'It isn't,' she says. 'It's not boring, it's good.'

'You only think it isn't boring because you're used to being bored, because you live here in Dullsville.'

Which is what it is, Blackball. It's Dullsville. It's Squaresville. It's the backblocks. It's the sticks. It's had it. It's out. And I don't mean far out. Blackball isn't shooting into the Space Age. It's skidding back towards olden days. Black beech. Grey lichen. Red rust. All the paint's peeling off. Yards are tangled. Gorse, wiwi, dock. Blackball is poor, rundown, grubby, smoky. It's slinking back into the bush. It's like someone who wasn't thinking dropped an atom bomb on the most gruesome slums in South Christchurch. You know, the soot and iron dumps where Mum and Aunty Ikey and Aunty Bella were dragged up. And it's like the bomb flung a few scraps of blistered weatherboard, with a coal bin or two, and twisted sheets of corrugated steel, so far up into the sky that they flew over the Alps.

And after, dropped like dirty pick-up-sticks at the bottom of some wet, lost, dead-end valley.

A coaly old cul-de-sac.

Why has it taken me so long to see how it's so square, Blackball? Why did I come on this stupid holiday? To take a walk, just a little walk. Blackball's blurry. It blurs into everything. Only say that you'll be mine, in no other's arms entwined. Black is the colour of my true love's hair. Blackball is trees, and mist, and creeks, and coal, and cock, and pig trotters, and milk, and moss. The handsomest face and the strongest hands. I love the ground whereon he stands. I love that man and well he knows, I love the ground whereon he goes.

Blackball isn't right. It's wrong.

It isn't contemporary.

TUBECHROME

And now it's a bright sunny day in Olivine Street. Which is great. It's fabulous being back in East Midland. I'm standing in our bedroom and I'm looking out through one of its picture windows. I'm looking out through the clean new glass. New pink Windolene, now with DDT. No speck, only sparkle. I'm looking at the new black tarseal. I'm looking at the new concrete kerb. I'm looking at our cool cul-de-sac of fourteen brand new bungalows. Red brick. Summerhill stone. Tiles. Glossy wood. Glossy steel.

Bermuda, sky blue, turquoise, caprice yellow, flamingo.

And it's really great.

Pink pig trotter.

Black dog.

Milk.

And happy days follow one another, one by one. We go to school. It's spring. They get a new president in the United States. Mr Kennedy. He's modern and young. So that's cool. I turn eight. The magistrate's sentence was not excessive, says a supreme court judge dismissing an appeal by Eric Elkis against a sentence of imprisonment imposed on eight charges of committing an indecent act on a male. We get a new prime minister, too. Mr Holyoake. He's not young. Also he's the leader of the National Party. So he's very square.

Labour stands for the working class and peace and fairness and democracy, says everybody. Only also they're a bit boring and sort of grey, Labour.

National are boring and grey, too. So the whole scene's not rocking, yet.

Not yet – but soon!

Travel the Caltex Way. Philishave Speedshaver de Luxe. The effortless ease of rotary action shaving, leaving your face smooth, smooth, smooth. Appearing for sentence on four charges of indecent assault on a male, William Pono said that at the time he did not realise the seriousness of the offences. A secret love inside my heart. A secret love waiting to be free. I told a glistening star, the way a dreamer will often do.

All I have to do when I feel blue.

All I have to do is dream.

And then it's summer. And then it's the summer holidays. Hooray! And the frontyard isn't weeds and seeds anymore. It's green mown lawn. And clean weeded flowerbeds. And the backyard isn't seeds and weeds anymore. It's green mown lawn. And green young veges in tidy rows. And we've got a modern new dining suite for the dinette. A shiny new dining suite. Tubechrome, you call it. That's the brand. A table with silvery legs. Steel tubes, chromed. A tabletop of yellow Formica. A swirly sort of yellow. Which is swinging. And the dining chairs have got silvery Tubechrome legs. And the chair seats and backs are lemon yellow vinyl.

So our dinette now looks very contemporary.

And we get venetians for all our windows. Venetians are also swinging. Tension headaches need the extra medication in Anacin. Venetians are blinds. Blinds of thin steel blades, white blades, curved like the wings of a plane. Or a row of white false teeth. Why limit yourself to aspirin alone which contains only one pain reliever and has no special medication to relax tension? You control venetians by tugging on nylon cords. Also, the nylon cords are white. So now when it's night you don't have to look at yourself in the glass, Windolene clean, with blackness behind.

You look at a blind, its thin steel blades, thin, curved, white, shimmering, slick.

'They're a bugger to dust, though,' says Aunty Bella.

'That's easy,' says Mum. 'Don't dust them!'

Anyway, like I was saying, it's now the summer holidays. It's summertime, summertime, sum sum summertime. Teacher, zip your lip. We're so happy that we could flip. John organises games for us to play in the backyard. We play cowboys. We play war. We play bar-the-door. Sometimes we start doing the twist. Go on baby, just do the twist. Baby, baby, do the twist.

And we go to the East Midland Museum.

I love the Museum.

It's a big dark grey stone building. The roof's black slate. Slate that came in ships from England. Or Scotland. It's startlingly interesting. We stand for ages looking at things from olden olden days. Maori things. Nets. And traps. And weapons. And a beautiful feather cloak. And we stand for ages looking at things from ordinary olden days. White people's things. Hoop skirts. Satin, silk. Mirrors. And rat poison. And a hansom cab. Or do you spell it handsome? And guns. And glass jars of drugs. And on another floor is what I love most about the Museum. A diorama of East Midland. A massive modern diorama. You stand at a wall of sloping glass. You're looking out an airliner window. You're on a flight descending to East Midland. Your silver wings are swooping. You see blue. It's the Pacific. You see gold. It's a sweep of golden grass and city glass. A vast province, always and forever, from the days before olden days right up to modern days – and onwards to Tomorrowland!

You know, Walt Disney's Tomorrowland. At Disneyland, Orange County, California. Which I'd quite like to go to, if we had the money.

Of course we've got nowhere near the money.

You know, to go to Disneyland.

Anyway, the gold and glass bowl is sealed on top. Sealed by an upside down bowl of blue sky. And the two bowls make a ball. A ball of sky blue, Pacific blue, gold. And glass. A bright brilliant ball of gold and blue which is the exact opposite of a sooty dark black ball. A coal ball. Or in other words Blackball. So I peer harder into the diorama. I squint towards its rugged back. West Midland. Dark. Sawtoothed dark ranges shaggy with black beech.

Dog.

Black moleskins.

Dog up on his hind legs.

West Midland, wrong, wet, dark.

Midland, dry, bright, right. Cathedral Square. Cranmer Square. Latimer Square. Victoria Square. FitzGerald Avenue. Bealey Avenue. Moorhouse Avenue. Rolleston Avenue. Oh, what a beautiful city! Twelve gates in the city.

Alleluya!

So in other words what I'm seeing from my silver plane isn't only East Midland. It's all Midland. The land of the Midland Line. You know, the railway. The transalpine railway. I know quite a lot about the Midland Line. We did it in a project at school this year. They made the railway in olden days. They laid it across the East Midland Plains. They dynamited a way for it through the Southern Alps. Which is why you say transalpine. And they laid it all the way to the seaports of West Midland. Greymouth. Also Westport. Hokitika.

So it was the Midland Railway of the Middle Island.

Which is cool.

I can dig it.

We go with our aunties and our cousins. You know, when we go to the East Midland Museum. And we go lots of other places with our cousins and our aunties. We go with them because we're a clan. We're Ilk of Forbes. And nearly everyone of our ilk is rough and rowdy. Aunties turn up on our doorstep with carloads of kids. And they bring armfuls of stuff that's fallen off the backs of lorries. And they yell, and joke, and scratch their bums. Seven scruffy sisters, poor, with a jaw. Gift of the gab. Seven Sisters sprogged by South Christchurch.

Mares eat oats and does eat oats. Don't fence me in. Run rabbit, run rabbit, run run run.

I love listening to them singing, even though their old songs are silly.

Also, they talk. They talk. And they talk. And they talk. They talk about husbands. They talk about kids. They talk about Grandma Forbes. Who when they think us kids can't hear they call Vinegar Tits. And sometimes they talk about a person they call the Old Man. I think he lives in Kaikoura. I've never met the Old Man. He left Grandma Forbes about thirty years ago, say the Seven Sisters. And she hasn't seen hide nor hair of him all those years, they also say.

I love them talking.

It sounds like reality. You know. The life they lived in olden days sounds like reality. The things they say and the way they say those things make you think about this side of the glass not being reality. Only somehow you sometimes go on to think, don't you, that if things on this side aren't reality perhaps even things on the other side of the glass aren't reality? One side must be reality. Mustn't it?

It must be one or the other side. Reality. Mod. Now.

Not olden days.

Mustn't it?

Other days we go to the beach with some of the Ilk of Forbes. We spread tartan woollen blankets on top of dry needles banked under big shady pines in the sandhills. The dry pine needles are slithery. And they're the colour of prairie rose and sandalwood. We sit on the blankets and happily chew sandwiches. We gaily drink orange cordial. After, we play in the sandhills. And we go swimming. We jump over breakers. We dive under breakers. We lie on hot sand.

Teenage girls are wearing bikinis.

Which are in. Itsy bitsy teeny weeny yellow polka dot bikini.

Only I don't look at teenage girls. It's rude. I look at teenage boys. I look at their togs. A few of them are wearing baggy togs. You know, the old sort of togs that look like shorts. Which are out. Other teenage boys are wearing with-it togs. Skimpy togs tight over their bums. Also, tight over their cocks. Shiny togs. It's hard not to look at their cocks. Tight togs in lots of bright colours. Delphinium blue. Daffodil yellow. Orient red. Miami orange. I really like looking at those togs. I wish one of the big boys in tight shiny red or orange or turquoise togs would come over and talk to me, and ask me to come into the sea with him, and jump waves with him, but no big boy does.

And some days we go to the pictures. Which you watch at picture theatres. Which aren't operating theatres stacked with stainless steel trays of sterilised knives, bright with fluorescent light, like at Christchurch Public Hospital, or Burwood Hospital, or St George's, or Princess Margaret, or Calvary. The names of the picture theatres are Savoy, Avon, Tivoli, Vogue, Mayfair, Majestic, Metro, Empire, State, Century, Plaza, Rex, Roxy, Crystal Palace, Hollywood, Harbour Light.

I love going to the pictures.

They're a bit like books, only not quite as good.

One day when a hot norwester is blowing John takes all of us, except Peter, to the pictures in Cathedral Square. Peter's still too young. He's our wee brown berry boy. He's two. He's a cheeky monkey. After school you go into our bedroom and find him making car noises while he rolls the little black rubber wheels of his little red plastic car over the bare rimu floorboards.

Vroom vrrrrooooom.

Caltex. Atlantic. Europa. Shell. BP.

Anyway, John minds the money. We've only got enough for the bus there, and the cheapest tickets, and then the bus back. And not a spare penny.

'Can't we have money for an ice cream, Mum?' says Sissy.

'No! Get cracking!'

Get cracking means that we shuffle through the door and slope off to the bus stop, complaining all the way.

'It's not fair,' says Sissy. 'Other kids get ice cream. Why can't we get ice cream?'

We stand at the bus stop in Voss Street. We wait for the big stinky red bus. We get tired waiting. A bus comes. We get on it. The bus takes ages to get to the Square. Which is the dead centre of the city. It's black tarseal, and grey concrete, with mown green lawn, ringed with newspaper buildings, and hotels, and banks. And leaping out of the middle of the Square's a massive bronze statue of Victory. She's got huge bronze wings. And a grey stone and black slate cathedral sticks its glittering brass cross two hundred feet up into the sky.

After we get out of the bus we go from picture theatre to picture theatre, looking at adverts.

Columbia Pictures – Metro-Goldwyn-Mayer – Warner Brothers – J Arthur Rank –

Paramount Pictures –

Which whenever I see it makes me nearly stop breathing. Paramount!

Dad works for Paramount. At first he worked for Paykel Brothers. You know, when we first came to hip swinging Christchurch from backwards backblocks Blackball. Paykel Brothers sell oil and things. Jews, says Dad. Tight with their money like all their race, he adds. When he worked for them we had to rent a dark old villa by the big smoky, smelly, shunting and steaming, and banging and rattling, railway yards. You know, the railway yards in Sydenham. Sydenham is all old, and crowded, and ramshackle, and poor, and sooty bricks, and black steel tracks. Sydenham is right next door to the coal stacks, and smokestacks, of the railway yards. Sydenham is right next to the stinking steel tanks of the gas works.

Sydenham is not modern.

Sydenham is very, very, olden days.

Dad didn't like the job at Paykel Brothers. He was the office manager. He said it was just being a jumped up clerk. Which I don't know what that means. Anyway, he got bored. And the money wasn't very good. And it's dear in a city. And he likes working outside. That's what he says. He says he likes working outside because of growing up on the land. And going out into the paddocks and plantations. He says when he was a boy he always loved being out in the plantations and paddocks.

Down at de ole plantation. A dollar a day is black man's pay. Maori shearers.

Anyway, he doesn't work any more for Paykel Brothers. Dad. He works for a big building company. Paramount! Paramount Homes Company Ltd, Christchurch, Auckland, Hamilton. Which is why we've got our shiny new modern bungalow. Our home is a Paramount Home. Just released – another superb Paramount subdivision – choose your section right away in this sunny development close to bus stop, shops, school – and adjoining the beautiful green links of the Shirley Golf Course.

Dad isn't a clerk in the building company. He's what you call a precutter's orderman.

I don't quite know what that means.

I do know that he works with plans for new bungalows. Which you call blueprints. He unrolls the blueprints. He does sums to work out the wood needed for the bungalows. He works out how long, or how short, each length of wood needs to be. And how many lengths are needed. And what all of it will cost. He does sums in a book. Arithmetic just makes me sick. Next, he goes out to the timberyard. He measures up all the wood. After, he cuts it into its right lengths, using an electric saw. A massive, stainless steel, oily, shining, screaming, electric saw.

Working in a timberyard is hard work.

So – well, poor old Dad.

Wood keeps scraping, scratching, pinching, his hands. Which bleed a lot. After bleeding they get scabs. Which are red and black. And when a scab gets a bit better he knocks it against something sharp at work. And it starts bleeding again. He's always bleeding. And it makes me feel sick, and sorry, looking at his bleeding scabby hands.

Anyway – Paramount Homes.

Paramount Pictures!

We get tickets for a picture by Twentieth Century Fox. We scoot into our seats. The lights go down. They play the boring national anthem about god saving the queen. And you have to stand up. Which is stupid. Queen Elizabeth on horseback. Who cares? She's wearing red, and gold, and black. Queenie's an old square. After her, you sit again and watch cartoons. Woody Woodpecker. Mr Magoo. After, there's a documentary about Fiji. Dark plantation workers sweating in a hot sun. A sugar plantation. Colonial Sugar Refinery.

And then a documentary about spaceships.

Cape Canaveral. NASA. Boss!

After, it's halftime.

We sit in our seats watching the ice cream lady. We watch her every step. She walks, wearing a flouncy red and white uniform, very slowly up and down the rows of seats. We ogle her ice creams in the white and red striped box thing she's got strapped around herself, snug under her big bosoms.

'Gee, I'd love an ice cream,' says Sissy.

'You can't,' says John.

'It'd be beaut to have an ice cream,' she says.

'We've only got the bus money left.'

'Aw, we want an ice cream, John,' the younger kids start saying. 'John, why can't we have an ice cream?'

John gives up, gets out of his seat, goes over to the ice cream lady. He pokes around in his pocket. He buys six cones. He comes back to our seats and hands them out. We grab them greedily. He hasn't got a cone for himself. I feel guilty.

'Aren't you hungry?' Sissy says to him.

'No,' he says.

'I am!' she says. 'Yum yum!'

And the lights go dim. And the picture starts unreeling. Flaming Star. Elvis is the hero. He's a cowboy. He lives on a ranch in Texas. His dad's white. His mum's Dolores del Rio. She's Indian. She's from south of the border, down Mexico way. You know, like Joan Baez. And there's a war between ranchers and Indians. Which means Elvis has to work out which side he's on. It's awkward. It makes me think about that song on the charts. You know, about two young Indians. One is a brave, Running Bear. The other one is a maid, White Dove. They love one other. They want to be together forever. Only their two tribes are sworn foes.

I'm White Dove. Only a boy.

White Wolf.

Me and Running Bear are standing on the opposite sides of a

raging river. On the bank I hear him calling to me, to me. We jump. We start swimming towards one another. We meet in the middle of a powerful flow. And we – well, in the song they kiss but we're boys so we can't kiss. We cuddle. And then the raging river drags us down.

So we'll always be together, only dead.

When you listen to the song about two young Indians you want to be Running Bear. Or White Wolf. Only you want to be a cowboy, too, like I said already. And cowboys kill Indians. And Indians kill cowboys. So it's not only awkward for Elvis it's awkward for me too.

Me and you, whose side are we on, Elvis?

Cowboys?

Indians?

I try to be good. It's not always easy. Yesterday I was building a town out of toy bricks. The town was Dodge City. I was building a saloon. And it went all wrong. The saloon fell down. So I had a paddy. I smashed Dodge City. Which ended up red-brick rubble on lino pick-up-sticks. Jaipur pink, iris blue, regale blue, canyon coral. And of course it only made me feel worse, for wrecking my work.

The film is alright. It's got shootouts. The best bit is when Elvis takes his shirt off. He takes his shirt off because he's doing some hard work on the ranch, and gets hot.

He looks really handsome, Elvis. Glossy black hair.

Brown eyes.

Afterwards we walk, blinking, into petrol fumes and bright light. I feel flat and sad. Actually that's how you always feel after the pictures, isn't it? When you come out of the pictures you think for a minute that the pictures are more real than reality. You know, coming out, blinking, your eyes not used to the sunlight. And you know you have to shuffle back to the bus stop. And you know you have to wait again for a big stinky red bus. Only they're not. The pictures. They're not more real than reality.

Reality is reality.

We've been talking about that quite a lot, haven't we?

Anyway, we come out from watching Elvis and Dolores and I'm feeling flat and sad and that's not all. I'm feeling scared, too. I'm feeling scared because I'm thinking about what we did with our bus money.

'How much have you got left?' I ask John.

He pulls a few threepences from his pocket.

'We'll divide our forces,' he says, which is what they say in war comics. 'Alan, you catch a bus with the little kids. The rest of us'll hoof it.'

'I'm not hoofing it!' says Sissy.

'Ross and Jan, you go with Alan. Sissy and Stevan and Noel, you come with me.'

'Bite your bum!' says Sissy.

'Bite your own bum,' sighs John. 'We're walking.'

It's three-and-a-half miles of long straight streets from the Square to Olivine Street. And it's hot. We're soon really thirsty. John says we'll stop for a drink of water at Grandma Forbes's. Which is in quite a poor street. Grandma Forbes will give us something to eat, too, John says. He says she'll give us something to eat so we'll have more energy for the walk. We get to her dump. John opens a rusty little iron gate in a corrugated iron fence. We follow a tarseal path past hydrangeas and a clump of silverbeet run to seed. I look at myself in a warped old window. I look behind the glass and see bunched lace curtains. The big front door is painted maroon. The paint is blistering.

John knocks.

The door flings open.

A little angry woman in a limp dark frock.

'Who're yous kids?' she raps. 'Are yous kids Darkie's kids?'

John says we are. And he says we're walking home from the Square. And he asks if we can have some water to drink. And all she says is hmf! And she thumps off down the passage. And she comes back with water in a glass. It's an old jam jar. And only one old jam jar. Also, she hasn't brought us anything to eat. We take turns sipping water from the jam jar. Grandma Forbes still doesn't say anything.

'Thanks, Grandma,' says John.

'Hmnf,' she says.

And off we go.

Grandma Forbes pays for her dump from a pension, which is money she gets from the government. Money she gets for being old. Dad, one day, says to her it's good the state keeps the wolf from your door, Barb. Which is her name. Barbara. A better name would be Banshee.

And she lets out a grunt.

'Hmf,' she says. 'When I get back what men, and kids, and landlords, and shopkeepers, have taken from me, I'll bloody dance the ragtime to Rangiora.'

Next day we go to North Beach. We go with Aunty Bella and her kids. Next day we go to Woodend Beach. And – well, the days are flying by. That's what the olds always say. The days fly by. Today becomes yesterday. Tomorrow becomes today. Sort of scary. One day there's going to be no more tomorrow. Which means there's also going to be no more yesterday. Or today. Anyway, days fly by. Kids. Cousins. Aunts. Tea. Talking. Car, river, canoe. Picnic, paddling, swimming. Sea. Surf. Li-lo, lupin, marram, macrocarpa, picnic, pine. Aunts. Tea. Cigarette, tar, car, lead. Sweat, beer, beetroot, tomato, egg, chive. Chesdale, cordial, pikelet.

And now it's our first day back at Quinns Road School. We walk south along Quinns Road. We come to the one gate in the west. We walk into the grounds.

My teacher this year is going to be Clarrie Jack.

Only his real name is Mr McLaren.

Clarrie Jack's famous in our school for blowing his jets. Also he's famous for being great at reading a story. Which makes me think that being in his class is going to be interesting. Clarrie wears bright goggling glasses. And actually everything's pretty ordinary in his class till the last hour or so. You know, the last hour or so on this first school day. Which is when he starts reading us a story. I can dig it! He pops a wee wooden chair down in the middle of the classroom between our desks.

And we settle ourselves. Settle yourselves, children, is what teachers say.

Clarrie Jack then shows us the story.

Jansson. Comet in Moominland.

And he starts reading.

MOOMIN MIDLAND

Strike me pink! The Grigg family have been living for well over a year in a new modern Paramount Home in a new modern cul-de-sac in the beautiful modern suburb of Shirley, Christchurch, Midland, Middle Island, Oceania, World, Solar System, Milky Way, Universe. A universe with lasers, and plastic, and television, and a space race, and deodorants, and civil rights! Well, in our family we don't use deodorants.

'Nothing wrong with just giving your armpits a bit of a soaping when you have your weekly bath,' says Mum.

Only when I grow up I'll use a deodorant. And I won't have a weekly bath.

I'll have a daily shower the modern way.

Mum's not very in. Well, she's really out! Dad, too. Dad says why we haven't got a television yet is because we're going to get one as soon as we can see our way to scraping together the wherewithal. He sometimes talks like a book, Dad. It's supposed to be funny. Poor old Dad. Poor old Mum. Well, they're old. They're really old.

Mum's thirty-two. Dad's nearly forty!

Isn't it extraordinary?

Stephen McKenzie, age seventeen, rubber worker, two charges of indecent assault on a male, remanded to Sunnyside Mental Hospital. Albert Kyle, age thirty, fined twenty pounds for indecent assault on a male. Ian Davies, fitter and turner, sentenced to imprisonment for nine months on a charge of attempting to commit an indecent act on a male. William Jackson, age nineteen, fined twelve pounds.

Anyway, you need to stand for a tick gazing at our suburb.

Perhaps you feel spellbound by the sight.

Yes, truly a wonderful suburb. A flowering colourful suburb of violet hyacinths, yellow pansies, violet pansies, primroses, red, yellow, pink, purple, pink, pink, pink. Tension headaches need the extra medication in Anacin. A glassy block of concrete shops painted lolly colours. Black tarseal, white stripes, yellow arrows, brick rectangles, Four Square. Geometry. Shiny cars sprayed red, yellow, white, green, blue. Ipana toothpaste with hexachlorophene. Kids sucking lime iceblocks. Or lemonade. Steel manhole cover. Cadbury's Chocolate. Red phone booths. Peter Stuyvesant Miracle Filter. Garden sprinkler. Sprays. Rays. Insecticide. Herbicide. Knowledgeable people smoke du Maurier. Mortgage. Family. Happy. Family family family family. Happy happy happy happy happy happy happy. And spinning on our new teak radiogram the cool but hot sound of the Shadows.

The Frightened City.

Actually it's teak veneer. Glued to hardboard.

Do you know something? If we could fly, if we flew straight up from our cul-de-sac, we'd come to where it isn't sky blue any more. Trevor Way remanded on a charge of indecently assaulting a male. Also, you don't need even to fly very far, in reality. Not even as far as the rings of Saturn. Let alone Alpha Centauri! All we'd have to do is go only two thousand miles up before finding it's not sky blue but black.

In the daytime, too. Black.

Nothing.

I don't want to make plaintive noises about such things.

So I won't. And anyway, a far more extraordinary thing is that Clarrie Jack has turned out to be an extraordinary teacher. The Moomins are fabulous. And as for Clarrie Jack, he's extremely, extraordinarily, expert at reading a story. I love him. Well, he gets crabby some days. When he does he scowls. And he yells. And he does chuck chalk at some of the cheeky boys. But I still love him.

I love him because he's loveable! And clever. And a storyteller.

Glinting, winking, gleaming, goggling glasses.

Clarrie reads us every single Moomin book that's ever been written up to today. And he tells us about the lady who writes the Moomins. Tove Jansson. She lives in Finland. She writes in Swedish. Not Finnish. Did you know many Finns speak Swedish? I wonder why. It's interesting. If I was a poor Maori boy living in a wooden shanty with a red rusty roof somewhere in the backblocks up north would I be writing this story in Maori? Writing it somewhere wet and grey, frilly with ferns, crammed with dairy cows, in the backblocks of one of the many towns up there whose quite long names on the map nearly always seem to start with T or W then go on to iti or nui, or wai, or ra, or papa.

Also, wouldn't it be boss writing in Maori?

I think hardly anyone can read Maori. Or can they?

Anyway, in summers, which are short in Finland, Tove Jansson and her best friend, who's an artist lady, stay together on a rock island. A tiny island like a tiny boat. A boat of old rock. A best-friends-size island. Not a new steel ship. And the writer lady, and the artist lady, live together in a wooden shanty. The two of them side-by-side on the old rock island. Also, the Maori boy up north has got a best friend, too. A white boy. And the two boys also live on a tiny island like a tiny rock boat. Swimming together the warm days. And talking together. And reading together. And sitting silently. And listening. And drawing. And swimming some more, and fishing, fossicking. At night they sit together looking at a flat black sea and white stars.

On their tiny rock boat, which doesn't float, they look at the Gulf of Finland.

I've got two friends, now.

Which is great.

One of the friends is Eric Wright. We talk about things like maps. And sit-ins. And motorways. At his house after school we play with his electric train set. And his mum gives us milk and two of her home-made biscuits. Eric and me made friends last year. He's a very skinny boy. And he's ugly. His head, white and bony, looks like it's been squashed by a vise from the ears inwards. And after the vise squashed it, someone peppered it with freckles. One of the freckles is as big as my thumbnail. He's clever. I quite like him. We're always talking. We're always mooching around together.

Only sort of I don't like him, too.

He's a bit of a know-all and sometimes he talks to me in a rather superior manner, I think.

And the other friend is called Filip Gama. And he's not ugly. Actually he's quite a cute boy, Filip. He's got smooth skin. Which is sort of copper colour. And when we're outside in the grounds he sort of shines in the bright sunlight. He's Indian. Not red Indian. Not like Joan Baez. Or Running Bear. Or Dolores del Rio in Flaming Star. Also Elvis. Filip's Indian Indian. His mum and dad are from Goa. And he always looks happy. And when he smiles, which is lots and lots, you see he's got buck teeth. Which is sort of cute, too. And his hair is black and glossy. And he's got beautiful, beautiful, brown eyes, eyes so brown they make you stare, the handsomest face and the gentlest hands.

And he's just as clever as Eric. Only he's not a know-all. He's modest, Filip.

And in playtimes us three hang around together, talking. Which is cool. And sort of tagging along is Noel.

We're a little gang of four boys.

Andrew Harris, sentenced to five years' imprisonment on each of six charges of indecent assault upon a male; the sentences to be served concurrently. A man, name suppressed, remanded on bail on charges of attempted indecent assault on a male. Melvin Anquitel, age twenty, remanded on bail on a charge of indecent assault on a male. A youth, name suppressed, placed on probation for indecent assault on a male; the magistrate says the crime was a result of immaturity, ignorance, and a bad environment. Graham McGavin, age twenty-five, plasterer, remanded to Sunnyside Mental Hospital after pleading guilty to a charge of indecent assault on a male. Albert Kemp, two years imprisonment on five charges of indecent assault on a male. Eric Maynard, radio technician, inducing another male to act indecently. Derek Legge, age twenty-three, storeman, attempted indecent assault on a male. Donald Evans, age twenty-one, salesman, permitting a male to do an indecent act on him. A man, name suppressed, permitting an indecent act by a male. Dale Hill, age twenty-eight, plasterer, indecent act on a male at New Brighton.

We walk around the mown green perimeter of the grounds, me and Eric and Filip. Also, Noel. We talk about sparrows. Eric knows a lot about sparrows. We talk about Esperanto. We think everyone should learn Esperanto. We talk about the United Nations. We talk about Venera I. That's the latest spaceship. It's been launched by the Soviet Union. It's on its way to Venus!

We talk, now and again, about olden days.

Clarrie has been showing us how to make a diorama of the olden days. A diorama like the massive one in the East Midland Museum. Only tiny. A mini diorama, says Clarrie. You get an empty shoebox. My box says Women's Bata Flats, White. Eric's box says Men's

Bata Bumpers, Black. On the inside of your box you crayon a few clumps of cabbage trees and raupo and flax. Also the Avon. After, you cut out bits of cardboard. And you glue the cardboard bits together to make the first houses that they built here in olden days. You know, white people from England. And Scotland. Ilk of Forbes! After, you make cardboard carts, cardboard men, cardboard ladies, and sheep. And you place them in position between the buildings.

And you've got your diorama about the olden days in East Midland. Oh, what a beautiful city!

Alleluya!

Twelve gates in the city.

I look at my diorama too overcome to speak. It must have been really exciting coming all the way from the other side of the world to start a whole new province and city.

Anyway, our little gang talks and walks round and round the perimeter of the mown green grounds. And the bells ring for the end of the break. And we queue outside the classroom. And we march inside. And it's spelling which is easy but boring. Or it's arithmetic which makes me sick. And the schooldays go round and round. Though while they go round they always stay straight. Really straight. A dead straight line from where to where? And summer becomes autumn. Mr Kennedy says the United States is going to land men on the moon before the end of the decade. Well, perhaps the Soviet Union will beat them to it. Autumn becomes winter. BP. Shell. Atlantic. Travel the Caltex Way. Tubechrome. Philishave Speedshaver de Luxe.

Winter becomes spring.

The effortless ease of rotary action shaving.

And me and Eric and Filip and Noel, we keep walking round the mown green perimeter of the grounds. We keep talking. We keep walking. We keep talking. We talk about Moomins. We talk about heart transplants. We talk about Mr Khrushchev. I like Mr

Khrushchev. Eric doesn't. We talk about why grass is green. Chlorophyll, says Eric. Only isn't that a chemical in toothpaste? You know, for bad breath? We talk about stamps. Filip's got thousands. He keeps them in a stamp album. I wish I had a stamp album. And we talk about modern days. And we talk about democracy. And we talk about lots and lots of things – an extraordinary lot of things.

'I'm thinking about you and me going on an expedition that will be the longest we've ever had,' I say to Filip one day. 'We're going to walk all the way up Marshland Road to the Crossing – you know, where the road goes over the Main Trunk, just before the junction with State Highway One.'

'You mean the Crossing at Chaneys Corner?' he says.

'Yes, we're having a sit-in at the Crossing.'

'Are we? Why?'

'We're showing our support for Goa.'

Goa's a colony. Portugal, which owns it, won't give it independence and democracy. It's been pushed around by the imperialistic Portuguese for hundreds of years, says Filip. Luckily the time is not far off when they shall be able to achieve their liberation. The Press says.

Filip and me are both disgusted with Portugal.

'Portugal isn't democratic,' says Filip. 'It's a dictatorship,'

Goa needs the help of the world's biggest democracy. Which is India. Which I didn't know till Filip said. All the adults seem to think the world's biggest democracy is the United States. So that's very interesting. So we get busy. We make a protest sign out of two yards of old wallpaper which we paint with a red slogan. Democracy for Goa! We roll the sign around two sticks. Which are cricket wickets. Which nobody's using for cricket right now because it's only the start of spring.

We agree to set out early for the Crossing.

It's a long way.

Filip brings provisions in his school satchel. You know, one of those leather satchels the colour of toffee. Shiny toffee leather, snapped shut with shiny toffee leather straps. And buckles of brass. Stitched with thick yellow yarn. Riveted with nickel studs. Or are they steel not nickel? Anyway, the sort of satchel most kids take to school. Filip wears it strapped to his back. He stands in our kitchen while I wrap up my own provisions. Marmite and butter sandwiches, and gooseberry jam and butter sandwiches. I stow the provisions in my own school satchel. Which is exactly the same as Filip's. Only older and more beaten up. And when you unbuckle the straps and open it out inside it's like suede.

Only it smells of apple cores, and old tomato sandwiches, and pencil leads.

The inside of my satchel would make a good rat nest.

Which would be interesting. Rats must make quite good pets, mustn't they? They've got nasty front fangs but they're pretty brainy. Anyway, I strap the satchel around my shoulders the same way as Filip.

'What's the bully with you two up at sparrowfart?' says Mum who comes scuffing past in sheepskin slippers on her way to the toilet.

I roll my eyes at her humorously.

'Oh Mum, remember I said we're walking to the Chaneys Corner Crossing?'

'Oh, right,' she says, also rolling her eyes humorously.

After she gets to the toilet she has quite a noisy wizz. Which we hear easily from the kitchen even though it's two doors away. I think perhaps I get a little pale about the nose from embarrassment. After, the toilet flushes and her and her sheepskin slippers come scuffing through the doorway. Scuffing to the electric stove, where she switches on the electric jug. Scuffing to the kitchen bench, where she picks up the tea canister. And unclicks its lid. And scoops out a few teaspoons. And flings them into our big, dented, aluminium teapot.

After, she picks up her purse. Which is maroon leatherette with a brass snap lock.

'Get's something on the way back,' she says.

Her big red arms and her big, loose, streaky, pink neck are poking out of a teal coloured nylon nighty. And two big indigo varicosed legs, looking like slabs of blue vein cheese, poke out of two cocoa coloured sheepskin slippers.

She hands me a florin and a shilling.

I look down at the florin, which shows tails.

Which on a florin is a kiwi. The kiwi looks like a swollen weasel with a beak. A nasty long beak. A bloated beaked weasel standing on two bony scaly legs with claws. I wish she'd wash her hands after going to the toilet, Mum. She never does. It's unhygienic. She could spread germs.

'What's this for, Mum? Lollies?'

'No. I can't afford that. Get us some apples and pears from an honesty box. You can do it on your way back. Your satchels'll be empty. Get's a good bag of apples and a good bag of pears. Watch they're good. Not windfalls. And get's as many as you can carry. And pay half what they're asking.'

'Alright, Mum.'

'And watch you don't get run over.'

'Alright. I'll watch out. See you, Mum.'

'Hooray.'

And leaving behind the hot hiss of steam, and the tarry reek of the first tailormade of the day, we open the back door and trot down the back steps and start off on our adventure! My longest ever expedition only by myself with a friend!

A bleak, cold, early spring day.

We have to walk nearly six miles to get to the Crossing at Chaneys Corner. Which will mean nearly twelve miles before we're back. Although arithmetic makes me sick, at least I can multiply by two. And all those twelve miles we'll walk straight along Marshland Road. And do you know why it's so long and so straight? And so long? Marshland Road. So long and so straight that in the end they made it into an arterial road? Well it's meant to be a canal. A canal to float paddle steamers across the plains. In olden days. Only the canal was never cut. They cut the land up into little farms instead, to grow cabbage, and apples, and grass.

And it was a swamp.

Marsh Land.

Perhaps you already know that in olden olden days the whole city was swamp, nearly. Swamp rich with reeds. Swamp thick with flax. Flax, reeds, stirring in a breeze from a bayou. A zephyr over swamp whirling with flocks of parakeets. Creaking with rails. Croaking with frogs. Booming with bitterns. Raked by the odd hawk. Anyway, in the end they drained the swamps. They dug races, deep. Workers did the digging. And after a while they embanked a highway.

And it's a highway you can only roll along two ways.

You can roll along to the north.

Or else to the south.

Marshland Road, long, banked, straight, squared, tarred, metalled, painted, signed, signalled, flat. Don't you reckon it would have been fabulous if we had a canal? Think about an olden days canal carrying paddle steamers across the Plains! Steel smokestacks, painted, piped, spouting white steam and black smoke into a sky blue sky. Wooden paddles thrashing the brownish water. Whistles shrieking.

De ole plantation, de whistle o de steamboat coming round de bend.

The water was brownish because of the swamps.

Sour water, you call it. Dad says.

A zephyr off the bayou. A spruce gentleman in top hat and stovepipe trousers strolls along the hurricane deck. He holds a lacquered cane. A lady in silken skirts touches his elbow with kid gloved fingertips. The kid gloves are lavender. The lady looks through a lorgnette at the gardens, parks, paddocks, plantations of East Midland. White wooden mansions. Red brick stables. Waxed and painted carriages. Highstepping steeds. Dove grey gravel driveway. Green sweeping lawn. Maori shearers, sweating. Stripped Negro slaves. Black coal. Boiler, furnace, stoker. Soot. Whistling, sweating. Coal black. Sooty shovels. Fire. Red. Black. A roaring red fury.

Let the steam whistle cry! Away along the wide Missouri.

Roll on, old mighty Mississippi.

Toot! Toot!

Only all that's really happening is that me and Filip are walking, one foot in front of the other, due north on the shingly verge of an arterial. And the paddocks aren't interesting sheep paddocks or horse paddocks. They're boring market gardens and orchards. Also, poplars. Poplars in straight rows. Poplars with their tops lopped off. And in the most alarming way when you set off to walk for nearly twelve miles from the suburbs out onto the Plains and back you realise you forgot till now how very flat they are, the suburbs and the Plains.

And you forgot how absolutely everything is straight!

Crewcut hedges. Drains. Painted wooden gates. Hardwood fenceposts.

Barbed wire. Concrete culverts. Stopbanks.

And even more alarmingly you forgot that highways are for cars and lorries greased with oil, exploding petrol, whirling on big black rubber wheels, travelling the Caltex Way. Highways are most certainly not for small walking boys.

'Let's sing to keep up our spirits,' says Filip.

'Alright,' I say.

'That latest song by the Marvelettes?'

'I have every respect for your opinion but instead of Please Mr Postman, why not Will You Still Love Me Tomorrow?'

'Perhaps. Only why a song by the Shirelles and not the Marvelettes?'

'Will You Still Love Me Tomorrow is easier to sing.'

'Alright,' says Filip.

So we begin singing the song by the Shirelles.

'Is this truly treasure, or only fleeting pleasure?' we sing. 'Will you still love me tomorrow?'

I want to be a pop star one day. Oh, you know that because I've told you already. And do you remember that's why neighbourhood kids call me Singer? We don't see neighbourhood kids so much these days. Now that the high paling fences are up. After, we sing Poetry in Motion. Filip and me. Next, we do that Elvis song. Are You Lonesome Tonight? Corny. Elvis isn't cool the way he was a while ago. He's become sort of the living dead. Zombie Elvis. Anyway, we're all the way out in the market gardens. And there's no footpath any more, just highway. And brown earth behind green verges. And the veges and even the earth are in straight rows too. Rows of carrots, lettuces, beet. And more rows of lopped poplars. And we sing that song by Cliff. You are the theme for a dream, a warm and loving dream. Cliff has become sort of the living dead, too.

Or a robot.

Actually, he always was.

'It's been somewhat boring so far, our expedition, but I like it,' I say after we've stopped to take turns reading out loud the names of dead men on a memorial gatepost. 'Do you?'

'Yes,' says Filip earnestly.

'Filip, I like you.'

At first he doesn't say anything. He just gets very pale about the nose.

'I like you, Stevan,' he says finally.

And I think I must get very pale about the nose, too.

And we turn away from one another, and from the dead men's names carved into grey stone in straight rows. Men from here killed in one of the wars. Brown. Bussell. Cox. Chidgey. Grey stone set in the red stone of the gatepost. Dass. Dobby. Delamain. Dempsey. Red stone. Madder stone. Indigo stone. Ellemers. Faulls. Head. James. Jackson. Martin. O'Callaghan. Stanbridge.

'Why aren't there any German names?' asks Filip pensively. 'A lot of the market gardeners here were German, weren't they?'

'Yes,' I reply. 'Perhaps we wouldn't let them join our army because of loyalty?'

'I wonder how we could find out if that's why?'

'We'll ask Clarrie.'

Opposite the stone gatepost is a twin gatepost. Also red, madder, indigo. And between the gateposts is a gateway. Two gates in the west. Ian Mulligan, driver, tried for indecent assault on a male and permitting a male to commit an indecent act on him. Or is Dass a German surname? Three gates in the east. Weeds in the gateway. Muss i' denn. Mein Vater war ein Wandersmann. We start walking away from the gateposts. Ach, mein Papa. Papa, auf wiedersehen, auf wiedersehen! Neville Sands, toll operator, indecency with a male at New Brighton. A man, name suppressed, indecent assault on a male. Another man, name also suppressed, permitting a male to commit an indecent act on him. We keep walking away.

We see boxed water races, lopped poplars. We see carrots in hoed rows.

And beet.

We keep walking.

We walk, and walk, and walk.

'According to my calculations we should be there by now since it's already after eleven o'clock,' wails Filip. 'And I'm thirsty!'

'I think the Crossing might be that bump in the tarseal up ahead,' I say consolingly.

'It is! I can see the railway signals and they're – oh, oh!' he cries eagerly. 'I hear quite unmistakeable sounds of steel wheels on steel tracks!'

We strain our ears excitedly.

'Yes! A train's coming!' I scream to Filip.

'We have to stop it!' he screams back. 'Stevan – run – run – run like the wind!'

And we do, but we're only boys. And the train's got huge steel wheels. Wheels with steel flanges. Wheels spinning on the shiny tops of strong steel tracks. So of course we miss it by a long way. It's a goods train. Flatbed wagons. Wagons that da-dack da-dack across the Crossing. And fade away. And we're still running. And we're puffed out by the time we get to the Crossing.

Two white crosses stick out into the sky on top of two white and scarlet striped posts.

The crosses say Crossing.

Also, two scarlet and white striped wands are being drawn up from the black tarseal. Bells are ringing. Clang! Clang! White and scarlet wands hinged on scarlet and white striped posts. After the wands go up all the way, black rubber tyres of cars begin bumping over the black tarseal, over the straight, twinned, shining, oily, steel, tracks of the Main Trunk.

I look at Filip, who seems somewhat crestfallen.

'Never mind, another one will come soon,' I say consolingly.

'Already it's half past eleven,' says Filip.

We look around us at the Crossing. We see black tarseal, glossy cars, white paint. Marshland Road. We see grey stones, grey sleepers, shiny steel tracks. Main Trunk. And over to the east we see a low railway station painted red and yellow. A station from olden days. A row of cattle cars sits silently on a siding. It's waiting to be shunted. All around are dark pine plantations. Carry me back to de ole plantation, de whistle o de steamboat coming round de bend. Magpies in the pines are singing. Quardle oodle ardle wardle doodle. Clarrie reads us poetry.

Cars are streaming along, brown gas and orange spit squirting out of their exhausts.

Filip and me stop on a shingle shoulder of the Crossing.

We unfold our banner of old unrolled wallpaper painted with red words. We poke the two cricket wickets into the gravel under the railway tracks. It's quite hard work. The gravel's packed really tight. You call it ballast. Afterwards, Filip sits on one railway sleeper. I sit on another railway sleeper.

Democracy for Goa!

We sit-in, and we sit-in, and now and then a magpie comes to take a look and wonder what we're doing. And hop a bit closer because perhaps there's food in it. A white and black magpie. A boy. He's very curious. He's very strong. The black tip of his thick white bill pokes in and out of the grey railway ballast. Quick red eyes. His mate will be nearby. You sometimes see two boy magpies who're mates. I know about magpies because I watch them a lot. You're never lonely if you're near a pair of magpies.

Also, gulls are wheeling overhead and looking down at us and wondering, too.

And we sit-in, and we sit-in.

And no trains come even though we've now been sitting-in for half an hour. We can keep tabs on the time because Filip's got a silver watch. He's quite proud of that watch, I think. A silver watch with luminous hands! Only they don't need to be luminous right now since it's the middle of the day. It must look really good at night. I wish I had a luminous watch.

We can't afford it.

Anyway, we sit-in till a man yells at us. A stumpy man who's standing on the stubby little platform of the yellow and red railway station. A stumpy red man bulging out of a black railways uniform. It's got white piping. Sort of like the Gestapo. And the man's wearing the Nazi sort of hat you wear if you work for the railways. A flared black hat, flat on top. With a shiny black beak.

'Get off the track, yous boys! Get yourselves killed!'

We stand up, go over to a pine tree, sit under it, and pretend to be thinking about something important.

'Take no notice of him,' I whisper. Out loud I say, 'Good spot this, isn't it Filip?'

'Yes!' he says. And then he mutters, 'Wretched wretch!' and looks pointedly at the red and black railway man.

After a while we decide to eat our provisions. So we unpack our satchels. Filip's lunch smells spicy. It's because of Goa. And mine smells jammy. And then there's silence for some minutes while we munch happily. After which we decide to get up and walk to the Waimakariri. It's only another half a mile or so. Cars are flying by. It's quite interesting. When you get to Chaneys Corner you see a row of petrol bowsers in front of a station. Not a railway station. Not a sheep station. A service station. Chaneys Corner is only a junction with State Highway One. Not a township or anything. At the service station you can buy oil, anti-freeze, hi-octane, chocolate bars, electric torches and steel chains.

The chains are for winter snow.

And next to the service station is a bungalow.

And then we walk some more and talk some more till we're alongside a modern sawmill owned by Christchurch Timber and Box Company. Which is also interesting. And we talk and walk some more till we're alongside a factory owned by Unit Concrete. And after a few hundred yards we come to a big gravel yard. Which has got lots of roaring diggers and lorries. After that it's only another hundred yards or so and we get to the stopbank on the southern bank of the Waimakariri. The stopbank looks like the wall of a lost city. Or a lopped pyramid along the Nile. Grass grows all over the sides of the stopbank. And on top grows a towering row of unlopped poplars flickering green with the first tips of spring leaf.

A beautiful city.

We climb up the stopbank.

We stand under the towering poplars and look down at the Waimakariri. Which is about a quarter of a mile wide here. Which is where it's at its narrowest! Along this reach in olden days they straightened and walled the river to build twin bridges for State Highway One and the Main Trunk. Anyway, half the riverbed is swirling shingle banks fuzzy with yellow flowering lupin. And the other half is green meltwater, icy. A chilly glittery sparkling torrent that rips its way from the Southern Alps across the plains to the Pacific Ocean.

You call it a spring fresh. Dad says.

And the meltwater green torrent is growling. Stones are rolling down the riverbed. Thousands and thousands of stones. And rocks. All getting dragged down the riverbed. Overhead the river birds are wheeling. And swooping. And the sea birds. And the cold meltwater keeps threshing, thrashing. No paddle steamer would ever be able to make headway against the Waimakariri.

It's so powerful, the Waimakariri.

It's a river of overwhelming matchless splendour.

We sit. Filip and I. We gaze at the wondrous Waimakariri. We gaze solemnly. We gaze spellbound. And it's a mystery. White Wolf and Running Bear sit on the bank of a raging river. On the bank I hear him calling to me, to me. We jump into the river and start swimming.

We cuddle one another in the tow of the ice cold flow.

The raging river drags us down.

'I wish we could sit here looking forever, without anyone ever disturbing us,' says Filip.

'Me too,' I say.

Unluckily, a train comes flying by on the railway bridge while we sit on the stopbank. A passenger train. Red carriage – red carriage – red carriage – red carriage – coupled together behind a big black engine roaring over the railway bridge.

Da-dack da-dack da-dack.

With a howl of anguish, Filip leaps to his feet.

'Bother!' he says. 'We should have stayed at the Crossing so we could stop that train with our sit-in.'

'Another one will come soon,' I say again.

He grins at me gratefully.

We set off back to the Crossing. We walk past grunting diggers and lorries at the gravel yard. We walk past Unit Concrete. We walk past Christchurch Timber and Box Company. We get to the Crossing. We look down the railway tracks. Not a trace of the stumpy red man from the Gestapo. So we unroll our protest banner and sit on one of the shingle shoulders.

No train comes even though we sit-in for nearly an hour.

'I've just about had enough of this sit-in,' says Filip plaintively. 'I want to go home!'

'I think I've had enough too,' I say disconsolately.

So we stand up and set off south along Marshland Road.

Columns of cloud roll endlessly across the sky. And below us the earth lies waiting. As we walk farther and farther south we become melancholy and quiet. The highway stretches away in front of us getting smaller and smaller. It's like a nightmare. A black tarseal nightmare inside a strange false landscape of straight flat rows of vegetables and fruit trees in flat straight ploughed ridged paddocks and tall straight stalking rows of lopped poplars.

'Oh dear,' sighs Filip deeply. 'Isn't this jolly road ever going to end?'

I sigh deeply too.

And there doesn't seem to be anything to say. So we keep trudging along the darkening highway, each of us wrapped up in our own gloomy thoughts, two subdued silent boys.

'Not one adventure in a whole day,' says Filip ages later. 'Just grey road, grey road, grey road and nary an adventure.'

'Cheer up, be cool, I know how to make ourselves happy,' I say. 'And if you want to know too, you must repeat after me may the ground swallow me up, may hags rattle my dry bones and may I never more eat ice cream if I don't dutifully and zealously guard this secret with my life.'

'Alright, may the ground swallow me up, may old hags rattle my dry bones, and – etcetera.'

'Well, once upon a time I used to stand before the glass and look deep into my own unhappy eyes looking back at me and heave sighs such as: Oh cruel fate! Oh terrible lot! Only it turns out it's pointless. You know, heaving sighs. Nobody ever hears your sighs. Or wants to hear. So you have to stop. It's boring. You have to stop. And then you can be hip. You'll be in. Not out. Strike me pink and purple, you're the first person I've told!'

'Thank you for telling me,' says Filip wriggling with embarrassment but giving me a shy little bow.

'Thank you for saying thank you,' I shyly bow back.

'Stevan, I like you a lot.'

I probably get very pale about the nose.

'I like you a lot too, Filip.'

And then we have to get apples and pears from an honesty box. Marshland Road orchards nearly always sell fruit by the bag from roadside honesty boxes sitting on wooden struts. We select a box. I take more bags than I'm going to pay for. I put a florin in the slot.

I keep a shilling for myself.

Filip looks shocked.

I explain how Alan taught me that when you buy fruit or veges from an honesty box and follow Mum's orders by cheating the orchardists or market gardeners out of some of their money, you also make sure to cheat Mum. Alan punched my belly when I said it's double stealing. He told me to stop being a pansy.

'Aren't you too afraid to steal?' earnestly asks Filip.

'Yes,' I answer solemnly. 'But if we're not afraid how can we be really brave?'

We stow the bags of apples and pears inside our satchels.

'Well, that was a wrong thing to do,' says Filip, 'but at least we've had an adventure now!'

After fifteen more minutes we get home to Olivine Street.

'Oh, Mum!' exclaims one of the little kids. 'They're back from the Crossing!' Whereupon all the kids gather round us two travellers with cries of astonishment and admiration. Mum, slightly flurried, comes running and we fall into each other's arms and Mum bursts out: 'My darling child, I thought I'd never see you again!' And she looks with her green eyes into my green eyes. And with one of her red, freckly, fat mitts she strokes my soft brownish hair. And then she tells us there are some fresh gingernuts. And she starts putting out the new coffee cups with roses and lilies on them, even though we're much too young to drink coffee.

'Mum,' I say, 'is it all over now?'

'Yes, it's over, my little Stevan-child,' says Mum consolingly.

'We're quite startlingly weary, Mamma,' I say, opening my jaws wide in a most tired yawn.

'Ttt, everything is alright, I'm going to sing you a lullaby.'

And this is what she sings:

'Smoke gets in your eyes. You asked me if my love was true. You said someday you see venetian blinds.'

One has to discover everything for oneself. And get over it all alone. Of course that last bit is a story. The bit beginning with one of the little kids exclaiming 'Oh, Mum!' We haven't got any coffee cups, new or old, with or without roses and lilies. Filip and I in reality say goodbye at the corner of Voss Street and Olivine Street. He's still got another quarter of a mile to go. Poor weary Filip. William Bell, commercial traveller, sent to gaol for six years for indecent assault on males. Geoffrey Roff remanded for indecently assaulting a male. Ronald Sinclair imprisoned for three years on a charge of indecently assaulting another male.

After sitting-in at the Crossing we go on no other adventures, Filip and I.

Ian Harper, age eighteen, underpresser, indecently assaulting a male in New Brighton.

All we do is mooch at school, talking, walking, talking, looking at green caterpillars on the leaves of the red and white geraniums in front of our classroom, walking, talking, talking and walking. And it's nearly always Eric too. And Noel.

Our little gang of boys talks, and walks, round and round the perimeter of the mown green grounds.

And the bells ring.

A man, name suppressed, attempting to induce another male to do an indecent act at New Brighton. And it's spelling which is easy but boring. Or it's arithmetic which makes me sick. John Rumble, plastics factory worker, convicted on five charges of indecently assaulting a male in Spreydon Park; remanded to Sunnyside Mental Hospital. And the world goes round and round. Travel the Caltex way. Speedshaver de Luxe. The effortless ease of rotary action shaving.

I've got a girlfriend now. I often have a girlfriend. I had my first girlfriend after our family shifted to East Midland. Her name was Vicky Klein. My girlfriend now is Heather Newman. Heather's got blue eyes and flaxen tresses which she ties back from her pretty face in quite a long ponytail. She likes talking to me. Girls nearly always seem to like talking to me. Heather talks about her secret hiding hollow under a cabbage tree near Horseshoe Lake. One day she kisses me shyly on the cheek.

I probably go very pale about the nose.

Is this truly treasure, or only fleeting pleasure?

It's great having a girlfriend because if you're a boy you've got to have a girlfriend. My lady love she stands awaiting. On the banks I hear her calling. I live for love. I live just for my true love to see. Hand in hand we'll find love's promised land. I asked my love to take a walk, just a little walk. Will you still love me tomorrow? You get a girlfriend and when you both grow up you can marry. And buy a bungalow. And then you'll be really happy! Nobody but you. Sweetheart true. Cling close.

It's you I adore. You're my all. That's amore.

Mystery. Ecstasy. Trance.

Get in the groove!

And spring becomes summer. Oh, yes I'm just a pretender. And so on. Only it doesn't matter, my life is very good, in reality. Too real is this feeling of make-believe, too real when I feel what my heart can't conceal.

And now it's the summer holidays. It's hot and sunny.

Also, the Indian army has liberated Goa.

Democracy for Goa!

Filip must be happy. Only it's holidays, so I don't see him any more. Nor do I see Eric. I don't miss Eric. At home all us kids play on our back lawn. Our feet are really hard on the growing grass. Dad says. We're an eight-kid herd of heffalumps, he adds. The lawn's become hard beaten dirt. Anyway, John's still our hero. And Alan, he's still – well – to tell you the truth about him, he's a bully. Alan. A fat, farting thug. And Sissy's skinny and selfish and wild. And Noel, he's pulling wings off flies. And Ross sits alone a lot of the time and rocks backwards and forwards. And Jan gets teased and starts crying.

Sissy teases her a lot.

And also Alan.

Noel, too.

As for our wee brown berry boy, Peter, he's three now.

And we get in our car and go to the beach with some of our cousins and some of the Seven Sisters, Ilk of Forbes. We go to North Beach. We go to Woodend Beach. We go to South Brighton, Spencerville, Corsair Bay. And we've got a new car. Well, it's an old car. An old Dodge. It's twenty years old. How embarrassing. A car with a little chrome goat. On the bonnet. So we call the car the Silver Goat. And we don't only go to beaches, sometimes we go for walks in the Port Hills. We walk up the Rapaki track to the yellow tussocky saddle and then down to Corsair Bay.

Where we go swimming.

Or we walk up the Bridle Path to another yellow tussocky saddle and then down to Corsair Bay.

Where we go swimming.

And then you feel a wind getting up, and now and again a strong gust shakes the trees turning their leaves inside out. And you notice an army of clouds massing on the horizon before they march up the sky. Soon the bell will ring and the two gates open upon Term One at Quinns Road School.

What adventures will a swinging new 1962 bring?

Western Samoa gets its independence from us on the first day. One more democracy in Oceania! Let there be drums! Mr Eggleston is my teacher this year. He's alright. He's not marvellous. He's not Clarrie Jack. For example, he doesn't love Moominland. He likes Gilbert and Sullivan. And he doesn't sit us down for a story. He sits us down for The Mikado. Three little boys from school are we. Eric. Filip. Stevan. Mr Eggleston wears a fawn suit. And also he's got crinkly brylcreemed hair like Gladstone Gander.

So everything's alright but ordinary.

Eric. Filip. Stevan.

If you want to know who we are, we are gentlemen of Japan. On many a vase and jar, on many a screen and fan, we figure in lively paint. Our attitude's queer and quaint. Three little boys from school are we, pert as a schoolboy well can be, filled to the brim with boyish glee, three little boys from school!

Eric. Filip. Stevan.

Life is a joke that's just begun!

And we run outside to play. And our little gang of boys talks, and walks, round the perimeter of the mown green grounds. And the bells ring.

And we queue. And we march to our desks.

And we sit at our desks. Spelling, easy but boring. Arithmetic, makes me sick. Eric, Filip, I. And the bells ring. And we run out to eat our sandwiches and play. And we walk round the perimeter of the mown green grounds and talk, and walk, and talk. We talk about the new superliner, the France. She's chic. Dad says. It's French for smart, he says. A man's being tried for indecent assault on a male in the service station at Marshland. His name's been suppressed because he's got kids. She's the longest ocean liner in the history of the world.

After, we talk about the American astronaut who's taking the first ever space flight around our planet.

We really are in the Space Age!

Far out!

Only there's something wrong with Mum. She's going to have a baby. Which will be exciting. A little baby brother or sister to squeeze and cuddle! Only she doesn't seem to think it's very exciting. Mum. And she's worried about money. Dad brings home his pay in a brown paper packet. And him and Mum sit down at the yellow and silver Tubechrome dining table to talk about what to do with the money. Which is never enough to cover everything. Which is what they say.

'If we don't watch out we'll slip backwards,' says Mum.

'Things'll look up shortly,' says Dad. 'We'll be right enough in the long run, darling.'

Mum says: 'It's the bloody short run's got me stewing,'

Only she makes a snorting noise to show she's joking. So I don't need to worry. I think. And it's alright because Dad's doing lots of overtime to get us more money. He works nine hours every weekday. And he works six hours every Saturday. At Paramount Homes. Also, he gets paid for the time he travels to work. Which he does by riding a Puch.

Which is a power bike. It's made in Germany.

German workmanship is very good. Dad says. Also, he says, the power bike is economical to run, unlike the Silver Goat.

Only it can be hard to start the Puch.

One morning, up early, I stand quietly at the dinette window and watch Dad. He's outside in the backyard. The backyard is still dark. I feel sort of sad. It's the May holidays. At least, for us kids. It's hardly ever holidays for Dad. He's muffled in a weatherworn army coat, and a brown balaclava, and mittens knitted by Mum from carpet wool that she got cheap from someone who knows someone who works at a carpet factory called Feltex. Dad lifts the bike off its stand. He flicks the stand up. He climbs astride the vinyl saddle. And, rolling the machine down the drive, balancing himself upright as he rolls, he tries to start the motor by pedalling like hell.

The motor coughs, then stops.

Dad keeps pumping its pedals, working to make its motor kick over. To help him, I squeeze my eyes shut and try to will the motor to work.

Then, issuing wisps of blue smoke, off he putters.

'See you, Dad,' I whisper shyly.

Next time I see him is when he putters back up the drive for his tea. Dinner, I mean. And by the time he does, Mum's moody. As you know, she's often moody. Only now with the baby in her womb she's always snapping and snarling. That's what she says. Me with this baby in my womb. She snarls and snaps at us kids. She snaps and snarls at Dad. She says he rots his brain with boozing. And she says booze costs good bloody money. Well it's true Dad does like to stop in at the pub for a beer or two after work. And when he gets home his eyes are his usual eyes so brown they make you stare, only different, sort of shining. And when he walks into the kitchen you can smell his beery smell layered on top of cabbage and onions and boiling saveloys.

'Come on, Val,' he says, reaching out with one of those red, raw, scabbed hands of his, red and raw from working outside in the timberyard. 'Give us a cuddle.'

Mum doesn't like that. She shrugs him off.

'Leave me alone and eat your tea,' she says.

'Give us a kiss,' he keeps saying. 'Give us a cuddle.'

Mum just keeps silent and clenches her jaw. Dad asks what's for tea, and says something about what an appetite a man has, and what tasty dishes his beautiful wifey always has waiting. And what a tasty dish she is herself. Mum looks black. And poor Dad, I'm thinking. Why can't crabby old Mum leave you alone? You work hard, you need a beer.

'Give us a kiss,' he keeps saying, smooching the air as she snarls past.

At last, she's had it.

'You bloody pisshead!' she shouts. 'Pissing every bloody penny against the wall!'

Dad starts jumping round the kitchen, ducking and weaving, making a fool of himself in front of everybody.

'Give us a kiss, Val. You know I love you, give us a kiss.'

She hits out at him with one of her big freckly mitts, but he keeps weaving and ducking.

'Get out of it!' she starts roaring. 'Piss off you piss-brained boozer! Coming home all piss and wind. If you're so bloody fond of your boozer – '

'Give us a cuddle! Give us a kiss!'

She stands there, full of fury. She wants to kill him. You can see it. She wants to smash his face in. But she does nothing. She turns. She slams out of the kitchen. She bangs down the passage. Dad stands in the kitchen looking sort of stupid. Us kids have to take charge of things, finish getting the dishes washed and the rest of it. And at last Mum turns up again all red in the face after fifteen minutes or so smoking in the master bedroom.

'Fine life for some,' she mutters, slamming across to the electric jug. 'Fine bloody life!'

I write a story about money. I write a story about money and our family. Only I don't want to embarrass anyone in our family. So I call us the Browns. The story's called The Brown's Money Worries. The Browns live in a modern brick bungalow, in a modern street, in a modern suburb, in a modern city. Brian Brown is my name in the story. And our life is great except we've got two mortgages. So we're really short of money. Well we've got no money, hardly. Only the narrowest screw the shysters can be bothered flicking at us to keep us breathing, says Mrs Brown. And keep us breeding, says the eldest daughter sarcastically. Watch your cheek, you, says Mrs Brown. We'll have a family meeting, says Mr Brown. So we do. And we discuss ways to solve the problem of being short of money. And we start a lemonade stand. I get the idea from Huey, Dewey and Louie. Only we don't make any money selling lemonade because lemons cost money. So we give up the stand. And then one day we're looking in our loft. And, curiously enough, we find an old box that nobody ever noticed before. And it's full of jewels.

So we're rich. So we don't have money worries any more.

And we all live happily ever after, for ever and ever.

I write a full stop at the end of the story.

I turn the page.

I start writing another story.

I write the family newspaper too. It's called the Grigg Gazette. I write it on two-sided sheets. I lift the sheets carefully from the middle of my school exercise books. You need to be very careful indeed not to rip those flimsy white leaves of paper on the gleaming steel staples. White leaves lined with thin blue lines, horizontally. And one red line, vertically. Two-sided sheets hip for story writing since they're already sliced up into lots and lots of neat, straight, white, oblongs. I mark some of the white oblongs with stripes and dots. Other white oblongs I leave hollow.

Which is what a story is, isn't it?

A story is dots and stripes inside hollow, white, dry, oblongs.

John taught me vertical and horizontal. You need those two words for geometry. I already knew oblong. Anyway, my Grigg Gazette stories are mostly about the family. I write about what John's been doing lately. You know, delivering groceries for Four Square. Delivering tins of poached peaches, packets of sugar, cigarette packs, on his bike. I wish I had a bike. I tell my readers amusing tales of customers he meets on the job. And I write about what the rest of us are doing. Sissy breaking the twist record in our family. She twisted one hour and six minutes and thirty-three seconds without stopping.

Also, I write about Noel doing jigsaws.

And Ross rocking.

It can be tricky work, you know, making everyone in the family sound interesting.

I write quite a long story about what name would be a good one if the baby turns out to be a boy. I think we should call him Philip Eldred Grigg. We've agreed on a girl's name already. Faye Ellen Grigg. Faye because it means fairy. Mum when she was a little girl wished she was a fairy. Ellen because it's the name of our lovely grandmother Grigg. Who's dead now. Also, in one edition of the Grigg Gazette I write a story about how fat Mum's getting these days. You know, how her belly's swelling with the baby like a line of washing in a southerly. I tell my readers that we'll have a competition for the funniest nickname to call Mum.

Sissy wins.

Mum's new nickname is Waddling Womb.

Sissy wins because it's not only funny it's got good alliteration. Glad Egg says. He says, mind you, it's pretty tough on your poor mother. And, he says, a word between the wise, best to keep it under your hat. I wouldn't say anything about that nickname to your mother or anyone outside the family. Childbirth can be very hard on mums you know, lad.

Of course I know. Also I happen to know it can be somewhat hard on lads.

Anyway, I gazette lots of things. Did you know you the word gazette can be a verb? Interesting, isn't it? One thing that I gazette, for example, is how we might have to concrete over the back lawn because of the grass dying. You know, because of the pounding feet of the herd of eight heffalumps. Concrete can be a verb too. Soon to be a herd of nine heffalumps. Also, I write about things happening elsewhere in the city. And in the whole of East Midland. And other provinces. And sometimes I write about things happening elsewhere in the world.

And the galaxy.

I flog my stories of world happenings from The Press. Nihil Utile Quod Non Honestum. I get my galaxy stories from a very cool picture book, with fabulous modern diagrams, you can look at in the school library. All I do is change the wording so that it's better. You know, the way the words go.

Father and son found guilty of receiving stolen goods.

Titan missile explodes in underground silo.

Christchurch city's parking needs.

The Jew's heritage.

Faye Ellen, our new baby sister, is born on a winter's day. Mum brings her home in the Silver Goat. She's snuggled up in a lemon yellow nylon suit. Faye, not Mum. And she's very pink. And she smells of milk. And a little trail of milky dribble's slithering down her pudgy little chin to drip onto the nylon. And we all line up to take turns holding her, which is quite scary because you have to be very very careful to hold the back of her head. Otherwise her neck might snap!

I love the new baby.

It's cool to have someone to cuddle. Peter's too big now. Also, a boy. All us bigger kids keep elbowing one another day after day to have a go cuddling Faye. Or squeezing. Or smelling the milk. Or patting to help her bring her wind up. Peter doesn't. He sits on the floor rocking.

At first Faye sleeps in the master bedroom with Mum and Dad. And then there's a big regrouping. Which is a word you find in war comics. Dad says we need to regroup with some urgency now that there's nine heffalumps in the herd. Soon we're all dragging beds and bunks. The bedroom with the cowboy wallpaper becomes the girls' bedroom, which means the cowboy wallpaper will need to be covered over with white and pink ballerina wallpaper. Or pink and white bunny rabbit wallpaper. Also, us four youngest boys are broken up. Noel, Ross and Peter have to shift into the dark back bedroom. A bedroom that never gets any sun. A south facing bedroom. And I have to shift into the sunroom with the big boys.

So, fabulous!

I'm a big boy now, like Alan and John!

Only I'm not, in reality. I'm only me. Anyway, John and I sleep in the steel bunks. He sleeps below. I sleep on top. Alan sleeps in a single bed. Its springs have gone. And the sunroom's a nice room and really sunny. Well that's obvious, isn't it? It's why it's called the sunroom. I've told you already how it's all rays of light. Rays lasering through glass. White rays. Not death rays. And it's great being with the big boys. Only now that it's winter the sunroom is really cold. All those windows on three sides mean that unless the sun shines it's freezing.

And the sun in winter doesn't shine very bright anyway.

Also I wish John and I weren't sharing the room with fat, farting Alan. Alan's sort of like a freckly fist. I don't know why. Why is he so rough? Although actually when you catch sight of him out of the corner of your eye you might notice that he looks lost. At night when the three of us are in bed and the light's still on because we're reading he looks sort of worried, hunched over a war comic.

I'm always scared he's going to thump me.

Which sometimes he does. Mum tells him to, sometimes.

Only it's alright because John will keep an eye out for me when he's not too busy looking after the little kids, and doing his grocery deliveries, and helping Mum. Which he does a lot. Also at least I'm not in the south facing bedroom. A few weeks after we regroup one of the boys in that room gets sick. Ross, who wakes up hot and sweaty. He's shaking. His teeth are chattering. And he says his elbows, and wrists, and knees, and ankles, are all hurting. They're red and puffy. Mum takes him to the doctor. The doctor says it looks like rheumatic fever, which is serious, he says. He says to take him to the hospital. So Mum does. Ross has to get injections and stay for a few nights.

And when he comes home from hospital he has to stay in bed and get more injections and be waited on hand and foot.

Which is what Mum says.

'Well seeing there's always more work for the usual suspect,' she adds meaningfully.

Mum's got Ross to look after. She's got Faye to look after. She's got all the housework. Cooking and washing clothes and all that for nine kids. And she's turned sort of sallow. Mum. I think she's sick. Has she got rheumatic fever too? She's lost weight. Not only from having the baby. Her skin's sort of puckering. All she does these days, when she's got a minute, is sit herself down in front of the kitchen incinerator, staring into the firebox.

She sits there looking at hunks of wood burning.

Staring into the fiery, fuming, sooty, steel, black, brittle, pit of the firebox. And feeling sorry for herself. We do too. You know, us kids. We stare into the firebox too. A black steel firebox with yellow and red fire at its sweating centre. Mum sits with a fag. Moaning. Too bloody many of us in this bloody house. Coming close to the end of my tether. Sappy sweating wood blackening into scorched ash, charcoal, soot, smoke, choke, can't breathe, can't breathe, choke, smoke, black dog, choke, pig trotter, don't squeeze me so tight, beaten, eaten burning biting fire blue white red yellow.

'Sorry you're so sick, Mum,' I say.

'Hmf,' she says.

'When I feel blue,' I start singing quietly. 'All I have to do is dream, dream – '

'Cut out that singing,' she snaps. 'Gets my goat the way you're bloody singing all bloody day long.'

'Sorry, Mum,' I say. 'I'll try not to sing.'

'Hmf,' she says.

I'm fed up with Mum. Also I'm fed up with Dad. They're adults. Why can't they be cool? I don't care when sallow loose skinned puckering moody Mum nags Dad. And also I don't care when beery hoppy Dad with his torn blistered bleeding dukes comes dancing through the doorway flashing a silly grin getting ready to be soppy and smack kisses at Mum.

No, I do not care!

I feel sick.

And then Peter starts wetting the bed. Which is the last straw. Mum says. Peter's no longer our little merry brown berry. He's crying, rocking. On the first morning after wetting the bed he tries to squeeze himself into a corner of the kitchen next to the airing cupboard. Watery snot runs out of his nose and drips off his chin. The way milky dribble drips off Faye's chin. The snot drips onto his jersey. Cheap. Warm. Scratchy. A jersey knitted by Mum.

Knit one, purl two.

Lincoln green shot through with heather purple.

Snot cupped in small, colourless, transparent balls on top of rough green wool. The snot looks like dew on weeds.

'I'm so-so-sorry,' sobs Peter.

And all of a sudden Mum's bellowing.

'Filthy little bugger! All I need on top of everything else, kid's piss!'

You can understand her fury, can't you? You know, how every morning he wets the bed she has to strip all its soaked bedding. She has to wash the worn cotton sheets. She has to squeeze the sheets through the electric mangle. She has to sponge warm water on the big wet blobs of wizz in the worn woollen blankets. She has to squeeze the blankets through the electric mangle. Cursing. She has to grab the box of pegs. She has to go outside and hang the whole lot on the rotary clothesline, which is new. It's a Suparotary. A super spinning wheel of slim steel spokes and a web of twisted wires. A wheel as wide as any three of the Seven Sisters if they were to lay themselves head to foot, flat, in the backyard.

Anyhow, Mum has to peg her way through the whole cold load.

The rotary clothesline, as soon as she lets it go, starts spinning. Flapping its deadweight of wet wool and clammy cotton. The effortless ease of rotary action shaving. Philishave Speedshaver de Luxe. Mum meanwhile drags the sodden mattress outside and leans it against a brick wall to try to dry it out. And it's the middle of winter.

Often as not she has to do it all again next day.

And then the day after that day.

And her rage is terrifying.

And Peter sobbing.

All of us other kids are watching. Wishing. Wanting to do something to make it stop. And knowing we don't know anything that will. Make it stop. One cold morning, Faye's got colic. Ross has woken up with his rheumatic fever a lot worse. Also the Puch won't start so Dad's taken the Silver Goat. Which leaves Mum with no wheels. She stumps into the south facing bedroom. She reaches out with her big meaty mitt. She gets a good grip around Peter's wee white neck. And she shoves him down on the stinky mattress. She rubs his nose into the stinky mattress.

Then she yanks him back up.

Peter's sobbing and sobbing, gulping for breath, his face all smeared and slimy and slippery.

'Stop blubbing!' she's shrieking. 'Shut your bloody gob, you little shit!'

She's scaring herself. I can tell. She's scaring herself witless. Which frightens me more than anything. Mum, till now – well she's always seemed sure of herself – she's always seemed to think, whenever things go wrong, that she's in the right. Not now. A look of terror. A look of terror after she yanks Peter up, scrags him up off the sopping mattress. Terror because she knows that she's not in control of things. Not even here, here inside our bungalow, in our cul-de-sac. Here, where we all thought that she was, more or less, in control – well, no!

She's not.

In control. Nobody's in control.

Mum's not only beside herself, she's beyond herself. Out in space. Away beyond Alpha Centauri. And we're here, us kids. We're trapped here inside our suburb of violet hyacinth, yellow pansy, extra medication in Anacin, Ipana toothpaste with hexachlorophene, Peter Stuyvesant Miracle Filter, Suparotary, steel manhole, insecticide, herbicide, radiogram, teak veneer, toll operator, age seventeen, two charges of indecent assault on a male, remanded to psychiatric hospital.

Anything can happen in our suburb.

In our cul-de-sac.

And it will.

'Essay topics,' says Gladstone Eggstone. 'Girls are to write about how to prepare a christening breakfast. Boys are to write about how to pitch a tent.' Which is typical of what he gets us to do. Gladstone's so ordinary. His lessons are nearly always very boring. We sit in rows at our desks. We sit in solemn silence in a dull, dark dock, in a pestilential prison, with a life-long lock. And we know that we're not even waiting for something excitingly nasty like a short, sharp shock from a cheap and chippy chopper on a big black block. All we're waiting for is to be bored some more.

'How to pitch a – ?' I say to Filip. 'Glad's so square he's a cube.'

Which is also more geometry. Filip rolls his eyes.

'Glad's a wretched wretch,' says Filip.

I've only ever seen a tent pitched once, when I went with Aunty Bella and Uncle Charley and them on a camping expedition to Le Bons Bay. You know, near where the French colony was in olden days. On the Peninsula. The main thing I remember from the expedition is Aunty Bella, swearing, laughing, squatting on a tussock, drinking whisky from a plastic cup.

'The first step in pitching a tent,' I write, 'is to seek out solid ground.'

Which seems safe enough.

'Hard or rocky ground is not suitable, nor is sand or light soil. You have to have a hammer to drive in the stakes. You need stakes and ropes to hold the tent up.'

What else?

'And then,' I write, 'you drive to a motel.'

Not that I've ever stayed in a motel, but I will one day.

'This is a funny little essay, lad,' Mr Eggleston says to me next morning.

He's sitting behind his big desk at the top of the class. I'm sitting behind my little desk in the middle of the class. He flicks my exercise book into the air. It falls with a smack on my desk. I look up at Mr Eggleston. He looks down at me.

I want to cry. I want to cry and cry and cry.

Please be kind to me, Mr Eggleston.

I don't cry.

'This is a funny little world and you're a funny little man, Mr Eggleston,' I say.

A second exercise book spins towards me. It bounces against my chest. It tumbles into my lap.

'Don't you get smart with me, lad,' says Glad Egg. 'You might talk rubbish at home, but you won't talk rubbish here. You might think you're smart, but let me tell you, lad, I'll teach you to be smart.'

He stops. He seems ashamed. He looks over his shoulder. Perhaps he's thinks he's been seen by somebody. The headmaster, perhaps. Or the infant mistress. Although we're not her province. Her province isn't Standards. Her province is only Infants. Or perhaps Glad Egg's looking over his shoulder because he's worried he's been seen by a school inspector.

'You can't, sob, talk like that,' I say. 'You can't, sob, say things like that.'

Glad Egg bends down to me in an awkward clumsy sort of way. And he drops a hand on my shoulder. It's not heavy.

'Come on laddie,' he says. 'Cheer up now.'

'Sob,' I say. 'Sob, sob.'

'What's a few words between friends?' he says, giving me a pat.

'Get your dirty paw off me,' I say, and the hand's gone, and I keep talking in the voice of authority. I hope it sounds like the voice of authority. 'I'm going to see the headmaster. I'm going home to see my mother. You're a bully. I'm going to tell my father. He's a

Grigg. I'm going to have you sacked.'

Only somehow I think that the more threats you make the less they work.

So I shut up. And I stand up. My little chair screams as I scrape it across the green and brown linoleum. Desks hit out at me as I scurry towards the door. I swing the door open. I slam it shut behind me. Only what next? I'm in the corridor of the Standards Block. A long straight tunnel, varnished, polished, waxed, white-fluorescent-tube-lit.

I don't know what to do.

I look left along the long waxed corridor. I look right along the long waxed corridor.

Glad Egg comes flustering out of the classroom. His wavy hair is sticking out on one side where I think he must have been scratching it. Glad's been scratching those brylcreemed waves on my behalf. He thinks I'm the sort of boy who needs what they call special vigilance. I don't know why. Anyway, for some reason he does. So he'll put up with things from me that he won't put up with from other boys.

'Stevan,' he says, 'Let's see if we can't square things between us, son.'

Son! Yes, we certainly can square things. Good old Glad! I love you, Mr Gladstone Eggston! I want to grab you tight in my skinny arms and bury my hurting head and rest my hollow chest and the whole of me right into you. You're nice, even though you're not Clarrie Jack!

'Alright,' I say sullenly.

Marilyn Monroe kills herself. Which is hard to believe. Yesterday she was alive, Marilyn. And a star. And now she's dead. Which is scary. And exciting. The school grounds in winter are sort of bottle green and forest green and emerald and dark and lank and tufty. And a lot of worm casts. It must be very exciting to kill yourself. It must be much more interesting than walking, and talking, and talking, and walking, round and round the green grassy periphery of our grounds. And bells ringing. And desks in straight rows. Spelling. Arithmetic.

It makes me sick.

'An overdose of sleeping pills and chloral hydrate,' says Filip in a melancholy tone, but quite proud of being able to say the last bit.

'Poor Miss Monroe,' I say, also in a melancholy tone.

'Let's mark her sad decease with one minute's silence,' says Filip, stopping just before the west gateway.

One gate in the west. One gate in the east. Alleluya! If you look eastwards from the west gateway you see Standards Block, Primers Block, Infants Block. And if you look westwards you see a steel mesh fence at the boundary of the school grounds. And the black tarseal and white and yellow markings of Quinns Road. And a naked row of willows vibrating in an easterly. Willow wands in winter are cinnamon and orange and yellow. On the wands are fat buds the colour of teak. And on the other side of the willows you see a long winding row of two-storey state houses. A pink one, a blue one, a green one, a yellow one.

Gulls are flying overhead on the easterly.

And the sky is full of bright sunlight. Sky blue. Also the sky's full of smog. Orange. A light ginger. A faint amber. Specks of black soot. A silver plane, high overhead, layers a vapour trail above the smog.

Ross gets better from rheumatic fever. Peter stops wetting the bed. Mum starts fattening up. She gets her old colour back. Red! And her wee green piggy eyes are bright. And the sun's shining. And our windows are pink Windolene clean, with DDT. And flowers are flowering. And on weekdays it's not cold inside the house any more. And the twist's still twisting.

Also there's now the mashed potato. Crazy, man! Our whole scene's rocking!

And the locomotion. Everyone's doing a new dance, now. Baby, do the locomotion! Come on, Filip, do the locomotion with me! Yeah, it's easier than studying your ABC.

Australia. Bechuanaland.

Cuba.

The United States and the Soviet Union have worked themselves into a lather over Cuba. That's what they say, Mum and Dad. All the Seven Sisters. And the uncles. And other mums and dads. All of them think the Soviet Union and the United States need to grow up. And so do I. And all us kids.

'What about the nuclear missiles the Yanks have got in Turkey?' says Dad. 'Missiles pointed at Ivan!'

'Yanks are a mob of skites and know-alls,' says Mum. 'Mind you, some of their pop songs are good.'

Dad says, 'It's just two fighting cocks.'

'Wouldn't mind another world war anyway,' grunts Mum. 'Might make a change.'

And she's joking. And Dad says, 'Well it'd certainly be good for carrion eaters.'

And Mum grins and says, 'And rats.'

'Rats are carrion eaters,' says Dad.

And Mum says, laughing, 'Yeah, well you'd know because you mightn't be a Yank but you're a bloody know-all.'

Which is sort of true, to be honest. Only, getting back to nuclear war, well she's right. Mum. For once. A nuclear war would be exciting. I think about it a lot. Silver planes. Dove grey missiles. The beaks of the doves painted coal black, like lipstick on a black-and-white movie starlet in the Forties. Shiny warheads dropping like dew from a high blue sky. A new crop. Creamy mushrooms popping up. Puffily opening out.

Blood boiling in your veins while you're dying.

Crying.

Afterwards, a rust coloured toadstool, a cocoa coloured toadstool, doing the twist in the sky. Next, iron grey. Charcoal grey. Black. A nuclear war would hold us all spellbound. Nonetheless, I can't talk about it with anyone!

Not even Filip.

Instead I think about it secretly and darkly.

And we'd be alright. I mean us in Midland. Although it'd be horrible for the world. You know, those toadstools doing the twist over Leningrad and Washington and Tokyo and New York and Moscow and Peking and Berlin and Buenos Aires. It'd be really horrible for nearly everybody. Only we'd be alright. Midland. Also, after the warring nations lobbed their bombs and knocked one another out, the dust would settle and we wouldn't have to sit around saying nothing while listening to the adults talking about the old war. We'd have a new war to talk about.

And it'd be a much much more modern war than the last war, not to mention the war before the last war.

So that would be the coolest of the cool!

Filip, if I told him about these dark thoughts, would say something about how it's not kind. And he's right. It's not. It's coldhearted to think this way. Only I do. It's really hard not to. And it's really hard not being able to say so. Not being able to tell anybody. Always you have to keep your thoughts secret, don't you? Nobody will like you if you tell them about the secret you. If you spell out how your heart's cold, icy and green like a spring fresh in the Waimakariri.

And then I don't need to say anything anyway. The nuclear missile crisis turns out to be boring.

Nobody lobs bombs. Mr Khrushchev talks to Mr Kennedy. Mr Kennedy talks to Mr Khrushchev. And they see sense, says Dad. All the adults are saying how sensible they are, Mr Khrushchev and Mr Kennedy. Adults are sometimes very boring.

Almost always, actually.

We've opened our presents under the tree. My best present is a chemistry set. After, we're going to drive to Trevillick. We're going to spend the day there with the other Griggs. You know, our cousins and uncles and aunts and our Pop. Eldred Grigg. We quite often go to Trevillick to be with other Griggs. And before we go we have to get tidy. Mum says. All the cousins will be tidy, she says. She's not having them looking down their noses at us. We might be poor but we keep our noses clean.

Only we don't.

I think we're a bit dirty, in reality.

Also it's a battle to get us tidy. Mum wants us all to dress decent, for example. That's what she says. She should say decently. Anyway, she makes me wear my best grey shorts. And my best shirt. Which is an orange and lime green tartan. Quite a cool tartan.

'Clan McMadeup,' playfully says Dad.

'Oh, Dad, get a job,' I respond, rolling my eyes sarcastically.

Mum makes us line up to get our hair bashed. Which is what we say when she says she's going to brush our hair. After, she sits on the vinyl seat of one of the Tubechrome dining chairs to tug nylons over her varicose veins. And she grunts while she's doing it. And next she says ttt when she pouts her thin lips to smear them with bright pink lipstick. And she says nothing when she pats a bit of powder onto her veiny bony nose and her big red veiny cheeks.

She probably feels like swearing.

Only all the other ladies at Trevillick will be wearing powder and lipstick. And nylons. And suits. And what you call court shoes.

And strings of beads. Pearls!

And then we cram as best as we can into the Silver Goat.

Off we go!

Travel the Caltex Way. Jan's sitting on my lap. Her bum's a bit bony. We drive through the suburbs. The white lines of streets, and avenues, and roads, are flicking against the glass of the car windows. No speck. Only sparkle. I turn to the left. I see streets and streets, houses and houses. I look to the right. I see houses and houses, streets and streets. The countryside comes next, the flat dry paddocks and dry dusty plantations. Carry me back to de ole plantation, de whistle o de steamboat coming round de bend. And then hours of driving. Well it's not quite two hours, in reality. Only it seems ages. And the car stinks inside of petrol and cigarette smoke and baby.

'I spy with my little eye,' says Dad, trying to make us stop moaning about how it's too hot.

He grips the steering wheel tightly. He goes through the gears. He guns the juice. The Silver Goat careens down State Highway One, pounding the tarred black highway at an illegal sixty. No, now it's nearly seventy –

'Gun it more, Dad!' most of us kids are yelling.

We thunder along at seventy.

State Highway One!

The enormous Rakaia river glitters under a climbing sun, knit one, purl two. Silver water, turquoise. It's a wonderful vast river, a sister river of the vast wonderful Waimakariri. After which, paddocks. Green, hedged, gated, wired. At last, Dad starts slowing. He changes gear. We wheel off the tarseal. The black rubber tyres of the Silver Goat da-dack da-dack across a cattle stop. Dad changes gear again. And the black rubber tyres pancake in the grey gravel and white dust of a long straight driveway. We send up a white cloud like a mushroom cloud blown sideways. And our tyres da-dack da-

dack across another cattle stop. We pass through a lot of big trees. A wide lawn, scorched pale, swells ahead of us. A hiss of shingle as Dad swings the steering wheel of the Silver Goat. And we come to a crunching stop at the homestead.

Which is a house from olden days.

The Griggs are different from Mum's family. The Griggs have got money. Grigg. Gilbert. Eldred. Ellen. Treleaven, Trevillick. Almost every single acre of the province used to be owned by the moneyed with the sheep stations, says Dad. And, adds Mum pointedly, they were toffs and snobs. Often, Dad admits. Although, he adds, there was a certain rightness. Wearing whites while playing croquet. Or tippling at tea, or whisky, on a shady veranda. A certain largeness about being seated firmly, yet lightly, on a good well oiled saddle on the glossy back of a good mount in fine fettle looking at a baaing mob of wellbred sheep being driven in the dust of a hot norwester by shepherds with dogs and whips.

And before the olden days of the moneyed with the sheep stations, the name of the tribe living here was Kai Tahu.

You know, in the olden olden days.

Interesting, isn't it?

Anyway, now we've come to our hissing crunching stop at Trevillick. A bald, pink, old gentleman in a dark grey suit is sitting on the veranda. Pop. He's waving at us with his cane. He's smiling. Eldred, which is his name, which I've told you already, is an old, old, family name. Trevillick is an old, old, family name too. Pop's very, very, very, important in the County. He used to be chairman of the County. And chairman of the Ashburton Hospital Board. Also, president of the Upper Ashburton Agricultural and Pastoral Society.

Only it's extraordinary how boring it can be, Trevillick.

Pop and the uncles and aunts sit around with glasses and

cigarettes. Well, a pipe for Pop. And they talk about cricket. And they talk about sheep. And the roast lamb and roast fowl get taken outside and get set down on top of stiff white tablecloths on top of a long trestle table on the croquet lawn. And the peas with mint and gravy and mint sauce and new potatoes boiled in their skins. And all the rest of what you eat on Christmas Day. And afterwards the pudding. And the cake.

And you have to be very good.

And you have to wait.

You sit. You stand. Perhaps you think about strolling pensively through the plantations and out into the paddocks. Only you're not allowed to go out into the paddocks. Christmas Day is a day when we can't do interesting farm things. Or even play cowboys. All because of what we're wearing. We haven't brought a change of clothes and we can't stay overnight at Trevillick. Trevillick's got quite a few beds, but not enough for us Olivine Street Griggs.

Which makes us feel proud for being such a big family.

And ashamed for being such a big family.

And disappointed, because it'd be great to stay for a holiday at Trevillick. Griggs have owned the land here for years and years and years. Only they look down on us, I think. Aunty Audrey, for example. Who looks like Dad. She's his only sister. Quite snooty when she's had more than a whiskey or two.

Often, in other words.

Aunty Audrey speaks tartly when she thinks we can't hear what she's saying.

'Don't give Gilbert any more money, Pops,' she whispers after the cake cutting.

I'm hiding behind a clipped hedge. He can't have been giving a lot. Pop. I've never seen any of his money. Only it's worrying. How much poorer would we be if he hadn't been giving us money?

'Why not, Aud?' he murmurs. 'I worry about those kids.'

'No point chucking good money after bad,' hisses back Aunty Audrey. 'He's lost his grip, Pops. She's dragging him down. And he lets her. He's hopeless. He might be my brother but he's the author of his own sorry story. All those kids. And, insult to injury, theft as a servant, for christ's sake!'

Aunty Audrey is a well dressed lady, only she doesn't know what she's talking about.

Dad's not a thief. Dad's very honest.

Mum's the thief.

Anyway, as I was saying, Griggs have owned the land here since olden days. Not only Trevillick. We owned a whole estate in olden days. An estate well over two thousand acres, and five thousand sheep, and I don't know how many paddocks of wheat. And it was named after a famous and mysterious old tree that was really ancient and historic.

Which was the Single Tree.

A story about it was in a newspaper years ago. You can still see the clipping at Trevillick. A story written when Dad was a teenager. Which is an odd thing to think about. Dad as a teenager.

He probably even thought he was mod!

He must have been super square.

Anyway, the story says that the Single Tree looks old, indeed one would almost say dead. It is not a giant. It has no spreading branches. It has scraggy branchlets on a bare dark trunk. Yet every year a few leaves appear on its spare trunk. The tree gives no shelter. It stands in the way of the plough. The Griggs, however, let it stay. The Single Tree will see out her days. She is sacred. Maori relics have been found round the spot. Many legendary stories of the tree are told. The true name for the tree is Hine Paaka. The name of a high ranking chieftaness.

It's really extraordinary!

The Story of Hine Paaka in Days of Yore.

Only it's sad, there's no Single Tree any more. She blew down in a big winter storm during the war. Or right after the war. Anyway, when Dad and so many other dads were in the army. Fighting for bloody democracy and effing freedom. Which is what Mum always says about the war while rolling her eyes most sarcastically.

One day we should plant a new Hine Paaka.

It'd be cool, don't you think?

Anyway, the adults talk about the history of Singletree. Single Tree. Hine Paaka. And about our olden days properties in Cornwall. And about our modern days properties in East Midland. And about the district, which is Alford Forest. And about the township, which is Methven. And about the County.

Also they talk about horses. And sheep.

And more about the County.

Cricket. The Lakes.

Ice skating.

Cousins.

Crops.

And now it's New Year's Eve. Tomorrow will be 1963! Let there be drums! After sunset I go into our backyard and see, glittering under electric light, the twisted black wires and galvanized steel cylinder of the Suparotary. I think about how easy it would be to hang myself from one of those wires on that slowly spinning wheel. Admittedly, only while I'm a boy.

I'll be too tall to hang myself if I wait too long.

It would make quite a good story. A True Tale of Mod Days: Boy Hanged for Being Alive.

Only that's not my story, in reality.

Is it?

I look away from the Suparotary. I look up at the night sky. I see the six white stars of the Southern Cross. Can we cross the Southern Cross? Also I see what looks like the twinkle of a Sputnik. Strike me pink! And, looking even higher into the black sky, I see millions more white stars. And I think to myself even stars aren't the limit these days.

I'm young!

Nobody's ever been young before. We're the first.

We're so cool. We tell a glistening star, the way a dreamer will often do. All our nights we hope, we pray, a dream lover will come and stay. Police, prison, handcuff, fist, shackle, shekel, straight, square, spy, bully, money. A raging river pulls us down. Tapping down a street with rhythm in our shoes, tapping away our blues, Mr Tap Toe.

And in a few weeks it'll be time for the new school year and I'm going to Shirley Intermediate.

Far out!

It's exciting, bewildering and perplexing. I'm sick of being a little kid. It's not at all interesting. I want to be a big boy. A clever big boy like John. Not a thug of a big boy like Alan. Anyway, on the radiogram the Tornados are playing Telstar. Which is cool, and top of the pops.

INTERWAR MINERVA

You go south all the way down Marshland Road. You know, the opposite way from the way you go if you want to get to the Crossing at Chaneys Corner. You go south towards a busy point in our suburb where four arterial roads come together and cross. So it's also a Crossing. What a beautiful city! One arterial is Marshland Road. The others are Shirley Road, New Brighton Road and North Parade.

Four arterial roads in our quarter of the city.

I love the name North Parade. Although actually the parade goes south from the Crossing.

Why not call it South Parade?

Anyway, you go south for one mile from our cul-de-sac. You pass two rows of pink, and green, and blue, and yellow bungalows. Painted bungalows. Wood, brick, glass, steel bungalows.

Not bungalows made of ticky-tacky.

Two long straight rows of bungalows bowered in flowery sunburned gardens. Millions of flowers! Larkspur. Foxglove. Hollyhock. Marigold. Michaelmas daisy. Candytuft. Zinnia. Aster – orange asters – indigo asters – violet asters – carmine asters. You go all the way south past the hundreds of flowery bowers of bungalow until you get to the Crossing. A busy Crossing. Very busy. A glass and concrete warehouse. A concrete and glass service station. A brick and concrete and glass block of shops. A twin block of shops. And a brick and concrete Methodist church with a stubby spire. Cars zoom through all day.

Also at the Crossing you find Shirley Intermediate School.

Which is my new school. Which was built between the wars, Dad says.

'It's an interwar intermediate,' he adds.

Which you can tell he thinks is witty.

Which it is, sort of.

Well, to get back to the story, my new school is interesting. It's cool. It's a very extensive school. It's got seven blocks. Seven blocks in the school! What a beautiful school! And the blocks are long and low. And there's a huge assembly hall. And a huge library. And an underground cellar. Concrete. Which is where kids and teachers used to go during air raid drills. You know, in the war. Wouldn't it be groovy being at school in a war and having air raids!

You can give yourself the creeps thinking about huddling inside the cellar knowing that Japanese bombs would soon be dropping.

Robert Tiller, age nineteen, guilty of committing an indecent act on a male.

Sissy's also at Shirley Intermediate. Form Two. And Eric. In the same class as I. Filip's gone to Xavier College. It's because of his family being Catholic. So we're no longer three little boys from the seminary. We're only two little boys. Anyway, the entrance to the Main Block of Shirley Intermediate School has got eight white pillars. And above them, on what you call a pediment, is the name of the school in Latin lettering. All spanking white with glossy Taubmans. And because of the eight pillars, and long wide verandas on the long low blocks, the school looks a bit like an olden days homestead on a sheep station belonging to a moneyed family somewhere in the County.

And my teacher at Shirley Inter is startlingly extraordinary! My teacher is the remarkable Tory bluestocking, Miss Denise Blackman.

And the class is Form One A.

Which means the top.

Swinging!

One or two of the new words I wrote just now I only know because of Miss Blackman. Bluestocking. Bower. Denise Blackman likes being asked about words. And she likes me for asking. Denise B knows words the way Clarrie Jack says words.

Also she looks like a nanny goat.

A shrewd, sharp, smart nanny goat whose lips are narrow and crinkly. And whose white and pink skin is wrinkly. And she's a chain smoker. The brand she likes is du Maurier. Knowledgeable people smoke du Maurier. Eric says cigarettes are the reason why her lips and skin are crinkly and wrinkly.

'Aren't they like that because she's old?' I say pensively.

After a discussion, we agree that the reason she's crinkly and wrinkly is probably because of both things. You know. Smoking. Also, being old.

Kids from other classes when they talk about Miss Blackman say she's a crowsfooted old maid. A shrivelled spinster. However, when you're in her class you quickly understand that she's not. She's ardently wedded. Wedded to learning. Mark my words, class. Learning is the key to the world. Or, I dare say, the universe. Which may well be infinite, apparently. And it's my duty to learn you to learn, as my mother says occasionally when simulating yeoman simplicity –

Alison? It's Alison, isn't it? Alison Proctor?

Ah, good question, Alison. Yeowoman? No such word. Yeoman, countable noun. Also, adjective. Yeomanry, uncountable collective noun. My mother, elderly now, when young did yeoman service for the Red Cross in the First World War. My father fought in the East Midland Yeomanry Cavalry. This is an example of using the noun man to mean people collectively. We speak of man's progress when we mean progress brought about by all of us. All of us working together in an intelligent, efficient way. Men, women, girls and boys.

Well done, Alison.

Always ask, class. Ask, ask!

Resuming my theme, I pride myself on taking the very best care of my scholars. I know you are most intelligent youngsters. Additionally, you need to know that for two years, beginning this morning, you're going to be taught by the most intelligent teacher on the staff of this large school. Always alert. Often dry. Quick with words. Exact with words. Apt with words. I expect a great deal of you thirty young people who between you comprise the topmost new stream of Shirley Intermediate School. At the same time, you have every right to expect a great deal of me. We must always say what we mean, and mean what we say.

Dry nanny goat with crinkly narrow lips.

Cherry red lipstick.

I sit up smartly. I love Miss Blackman. I love her and I love our class. I expect a strong esprit de corps from you, class. Can anyone tell me the meaning of the French phrase I just used? Alison? Good try! Anyone else? No? Very well, how may we find the meaning of the phrase? Eric Wright? A dictionary? Correct! Eric, please stand and collect a copy of the classroom dictionary. And the rest of you, while your classmate is doing that little task for us, please look at the blackboard. I'll write the phrase for you.

Esprit de corps (Fr.)

Oops, isn't that wrong? Isn't corpse the right spelling?

Anyway, I love Miss Blackman. I love our class. I love Shirley Intermediate.

Nevertheless, I miss Filip. Notwithstanding, I've still got Eric. The two of us go to town together on weekends to watch movies or visit the East Midland Museum. One afternoon in early autumn, for example, we go by bus to the Square to see a matinée at the Tivoli. We queue at a booth to buy tickets for an Italian movie, It Happened in Rome. Rank Organisation. A loveable film crowded with loveable people, bright and gay. A blonde beehived laquered go-go girl-looking ticketseller sits behind a tinted curved glass hood sliding notes, coins, tickets, forwards and backwards.

'What do you think of Robot Cliff top of the pops yet again?' asks Eric.

I roll my eyes.

Summer Holiday is the boring name of the boring number Robot's just taken all the way up the charts to Number One. A song that sounds like the smell of green or yellow jelly.

Eric rolls his own eyes.

'You forgot to include the word farting between the and pops,' I observe drily.

Which is pretty racy by my standards, because unlike nearly every boy I seldom resort to swearing. Additionally, quite a few girls. Swearing isn't intelligent. Eric laughs. Upon which we change our theme and talk about the breakup of the Central African Federation. It was in this morning's The Press. After nine years the Federation is swiftly collapsing into an extraordinary morass of uncertainties. Instead of a cohesive multi-racial organism at the heart of Britain's former African empire, there will shortly be three divided territories, two dominated by black African nationalism and the third tending to bigotry of the kind made infamous today in South Africa. The collapse of the Federation must aggravate racial divisions, against which the moderating influence of the British presence will already have been lost, and may imperil the orderly development of all Africa.

'It's the racist whites in Southern Rhodesia who're to blame,' observes Eric.

'They're a drag, white racists, aren't they?' I reply coolly.

'Notwithstanding it's no great loss to the planet cause the Federation was a set-up from the beginning,' goes on Eric, swivelling his eyes sideways so he can peer at me bossily. 'They claimed it was a plan to unite three colonies into a mod democratic federal partnership, only it was – '

'One country for white tobacco farmers,' I cut in cause honestly who doesn't know about the constitution of the CAF! 'One country for white mineowners. One country to cram with white people's farmhands and mineworkers.'

'Wage slaves,' says Eric, aiming to set me right politically.

'Africans,' I say, setting him right in another way.

It Happened in Rome turns out to be alright but a bit weak. Luckily not as weak as Robot's Summer Holiday. Apropos, television's more interesting than movies in lots of ways. Movies were interwar. Tele's now. We've just bought an Autocrat. Every stay-home night's a time for fun with an Autocrat. We bought it on time payment. When friends say let's watch TV you'll show them an Autocrat picture so clear, so realistic, it takes you right there. John pays half what we owe on the tele out of his delivery boy wage from Four Square.

Additionally, Dad has started doing an evening shift at a factory. A bread factory. A factory in Essex Street. It makes SX Sliced. SX Sliced, plastic-wrapped white bread, one hundred percent white, pure, enriched, homecut. The difference between breakfast bedlam and kitchen calm! SX Sliced, distributed throughout East Midland.

SX Sliced, the adults seem to think, is somehow amusing.

Which is to do with the word sex.

Which is a male human and a female human getting seed and

egg together to make a baby. Or to feel good. A male or female of most other animal species, too. Also, trees. Sponges. And why should that be funny? Anyway, when you think about it, since the noun man can mean all people collectively can we say sex is man and man getting seed and seed together to make a baby?

Kinky.

Anyway, he does the shift once a week. Dad.

Also, Mum has started working as a charwoman. Which, needless to say, she's not happy about. And she doesn't mind telling you or anybody else about how she's not happy.

'We've got our bloody dream home,' she says scowlingly. 'And we have to skive our guts out to bloody pay for it.'

She cleans offices for the East Midland Hospital Board. It's somewhat embarrassing having a mother who works as a charwoman. Which is rough work. And pays poorly. She does it at nights after dishing us up our tea. Dinner. And when she gets home she nearly always brings what she says are her perks. Which is loot. Sheets of smooth white paper, which you call bond. And blue, red, black, green clicking plastic ballpoint pens. I like green best. And she brings home stainless steel paperclips. And rolls of white toilet paper. And red and yellow packets of Choysa tea. And anything else that's portable and not nailed down, as she says with a sort of hooting laugh when she's talking about it with some of the other Seven Sisters, Ilk of Forbes.

Olden days. Glasgow Gorbals. Ilk of Forbes. Free tickets to a new world. Steam across the sea, far away across the wide Missouri, back to de ole plantation, squeezed inside black, smoking, screwing, steel, riveted steamers, de whistle o de steamboat coming round de bend. Across the sea, the deep welling waters, all the way to an open breezy land, flat, fair, grassy, tussocks, lakes, wool, wilderness, gold. Work for all willing to work. Dock lambs on sheep stations.

Hump wool bales over wharves and break your back. Scrub floors. Hew coal. Tip out gentlemen's jerries. Skivvy. Get your mitts mashed by a threshing machine. Stitch yourself blind in a workshop sewing shoddy. Sick up your lungs from blackdamp. One dollar a day is black man's pay.

A sunny new territory.

Opportunity opening along the Midland Line.

All along the whole shining steel length of our old globe's newest trunk railway, lacing with blast-furnaced stays the wealthy waist of the Middle Island. Onwards, Ilk of Forbes, Glasgow Gorbals, South Christchurch! Tickets clipped here for the Midland Line of the Middle Island! East Midland to West Midland! West Midland to East Midland! Buy now, pay later! Best wage in the world. Coast to coast! Nothing succeeds like success. Travel the Caltex way.

Anyway, while it's a bit embarrassing to have a mother who goes out charring, it's fabulous when a deliveryman dressed in blue overalls comes one day and opens the back of a lorry and wheels out our Autocrat.

Which is silky and shiny and veneered with mahogany.

And the delivery man rolls it through our front vestibule and into our lounge. He's quite handsome, the delivery man. Eyes so brown they make you stare. And wearing black Bata Bullets. Actually, he's dreamy. If I was a girl, which I'm not, I'd like us to hold hands. He sees me looking at him. And winks! I think I probably get very pale about the nose. I look away from the man. I study the lounge wallpaper with great earnestness. The lounge wallpaper is rose grey. And pink roses in little green baskets. And it's carpeted now, too.

The lounge.

Although it's still pretty empty.

All we've got are a lounge suite and a china cabinet that we bought a year or so ago. The china cabinet is made from blond wood and sliding glass. Mum keeps it clean with Windolene. And behind its sliding glass, on lacy white nylon mats, sit a few bowls and saucers and cups. As for the lounge suite, it's Formfit. That's the brand. And it cost us eighty pounds. Which we pay off at one pound weekly. Or did Pop pay for it secretly? Additionally, it's upholstered with a cushioning synthetic made from oil. Superfoam. Mod! The colours are dark red and flecked grey. Also, it's contoured scientifically to fit the human form. And the corners of the suite are striped with smooth white piping. It's made to look like leather but it's vinyl. Which is also made from oil.

A lot of things are made from oil.

Man's progress!

And, until now, the suite has been sitting in a little group in front of the fireplace. And the cushioning synthetic, even though it's new, has started to get quite thin in some spots. And quite shiny. Also, already the white plastic piping has started to crack.

'Don't sit on those armchairs so much, yous kids,' says Mum, looking tired. 'You'll wear them out.'

'Where are we meant to sit, then?' says Sissy.

'On the floor. On your own fat bums.'

'We'll wear out our bums!'

Actually, our bums are all pretty skinny. Other than Mum's. Alan's, additionally.

The satiny new television makes the whole lounge seem to change shape, somehow. The Formfit couch and two armchairs sort of twist themselves away from the fireplace and turn towards the Autocrat. So does the china cabinet. The Autocrat, standing on its four chrome legs, draws everything into its big, blind, glowing, swelling eye.

'Good evening, viewers,' says a polite lady in pearls and a

beehive hairdo. 'Welcome to CHTV3.'

The polite lady, baring her teeth, aims her brassiere straight at our eyes.

We watch her fade. We watch the screen go blank. We watch credits roll up. I like best what you call situation comedy. Sitcoms about families living in city apartments and suburban bungalows. The Donna Reed Show. My Three Sons. Sitcoms about families who drive big finned cars and clown around with mod cons that play up.

The telescreen sitcom most in the groove is I Love Lucy.

Lucy's a shrill housewife and a dag. Viv, her best friend, is another shrill housewife. Also, a dag. They do no work other than the odd scrap of cooking or vacuuming. Which always goes wrong. And is funny. You laugh till you cry. Dig it, man! Lucy's a kooky redhead. Her eyes, when she works out something has gone wrong, will goggle. Uh oh! says a canned voice on the soundtrack. Lucy does a doubletake. After, it's nuclear kookiness.

Also, on our telescreen we watch the news. The opening credits are extraordinary.

The screen lights up.

'You know it's cathode rays, don't you?' Eric says.

'Naturally.'

Notwithstanding, I don't. Anyway, the glass screen lights up with a sunny sky. And a steel television tower. And electronic waves pulsing from a steel spike at its steel tip. And four white letters, N E W S, pop up from a point in the centre of the screen and radiate to the four corners. CHTV3 pops up, too. David Sutton, age thirty, company director, guilty of indecently assaulting a male at Avoca. Upon which, ladies and gentlemen dressed as if they're about to go out for a flash party in Cashmere tell us in plummy voices what the politicians have said, what the crimes are supposed to be, where the wars and disasters are.

'You'll get square eyes, you brainwashed gogglebox watchers,' says Dad in his droll way.

'Shhhh, Dad, you're spoiling it.'

I walk to Shirley Intermediate. I walk alone the whole mile all the way south to the Crossing. Guys wearing black leather jackets and oily greasy jeans are doing burn ups. You know, on their motorbikes. On the way to work at some factory. A burn up on their bike, that's what they like. All the other kids think I'm mad for walking. They ride pushbikes. I still haven't got a pushbike. I like walking. I like walking alone. It gives me time to think. It gives me time to think about writing.

You know, about writing this story.

Interesting how we make ourselves into a story, isn't it?

I don't care if they think I'm mad. Well, yes of course I do care. Only when they tease me about it you can tell they're sort of impressed, too. What they're thinking is that perhaps it isn't mad to walk a whole two miles every day when you could just bike. What they're thinking is that somehow I know something they don't know. I think that's what they're thinking.

However, I –

Miss Blackman pointed out to me that when I write a story I need to vary my vocabulary. Also, I mustn't use conversational language. I must use academic language. For example, the word anyway can be replaced by however, or nevertheless, or nonetheless, or resuming my theme, or picking up my thread, or be that as it may.

You've already noticed, haven't you, that I've begun varying my vocabulary?

'Moreover the meaning of the word or phrase you choose must not only be apt, Stevan,' she says. 'It must be true to tone and style.'

'Oh, I see. Thank you, Miss Blackman.'

Isn't she fabulous?

Resuming my theme, I walk every day. It's super walking all by myself. Cars, cars, a bus, a lorry, cars, cars, cars, green and flowery front yards. Primary school kids sloping along dove grey concrete paths. A mum in acid green slacks and lemon yellow cardy. A hen sparrow pecking. Cliff crooning out of a car radio. A carmine red Zephyr zapping past with open windows. A kindy kid in cobalt shorts smiling up at me from behind glossy pink pickets. I smile at him back. Gulls flying. Ants filing. A wee black and white dog sniffing. A marmalade cat sitting on top of an electric blue flowerpot.

And not only do I look at everything while I walk, I nearly always end up writing a story.

Only a little story.

Not a long story, like this story.

I write it in my head. It's curious. I walk past flowery bowered bungalows. I listen to cars hammering their way south or north, or about to turn sideways. I see boys in black leather jackets and oily greasy jeans doing burn ups. I see mums getting stuck in with new pink Windolene, now with DDT.

And the story grows and grows.

It's very curious.

At school as soon as I get into the cloakroom I open my satchel, get out my exercise book, squat on my hams and write down the story. After which I go and play with Eric.

Or else I sit and talk with my new girlfriend, who's Alison Proctor. She's clever and quick. Her eyes are green like mine, which is gear. Not many people have green eyes. And her hair is mousy brown, which additionally is like mine. Moreover, she's reasonably pretty. We hold hands in secret. And talk a lot. We talk about hit songs. Alison loves the Tornados and the Shadows. Also she loves Cliff. Which I skate around awkwardly by making out I can't speak because I've just swallowed a fly.

After which we talk about the fabulousness of Miss Blackman. I must be in love with Alison, I think.

I live for love. A secret love inside my heart. A secret love waiting to be free. Hand in hand we'll find love's promised land.

'Sweets,' she says one morning, giving me a slice of shortbread that she's taken from her yellow plastic lunchbox, 'for my sweet.'

Which of course is a line from that fairly cool new number by the Searchers.

I take the shortbread. I'm smiling shyly. I look inside my green plastic lunchbox. I see a little box of Sun-Maid Raisins. A little red and yellow box. Give 'em nature's treat. Sweet. Chewy. Full of energy. Rich in iron and other minerals. Gobblin' good! Arthur Ringdale, guilty of attempting to induce another male to commit an indecent act with him, fined twenty pounds. I pick up the little red and yellow box.

'Sugar for my honey,' I say, handing it to her.

Or in other words the next line from the disc by the Searchers. After which we talk about Chubby Checker. And the limbo rock. And about the Cascades. Who we agree are quite good. And about Skeeter Davis and Don't They Know It's the End of the World?

'Hey, what do you think of the Beatles?' suddenly says Alison.

'They're absolutely fab, aren't they?' says Eric half an hour later while the two of us stand in a queue of other boys waiting for the door to be unlocked so we can get into the Metalwork Block. 'The Beatles are the most.'

'They're not bad,' I respond calmly.

'They're the most!'

Eric always thinks he knows what's swinging and what's not swinging. He thinks he's really with-it. Additionally he thinks he knows not only what's in and what's out, but what's wrong, and what's right, and what's left, about every other thing. And furthermore, nearly everyone else has gone as ape as him – he? – over the Beatles. A pop group nobody heard about till now. Yet nevertheless everyone going ape! Twist and shout. And everyone's saying it's a new sound. A sound that's a bit like the Everly Brothers. Only it's something else as well.

It's a happening sound.

It's true, the Beatles are pretty good.

Moreover it would be neat if it does turn out that there's a new sound because a lot of hits in the charts right now are old sounds. Zombie Elvis. Robot Cliff. Hits like we listened to years ago. You know, rhythm and blues with a little rock'n'roll on the side. One group has just done a cover of a song that was a hit when I was still in my cot!

A love song sings of woe, ask me why I know.

Hi-lili, hi-lili, hi-lo.

A few new discs I do think are really cool. Frankie Vaughan has put one out called Loop de Loop. It's super. Mod pop. Loop de loop! Here we go loop de loop! Bop a bop! It don't mean a thing, but baby come and swing. Sex. And there's an even more super disc put out by the Rooftops. Walk right in! So mod, the Rooftops.

Do you want to lose your mind?

Baby, let your mind roll on.

So mod!

Sex.

Eric and I have started talking about the Rooftops because at last he's stopped going on about the Beatles. He says they're basically beat, the Rooftops. He says it's an old sound. I say it's a new sound. It's a cold sound. Eric doesn't know what I'm talking about. Nor do I. He steps sideways.

'Want to know the meaning of the words?' he says somewhat haughtily.

'What words?' I inquire wonderingly.

'The words of their latest song,' he briskly explains.

'Walk right in, do you want to lose your mind?' I say with calmness. 'Daddy, let your mind roll on?'

'Yes, it's a song about drugs,' Eric continues, trying to look important. 'Pot,' he adds informatively.

'Oh, I see,' I reply with continued calmness, although I don't know what people mean by drugs. Additionally, did he say pot or pop? 'Have you smoked, um, po – ?'

He squints at me trying to make me think he's Fidel Castro.

'Not yet,' he says darkly.

The metalwork teacher unlocks the door to the Metalwork Block. Not cool, man. I hate metalwork. All boys have to do metalwork and woodwork. Miss Blackman doesn't approve of her boys doing woodwork and metalwork. The notion, pretty picturesque when you think about it, that boys like you, who in the fullness of time are going to be doctors, lawyers, academics, need to know how to saw and glue planks of pinus radiata in order to make an ugly bookshelf badly.

DB can be so clever and funny.

Only she's not really right about woodwork. I quite like woodwork. I'm not handy with tools but I love wood. Furthermore, I've always loved wood. I love the scent of wood while you work it. And the colour of wood. And the grain. And well it feels sort of healthy and wholesome sliding a thin steel blade over white wood, and seeing, and feeling, and smelling, the peeling and –

'Good chap, manual dexterity developing,' says the woodwork teacher when he comes wandering by.

And, resuming my theme, metalwork is the opposite! I hate metalwork. Only it's not the metalwork teacher's fault. He's just not a very good teacher teaching a nasty type of work.

Steel strips. Steel wire.

Ugh!

Eric and I distract ourselves from metalwork by talking about the new Master Plan for Metropolitan Christchurch. It's going to be so super! Avenues will be turned into arterial. All the boring old oak trees will be cut down along FitzGerald Avenue, for example, to make space for six lanes of traffic. Additionally, old oaks will be felled and traffic lanes will be widened in Bealey Avenue and Moorhouse Avenue. Also, the planners want to SXSlice a new motorway through Hagley Park. Furthermore, other new motorways will carry people south of the city, north of the city and west of the city.

Of course many thousands of old fogeys are up in arms saying that the avenues are historic and that nobody may cut down the old oaks.

Which is silly.

'Hey, did you watch Fireball XL-5 last night?' asks Eric suddenly.

'What's that got to do with the Master Plan for Metropolitan Christchurch?' I reply coldly.

'I'm changing the theme,' says Eric.

'Oh well, yes of course I watched Fireball XL-5,' I say less coldly. 'Additionally, I saw XL-9 being attacked by death rays from that mystery spaceship.'

'Wasn't that so groovy?' says Eric. 'And Boris – and – what's her name again?'

'Griselda Space Spy,' I cut in eagerly. 'And they're plotting to steal XL-5 and fly it away to – '

And we talk for at least ten minutes about Fireball XL-5 while we drive drills into shrieking strips of steel. And we grip steel pliers to twist steel wire into spiny corkscrews. We then talk a bit about Denise B. Eric says that she reminds him of Minerva. He means the goddess. He probably reckons I've never heard of the goddess. He probably reckons this'll give him yet another chance to show how much more than me he knows about everything.

'Oh yes,' I say calmly. 'Miss Blackman certainly does resemble Minerva, goddess of wisdom, war, law, poetry, family, science, medicine, business and civilisation.'

He doesn't say anything.

So there mister smarty pants Eric Wright!

Upon which the two of us resume our earlier theme, the Master Plan for Metropolitan Christchurch. Motorways. Arterials. You'd think from the way the fogeys are wailing that parks are sacred or something. I like parks a lot. But they're only parks. Christchurch has got numerous large parks and numerous pocket parks. Almost every bungalow is inside its own little park. And we definitely do need a new network of arterials.

One weekend I draw my own plan of the Plan showing how cool the city and suburbs will look with all the new motorways. I draw it on the back of an old roll of wallpaper. My first task is to rough out everything in soft pencil. Afterwards, I ink it in with black ballpoint. A ballpoint flogged from the East Midland Hospital Board. I draw a row of oblongs. The colour key. I paint the oblongs, beginning with blue for water in the first oblong, ending with black for built-up in the last oblong. After which, I fill in the whole back of the wallpaper with black lines and washy watercolour. Paul Hanes, age seventeen, guilty of permitting a male to commit an indecent act upon him, and of committing sodomy. Upon which, I let the watercolours dry. Following which, I roll up the wallpaper. And, next morning, I stride eagerly towards school amidst the bowered flowering gardens of ice-cream-coloured bungalows.

I hold in my left hand my satchel.

And in my right hand I hold my plan of the Plan.

My plan is to show my plan of the Plan to our miraculous

Minerva of the Intermediate, our dear DB.

'Very pleasing work, neat and careful,' comments Miss B. 'Stevan, you're a reliable, intelligent, very promising pupil and the work you do, as a hobby, of towns and planning is most interesting.'

'Mbmbmrl,' I mumble, knowing I've gone very pale about the nose.

'You're rather diffident when speaking, however. Don't be afraid to exercise your lungs.'

I think I must get paler about the nose.

'I'm sorry, Miss Blackman.'

'And furthermore,' says Minerva, 'give your vocabulary an airing.'

'Certainly, Miss Blackman.' I speak up promptly. 'I'll try my very best to ventilate my vocabulary.'

DB gives a short, pleased nod of her nanny goat head with its wrinkled shiny red lips. A nod that makes the starched white cotton collar of her blouse give out a tiny rasp against the knit two, purl one, white green wings of her cardigan. And a little waft of scent and stale tobacco.

'You've made good progress,' she says. 'Your attainment is high for so young a boy.'

I feel happy!

I feel too happy!

I think I'll burst if Miss B keeps saying such wonderful things. I don't know where to look. Or what to think. Or what to feel. Or what to do when she says these things. I don't know what to say.

I have to change the subject!

'It's going to be super when we can drive anywhere really quickly on motorways,' I say clamorously. 'Why didn't they plan for motorways in olden days?'

Miss Blackman waits a beat before speaking crisply.

'And which days were the olden days, Stevan? Biblical times? The Twenties of this century? The Age of Enlightenment?'

I think I must go very pale about the nose.

'Oh, I mean, um – I mean the Forties of last century, Miss Blackman, when they first planned the city.'

Oh, what a beautiful city.

'Good. Now we know where we are. Very well. If you intend to specify events that occurred only during the course of that decade, then it's enough to name the years. Alternatively, if you're thinking of those events in a wider context, you could say the colonial period. Or if you're thinking of events in the context of the world, you could say the Victorian period. Or go further to specify early Victorian, or late Victorian, or mid Victorian period. Ditto as concerns the colonial period.'

'Are the Forties of last century early or mid or late colonial, Miss Blackman?'

'The colony was founded in 1840 and ceased in 1907 when we acquired dominion status. So what would you say?'

'Um, early?'

'Quite. Notwithstanding, history's an art not a science, Stevan. Thank heaven!'

So many super words need to be learned while we sit at the feet of our Intermediate Minerva. Additionally, super songs because there really is a new sound. A super new sound to be listened to on the turntable of our radiogram. Or over the airwaves. Or on the telescreen glowing like radium in the lounge. Furthermore, other super things on tele every night. Changing Asia. Johnny Devlin Show. Our Man in the Mediterranean. News from London. Think – before you light up! Cigarettes can cause lung cancer. Mervyn Chapman, age twenty-three, sentenced to three years in prison for committing an indecent act upon a male and one year in prison for attempted sodomy.

And it's winter, now.

Mornings not only cold and frosty but bright and sharp with spikes of yellow sunlight striking through the thin orange smog and hitting the chromed steel of cars and bouncing into my eyes while I make my way south on Marshland Road.

After, spring.

John says that for his fifteenth birthday he wants a blue denim Beatles suit. Which is jeans and a jacket. Which I think we won't be able to afford, unfortunately. He's already got a pair of black leather Beatles boots. Well, black vinyl.

On his birthday everyone crowds into the dinette and ogles a toothsome array. A yellow and silver Tubechrome tabletop laden with plate after plate of cream cakes, sponge rolls, custard squares, jelly, whipped cream, and a coffee and chocolate birthday cake. Whose fifteen candles are red, blue, pink, chartreuse, canary yellow. Mum brings in the birthday present. She's wrapped it in crumpled blue and yellow striped shiny paper. Mum's slapdash when she wraps things. Let's just say she's slapdash, full stop. Dad isn't home yet. Mum's baked the birthday cake and she's baked all the cream cakes. Now she hands over the present with her big red freckly fat dukes and watches him unwrap.

Excitedly, he tugs the paper away. We see that it's blue denim Beatles jeans and jacket.

How did we get the money? Pop slipped us it, probably.

'Flip, Mum!' says a moved John. 'It's beauty!'

We all feel very happy. Notwithstanding, we then start stuffing our gobs with cream cake.

After a while Dad comes wandering into the dinette and in a slightly beery style tries to kiss Mum. Who shrugs him away.

'I love you, sweetheart,' Dad says before turning to look at John.

'How's the birthday boy?'

John steps up.

'Thanks for the great birthday present, Dad,' he says, sort of very slightly bowing.

Dad holds out his right hand, which is bleeding and scabby from a day's work at the timberyard. John holds out his own right hand, which is white and pink. They shake hands. Dad looks at John through his beautiful brown eyes. John looks at Dad through his beautiful brown eyes.

Ach, mein Papa!

'And now,' says Dad, 'you'll want to buckle down a bit and start swotting for your School Cert.'

John goes somewhat pale about the nose.

'I don't want to stay at school, Dad,' he whispers a little hesitantly. 'I want to get a job.'

Dad steps back and stands for a while sort of swaying.

Which is only the beer.

'A job?' he says uncertainly.

'Yeah. A fulltime job, Dad. I've been asked if I want to be taken on as a sales assistant at the Four Square.'

Dad stands there in his boozy haze for a while before slowly understanding.

'No, you need your School Cert and afterwards your University Entrance,' he says helpfully as though he's talking to a spaceboy who just popped out of an interplanetary rocketship shot at us from an alien space base on one of the rings of Saturn. 'And you need to go to varsity.'

John looks down at the pick-up-sticks lino, which in spots is blobbed with whipped cream or streaked with squashed blackberry jelly.

'I don't want to go to varsity.'

'You can study law, or medicine. Or accountancy, like me. All I ask is that you set a good example to your younger brothers and sisters. You'll graduate, with a good degree. After you've been capped we can talk about getting you a job.'

'I'm sick of school, Dad. I'm bored by it.'

'School's designed to be boring.'

'I want proper wages.'

Dad seems less beery now. All of a sudden he seems to be standing very straight. And he seems to be – angry? Dad can't be angry. I've never seen him angry. Dad's not allowed to get angry. Mum's the one who's allowed to get angry. Additionally, if Dad gets angry – ?

'You're a top scholar,' he says coldly. 'Why be a wage worker?'

John's standing very straight, too.

'It's a good job working for Four Square. The boss says he's keen to take me on because he thinks I'm a quick learner and good with the customers and he can see me becoming a successful grocer with my own shop one day.'

'My eldest son, a grocer!'

Which is startling. Additionally, quite hurtful, in my opinion. Doesn't he care about his other sons? I don't mind if he doesn't care about Alan. I do mind if he doesn't care about Noel and Ross and Peter. They're just young. Furthermore, I do mind if he doesn't care about I.

'Well you're only a timber worker, Dad.'

'You think I'm happy working with my hands in a timberyard?'

'You never complain about it.'

'A man doesn't complain. He does his best to learn from his errors. Throw up study to work as a counter hopper and you're – '

Notwithstanding, he bites his tongue and doesn't say.

'I'm taking the job, Dad.'

'If you don't manage to make a fist of it at Four Square,' spits out Dad, 'you could always get an apprenticeship to a bloody plumber.'

We're all dumbstruck.

Dad!

Additionally, I don't know why he's so dismissive of grocers and plumbers. Grocers are rich, as everyone knows. And plumbers earn heaps and heaps. A Forbes plumber uncle's rolling in money. Mum says. She says he's coining cash fitting out new bungalow developments with copper pipes and chrome taps. Moreover, every family in our cul-de-sac is working class. Or so Mum says. Nevertheless, she's exaggerating. Three aren't. The dad in one family's a bookkeeper. Two are clerks. Admittedly all other dads in our blind street are drivers, drainlayers, factory hands, photoengravers, dental technicians, welders. Also, which is very interesting, nearly every family in the cul-de-sac has a surname that's English or Scottish.

'Nothing wrong with working in a shop,' mutters John.

And he's gone very still.

Very, very still.

Foster, Graham, Greig, Grigg, Hill, Hooker, Ramage, McLaren, Moore. One family has a Dutch name, Waterreus.

'Do what you damn well want, then!' says Dad.

And he's snarling!

At John!

Mr Waterreus is a bus driver. Another family has a Yugoslav name, Popovic. Mr Popovic works in a footwear factory. Also, another family we used to play with a lot, before the high paling fences went up, their name's Bang. Which I think is German. Mr Bang's a bread deliveryman. SX Sliced, plastic-wrapped, one hundred percent white, the difference between breakfast bedlam and kitchen calm!

And he stinks of beer, and cigarette smoke and sweat.

Dad, not Mr Bang.

And he stinks of being frightened and being angry.

And he sort of vanishes from the dinette. He vanishes like some stubbled overworked wizard without a wand who, if he was on stage, would be wearing thickly caked makeup with a cloak of richly sown – sewn? – glitter stars. You know, a wicked wizard in a pantomime about the christening of a princess. A princess who one day will be kissed awake by a handsome prince in a story once upon a time, a long time ago. Dad's scuffing down the passage in his holey green worksocks knitted in dozens by Mum from skeins of hocked wool. One of the Seven Sisters hocks them from a woollen mill where she chars. Dad wears workboots to and from the timberyard. And when he gets home he always leaves the boots outside to air on the concrete steps. So, when he's wandering around inside, the socks are always scuffing raspily.

It's because the wool is coarse, Mum says.

John doesn't say anything more but you can tell that he will indeed do what he damn well wants. Nevertheless he must be in shock.

We all must be in shock.

Well, I am certainly.

Dad – angry!

Or was he angry? Was he angry, in reality? Perhaps it was one of those many jokes he makes that are meant to be funny. Only they aren't. You know the kind of joke. Dad, I'm hungry. Pleased to meet you, Hungry, I'm Gil. Anyway, the next day, my birthday, he's his ordinary, kind, cheery, slightly irritating, silly self. I blow out eleven coloured candles.

Strike me pink! Only two weeks to go to the summer hols. President Kennedy has been shot. Quite a primitive nation in many ways, isn't it? United States of America. Get with it, young voters! Ads are saying. Ads for the National Party. This is the cigarette you've been waiting for – sweet, smooth, satisfying. Vast new industries for forest products, nylon, iron and steel, are going ahead with our progressive government giving young people better opportunity. Look for the smart modern pack! There's nothing like a Lucky! You taste and enjoy the man-size flavour that comes from the world's finest tobacco. Once every thirty minutes someone is killed or injured on our roads. National will take you into the Space Age. The statistics on our road deaths and injuries are the most terrible evidence of social tragedy to ever confront our nation. Our nation may be one of the first to develop the peacetime use of atomic energy – gamma ray sterilisation – in the interests of public health. Mobiloil Special offers you a top quality lubricant with an exceptionally low carbon-forming tendency.

Minerva of the interwar Intermediate continues to be miraculously marvellous and marvellously miraculous

We star pupils sit at our varnished wooden desks.

We sit industriously. Varnished desks with old indigo inkwells which we don't need any more because we use fountain pens. Mark my words, class, a good fountain pen makes for the best calligraphy. A ballpoint is barbarous. Be that as it may, we use ballpoints when DB isn't looking. I still like green best. And right now we're sweating, a bit, below the light violet shade of the high wide ceiling of our warm drowsy afternoon classroom of Form One A Shirley Intermediate. Next year, says our withered darling Denise, I'll give you two hours a week to learn the rudiments of French. It'll equip you with some grounding for your French in Form Three.

Man, can you dig it!

Esprit de corpse.

One more week goes by. Flintstones. Mister Ed. NZBC Newsreel. Scoreboard. Science Fiction Theatre. Laramie. Astaire Premier

Theatre. Weather and News. At a time when states are torn asunder by the passions provoked by racial discrimination, ours can set a helpful example, says Mr Holyoake, in a statement to mark the fifteenth anniversary of the Universal Declaration of Human Rights. Get in the groove with Teen 63. The United States Atomic Energy Commission has not disclosed the purpose of a nuclear powered satellite newly sent into orbit. Grandstand. Face To Face. Loop de loop. Bop a bop. CBS Television Workshop.

It don't mean a thing, but baby come and swing.

Daddy, let your mind roll on.

One more week.

And now it's the summer holidays. Summertime, summertime, sum sum summertime. No more learning history. Minerva, we're sorry, zip your lip. It's summertime. Summertime! Summertime, summertime, sum-sum-summertime.

It's so hip.

Watch me flip!

We grab towels and togs and stuff them and ourselves inside the Silver Goat. Upon which we head off to North Beach or South Brighton. Or Pines Beach. Victor Walsh, photoengraver, two years in prison for indecently assaulting another male. Or we go to the Groynes. We run under the willows. We eat cold ham and salad. We play bar-the-door. We go for swims in the cold streams. Moreover, we're always with one, or two, or three, of the other Seven Sisters, Ilk of Forbes. Additionally, their kids, our cousins.

And not witchy old Grandma Forbes.

She's dead now.

Hurray!

Mum and the aunties sit talking, singing, smoking, drinking tea on old woollen blankets spread on the dry grass. I love the smell of the dry warm grass. I love the smell of the warm dry earth. I love the slightly bushy smell of the tea. And the milk souring in the sun. And the Virginia tobacco. Carry me back to de ole plantation, de whistle o de steamboat coming round de bend. And the smell of river weeds. The Seven Sisters smoke, and sing, and laugh, and talk, and smoke, and sing. After it gets dark we troop into our cars and drive to our suburbs.

On the last day of the year we're sitting in the Square. Sissy, Noel, Ross, Jan, Peter, I. We've come blinking in the summer sunlight out of the Carlton. Which used to be the Crystal Palace. Only now it's been sheathed in shiny steel to look like a spaceship. Anyway, we're blinking. Stunned after sitting in darkness watching Sandra Dee in Take Her, She's Mine. A startlingly weak work of cinema. Sandra going through teenage growing pains. At first, a bikini babe. Upon which she flips and goes beat. And then fights for civil rights. She goes on a sit-in. And lands in gaol. Cinemascope Color. Twentieth Century-Fox.

We're waiting for the next bus to Shirley.

And while we sit, and wait, at the bus stop I understand suddenly.

I suddenly understand, in the most alarming way, how many hours of every day of every week of every year I stand, or I sit, waiting. Waiting for a red diesel bus. Waiting for a movie projector to start spinning. Waiting for school electric bells to shrill. Waiting for the slower kids to catch up. Waiting for cathode rays to start lasering their way outwards from the darkness at the heart of a big glowing glass eye. Waiting for ad breaks to stop. Waiting to get into the Metalwork Block.

When I don't even want to get into the Metalwork Block!

Do you want to lose your mind?

Mad.

And while I sit or stand waiting, I'm almost always looking at a white screen or white sheet or shiny desk. Reginald Jaggard, market gardener, three years in prison for indecently assaulting a male. Or looking up at a quiet, kind, sky blue sky.

At a round gold toadstool.

A shining white star.

Pig trotter.

Night.

'Let's twist,' I start singing. 'Yeah, twist –'

Sissy smacks my right cheek with her swift left hand.

'Stop being such a poof, people are looking,' she hisses. 'Why are you always such a poof?'

'I'm not a poof, I'm hip,' I say coolly.

'You're a drip. And why are you always sneaking into a corner to write weird things in those crazy exercise books you obviously flogged from the stationery stores at Shirley Intermediate?'

Yikes! Help! Help! SOS! SOS! SOS!

Nevertheless I keep calm.

'What exercise books?'

'Hah!' she says.

'Sissy, my exercise books are private.'

'Yeah, like anything's private in a family like ours where we can't even lock the toilet door because we're so useless someone went and lost the key.'

'We shouldn't have to lock our doors anyway. We live in a social democracy.'

'See – you talk like a poof!'

'Additionally, you shouldn't snoop at my private property.'

'Christ! You! Your bookwormy wee dream world! Making out nothing's happening when everything inside that sleazy dump in our blind street is so bad it's a wonder we're not all mad.'

Curious, isn't it, that she's thinking about madness too?

'Which we probably are anyway,' I try. 'Mad.'

'You especially!' she raps.

Notwithstanding, and picking up my thread, more often than looking up at the sky I'm looking down at my feet. When waiting. At the moment what I see at my feet is dry. Grey concrete dry. Dry dove grey. Also, marks in yellow paint. Yellow and dry. A colour of powdered mustard. The marks are arrowheads. Here! That's what they yell, those yellow dry arrowheads. Also they yell other things. There! Go! Stop! Turn! Slow! Additionally, at my feet, tarseal. Stone, tiny scraps of stone, sealed. Dove grey stonelets. Stuck black tar, black, dry.

Notwithstanding, I also make out tiny winks.

Black, tiny, white, sparkling winks.

Oily little winks.

Tar lights. White stars from black tar. White starlets of dead light shining from the slickness of tarred stonelets. Marilyn Monroe. Only she was a star, not a starlet. Furthermore, I can see a living thing. A lichen scab. A small silvery scab peeking from a concrete crack. The detective inspector commented that police observation of the accused did not disclose any attempts to contaminate young boys. A silvery lichen looking very sad and very lonely.

Only it's doltish to look at it that way.

Lichen doesn't feel anything.

Does it?

Apropos, do I?

Do you feel anything? We're great pretenders, pretending we're alright. Daddy, let your mind roll on. Collect a copy of the classroom dictionary. Knowledgeable people smoke du Maurier. Formica, practical luxury. Taste a Lucky, everything you want in a man's cigarette. Four Square. Four Seasons. Walk like a man. Twelve gates in the city. Talk like a man. Ten, nine, eight, seven, six – two, one – blast off, Fireball XL-5!

Mademoiselle Blackman plays us a record of Parisians talking to one another on a shining longplaying black plastic disc. A disc that she slides out of a glossy sophisticated slip. She bought the disc in France. Two nights in La Ville-Lumière. Which is Paris. Be that as it may, class, neon pulsing from many glass tubes may seem brilliant at first glance but anyone who chances to look down at their feet will note that few cities, when it comes to filthy footpaths, can trump the City of Light.

Un, deux, trois –

You speak through your nose a lot. Well, you grunt a lot.

Consequently, French is quite ugly. Which is disappointing. A further disappointment is that it turns out DB only knows a few hundred words. Which isn't many. Police state that lately there have been a number of what are known as queer-bashings, attacks on homosexual men, in Hagley Park. Additionally, I wish we were learning German. Denise says she thanks her stars she knows not one single word of German. Other than the words everyone knows. Waltz. Kaput. Goethe. Ach, mein Papa.

The Fatherland, says Miss B, was behind both world wars.

Of course almost everyone says so.

Which isn't interesting.

Notwithstanding, it's quite startling to learn that everything is either male or female in French. Even when it isn't! Female or male! Le crayon, for example, is what you say when you want to say pencil. A thing is male if you say le. Nevertheless, how can a pencil possibly be male? Furthermore, why do they call a pencil a crayon? What do they call a crayon? Minerva doesn't know. And a shirt is la chemise. Which is female because a thing is female if you say la.

Although who wears shirts?

Boys!

Want to be cool? Wear Continental sneakers! Allan Aberhart, shop assistant, beaten to death by youths in Hagley Park. Continentals – a high-class sneaker in hound-dog suede. A fab range of colours. Orange peel. Whippet. White nylon. Gold spice. Blood. Ming blue. Cinnamon. Butterscotch. Victim accused by youths of being homosexual. Ginger with raw wool. Raw wound. I ask Minerva why every noun is male or female and she says once more she doesn't know. Which is also disappointing.

'It just is, Stevan,' she says somewhat tersely. 'It's language, it's not rational.'

'I see, Miss Blackman.'

Nonetheless, I don't see.

Yes, quite definitely it's a disappointment. Français. Also, I don't see why languages can't be rational. Otherwise, if they're not rational, doesn't that mean they're irrational? Which is another word for mad! And although it's true the world's mad, as Sissy and I seemed to agree that hot dry afternoon at a bus stop in baking, tarsealed, concrete-kerbed, Cathedral Square, it's not true about words. Madness. Words are not mad. Worlds, yes. Words, no.

Words cannot be mad.

Other than words for madness.

You know. Loony. Moony. Batty. Bats.

Resuming my theme, somehow this year I've started to feel let down by Minerva. I know her ways. She knows my ways. And now she seems sort of stale. Well, to be quite frank she's deadly square. I still love the way she's spry, wry, National Party, Anglican, madeup, powder, blusher, crowsfoot, wrinkling, twinkling, lipstick, knowledgeable people smoke du Maurier. Promising work. Good work. Excellent Work. One so young. Minerva Interwar Intermediate.

L'homme noir is what they say for Blackman. L'homme means man.

Noir, as you've guessed already, means black.

So they say man black.

Not black man.

So we'd be saying Miss Manblack if our language followed the same rules as their language. Which it doesn't, fortunately. Blackman. An excellent word. Clever. Universe. Ink. Knit. White nanny goat. White green wool. Agate. Amber. Mother-of-pearl. Blackboard. White chalk. Powder. Compact. Plastic. Lipstick.

Anyway, not to labour my point, she doesn't get it.

About being swinging.

Esprit de corpse.

Pourquoi?

Mlle B doesn't understand that our generation know that things will go wrong if we don't do the twist. Mlle is the way you write mademoiselle. If we don't do the twist we'll spin slowly to a stop. Mademoiselle means miss. You can't breathe if you stop. Interwar Minerva is a dictionary definition of not mod. Baby, let your mind roll on. Daddy, do you want to lose your mind? I want to hold your hand. The Beatles. The Hollies. The Rolling Stones. Manfred Mann. Cilla Black.

Out of sight!

Six youths arrested for manslaughter of Allan Aberhart. A group of boys fifteen to seventeen years of age. We was bored. Attacked, kicked, bashed, robbed, left dying. Black is the colour of my true love's hair. Eyes so brown they make you stare.

Oh, what a beautiful city!

The Caltex Way.

Filip.

I start to cry. I cry and cry. I cry and cry and cry. Notwithstanding, it's alright. I'm not really crying. I'm dreaming. Dreaming, deeply sleeping, trolling the deeps of a moonless black night in the dark sunless sunroom of Eleven Olivine Street, Oceania. Sleeping in my top bunk, breathing slowly. John's breathing slowly below. Alan belches opposite. Only the more I cry in my dream the more I seem to need, somehow, to dream cry.

Why?

I dream cry and dream cry and cry and cry and cry cry cry cry cry –

A magpie, magpie, mad-pie, mad, mad – mad –

Quite frankly, it's somewhat scary.

If I keep crying I'll stop breathing. It's obvious. I'm just a lonely boy, lonely and blue. And it happens every night. It's been happening for years, actually. I've been dream crying for years and years. I was dream crying even when we lived in our old wooden house in Blackball. I go to sleep. I dream my dreams. Can't do nothing else, or so it seems. All my nights I hope, I pray, a dream lover will come and stay. Dream and cry and cry. Dream and cry and cry and cry and cry –

However, very fortunately it most certainly is not reality. As I've explained already.

The reality is that I'm safe and asleep in a sunless sunroom in a moonless night.

Consequently, it's alright.

I'm not crying.

I never cry.

Sheryll Blank is my new girlfriend. Her hair is black. Additionally, it's cut in a hairdo like Dinah Lee's. Do the blue beat. Blank is Dutch. Sheryll's dad comes from the Netherlands East Indies. You know, Indonesia. He's not an Indian. East Indian. A hairdo like a helmet on top. Reet petite. Mr Blank's white. He was a stoker on passenger liners run by the KPM Line. A Dutch shipping company. And, furthermore, a lacquered glossy point that stabs down each side of her head towards a slightly plump white chin. The Dutch were driven out by the Indonesians. Democracy for Indonesia! Sheryll's head is round, and white, with quick dark eyes. Also, she's very clever. She reads a lot, like me. And she writes stories, like me. And unlike me she belongs to a theatre group for young people called the East Midland Youth Players.

Which must be so fab!

'Yet here's a spot,' cries Sheryll, gripping her left wrist in her right fist and scowling. 'Out, damned spot!'

Our class are sitting at our desks looking on in awe while Sheryll rehearses her role as Lady Macbeth. Minerva asked her to. Sheryll can be a bit shy. Nevertheless, she can be brave too. So after going bright pink she stood up. And now she's gripping that wrist in front of the blackboard. And she's not Sheryll any more. She's a murderous royal lady in mediaeval Scotland. The theatre group and she are going to put on Macbeth for three nights in a row. They'll be putting it on in a school assembly hall in a suburb on the other side of the city!

'Hold the words, then spit them out,' whispers Minerva.

Sheryll holds, spits.

'Out, I say!'

Lady Macbeth is cruel. And she's cunning. She's talked her husband into killing his sovereign lord the King of Scots so she can become Queen of Scots. Seven Sisters, Ilk of Forbes. And now red spots of blood have started popping up on her skin. The red spots make her think of dead men's blood. And she's going mad.

'The thane of Fife had a wife: where is she now?'

Can she really see blood?

'What, will these hands ne'er be clean? All the perfumes of Arabia will not sweeten this little hand.'

'Good girl,' earnestly says Miss B. 'Very good.'

'Oh,' croaks Sheryll. 'Oh, oh!'

We all clap frantically after the scene is over and Sheryll gives a little bobbing bow.

'It's been a pleasure to watch you, Miss Actress,' says Denise.

Sheryll gives another little bobbing bow.

And then, when she looks up, she catches my eye.

And winks.

After school we hold hands on one of the tarseal basketball courts. Sheryll says she's not sure whether she wants to be an actress on stage or on screen. And she adds pensively that if in the end she does decide on screen she's not sure whether the best choice would be the movies or television. I tell her that whatever she chooses she's sure to be boss. Upon which she gives me a kiss on the lips. Only a quick little peck. Nonetheless it's my first ever SXSlicedy kiss on the lips.

Ever!

It's like being patted on the lip by a boiled brussels sprout.

A sprout boiled and left to cool till lukewarm. So that's not very exciting.

Notwithstanding, she's the most. Sheryll's super groovy. So aren't I lucky? Although her family isn't so groovy. The Blanks live in the Emmett Block. Which is state houses. Hundreds of state houses on tree-lined, twining, twisting streets and terraces and crescents. State house kids sit in the classrooms alongside us kids from private subdivisions built by Paramount Homes.

Also they play with us in the very extensive grounds.

And they look and talk like us.

Only somehow you always know who comes from a state house.
I can rattle off the names of all the state house kids in our class. I
feel sorry for those kids. I feel pleased, too. We might be hard up
but at least we don't live in a state house. At the same time, it's only
money. Isn't it? Gold spice. White nylon. Moreover, everyone in the
world is equal to everyone else in the world. The working class are
equal to capitalists. And the two sexes are equal, as everyone knows
nowadays.

Additionally, all races are equal. Be that as it may, Dad does say
that he's not so sure about Jews.

'Naturally,' he says, 'I never had any truck with Hitler.'

'Naturally,' says Stewey, a dad from next door.

'Mind you, one thing he did was spot on,' continues Dad. 'I only
wish he'd jolly well finished the job.'

Sheryll isn't a Jew. Her family are nothing. Mum's nothing, too. Dad
was brought up Anglican. A bishop gave him what supposedly was
a god's muscle and blood to eat and drink. Ugh! You call it
confirmation. Naturally it's nonsense, in reality. It's only a dry bit
of bread. And a sip of sour wine. It's not really oozing sinew and
damned spots. Dad was only pretending he was eating a god's
muscle and drinking a god's blood.

However, why would anyone want to do that?

Picking up my thread, when he was a boy he went to church
with his family because that's what families like theirs used to do.
Dad says it was all show. He doesn't go to church now. He says it's
silly.

'Why's it silly, Dad?' I ask one day.

'God in three persons, blessed trinity, and common sense out the
window – that's why!'

'Churches are just a racket,' says Mum.

Aztecs ripped out bleeding hearts from living chests before handing them over to Mixcoatl. You know, god of hunting and the night sky. Vicious. Nevertheless in every other way they were very quiet, and polite, and tidy. Aztecs. Anglicans are not unlike Aztecs. Anyway, Sheryll. My true love stands awaiting. On the banks I hear her calling to me, to me. Now I live just for my true love to see, to see. Resuming my theme, whenever I and she are by ourselves together talking in a very friendly way I don't really want another kiss. Or even to hold hands. I don't know why. And she doesn't try. Even though we both know very well that there's meant to be more to boyfriends and girlfriends than just talking.

There's meant to be Sliced. Plastic-wrapped, with lots of hot butter!

Candy man. My boy lollipop. Get in the groove. Twist and shout.

The whole scene's rocking.

Hippy hippy shake.

Marvellous Minerva tells us to team up to do group projects. Class, choose any disaster in our young nation at any point in its history. Any fire, flood, eruption, earthquake, shipwreck. Sheryll and I are in one group, along with another girl and another boy. We get out disaster books from the school library.

'Shipwrecks are cool,' I say. 'Why don't we do the Tararua?'

A steel screw passenger liner churning in darkness one cold morning of the late colonial period. A liner bound for Bluff. A huge liner, heavy. Steel bows slipping through swelling sea. Steam whistle shrieking. And ramming a reef off the Catlins. And sinking very slowly. Crowds clinging to rigging. Only the sea's very cold and by the time the ship slips below the swells nearly all the passengers and crew are dead.

Far out!

'Or the Wairarapa?' says the other boy, Roger.

Also late colonial period. A luxury steel screw steamship, one night churning through thick fog at almost full speed. A liner bound for Auckland. Sleek, huge, heavy. Tall steel smokestack. Painted, piped, spouting white steam, black smoke, into black sky. A spruce gentleman in top hat and stovepipes on the promenade deck. A lacquered cane. A silky lady in a bustle touches his elbow. Sweating Maori shearer. Stripped Negro slave. Carry me back to de ole plantation, de whistle o de steamboat coming round de bend. Boiler, furnace, stoker. Sweat. Coal. Fire. Soot.

Let the steam whistle cry. Away along the wide Missouri.

Roll on, old mighty Mississippi.

Toot! Toot!

And slamming into the cliffs of Great Barrier Island. Crowds clinging to rigging. Cold sea, wild. And more than half the passengers and crew drowning.

Ocean liners steaming onto rocks.

So exciting and so scary!

On Becoming a Man is a cheap thick book in a thick cheap cover showing a worried cleancut teenage boy walking in school grounds while wearing a khaki cardigan and navy blue jacket. Two teenage girls are ogling. All three kids don't look the least bit swinging. A book written by Harold Shryock, MD, who's not only a doctor but also a Christian. Nonetheless, I think his surname must be Jewish. Mum and Dad bought the book so we can understand about SXSliced. It's nice of them to try to help us boys.

Notwithstanding, it's very very out.

It says, for example, that teenage boys are masculine in their attitudes and somewhat rough and ready in their relations with the outside world. Teenage girls, on the other hand, are domestic in their inclinations, think feminine thoughts, and are fundamentally gentle in their relation to others.

Tell that to Sissy!

Sissy once burnt my foot with a red hot poker.

Additionally the book says that teenage boys, impelled by unwholesome curiosity, can fall into the habit of manipulating the sensitive tissues of the penis as a means of excitement. And that this is spoken of as masturbation. Which when it becomes a habit tends to rob a young man of his nervous energy. Moreover, the book says that if you're a boy and you like another boy it's a common and transient phase in your normal development. Any individual who develops an abnormal fondness for someone of his own SXSliced is described as being homoSXSlicedual. Which in its full-blown form involves the practising of certain physical intimacies between boys.

Which is against the law.

Furthermore, boys who behave homoSXSlicedually almost certainly have passed through some shocking experience when young. A healthy teenage boy will conscientiously suppress any fleeting youthful crush he may feel on some fit, healthy, hunky, sexy boy. Swinging guys relax in Sax Altman slacks. Sax Altman slacks cut sleek-hipped extra-low hip-hugging slimlegged woven with miracle new oil-based synthetic fibre Si-Ro-Set.

We're going to the chapel of love.

All I have to do is dream, dream – dream – dream –

Hiram Shylock MD says oracularly that reproductive organs in a teenage boy produce billions of spermatazoa more or less continuously. At the time parenthood is in prospect a boy implants those billions inside his wife's vagina. I have to look inside our biggest class dictionary. Subsequently, husband and wife together hope that one of those tiny billions will begin the miracle by which splitting cells invisible to the human eye slowly grow into embryo, foetus, newborn, baby, toddler, boy.

Sheryll isn't keen on the Wairarapa or the Tararua. Nor is the other girl, Annette.

'One of my aunties burnt to death in the Ballantynes fire,' she says plaintively. 'So can we do that?'

Upon which we talk for ages about the infamous Ballantynes department store inferno. A massive department store, very snooty. It killed lots of working-class girls. Girls who worked for the shop. Hundreds of girls worked for the shop. A holocaust. Girls killed by the bosses. Bosses locking them in to see to the money. Bosses will kill girls for money. Or so sing the Seven Sisters, Ilk of Forbes. Always a chorus croaks that the girls were killed by Mister Fat. Additionally, wassail our Sisters over cups of Choysa tea buy now price reduced fourpence per imperial pound, everybody in the streets was singing up.

Jump, yous kids! We stood down there helpless, held back by cops, and we sung up to the girls. Girls up behind glass in the high windows. Cause we could see what they couldn't see. It was coming.

What was coming?

Black.

And white. And red. Just jump!

Jump, girls! Everyone in the streets was singing it up. Girls, just jump!

So we hunt out stories about the holocaust. A story I like best comes from The Press. Nihil Utile Quod Non Honestum. A story they wrote on the day. Thousands of horror stricken spectators see screaming girls leap from third floor windows. One pregnant girl dies. Additionally, the fear that death has stalked among the flames is substantiated when the bodies of dead girls are seen in what was the furniture section display window. Moreover, more bodies are soon found lying in the smouldering ruins. High up on black steel girders molten bodies are hanging. The trapped girls got so hot their brains burst out of their skulls. And the brains went sugary in the heat. And furthermore, the blood boiled in their veins while they were dying.

A black steel firebox.

A lamb. A gallows. Scarlet blood. Yellow tallow.

Can't breathe coal steel smoke soot choke can't breathe can't breathe smoke choke black dog pig trotter can't can't help help help choke can't don't squeeze so tight beaten eaten burning biting fire red white yellow.

Mum with a smouldering fag.

Mum moaning.

'Too bloody many of us, can't bloody breathe for bloody kids,' she says one midwinter day, turning to me and snarling. 'And as for you, you lazy leech, you're nothing but a stuck-up prick.'

At home one day, when everyone's out at some uncool sports thing, I sneak into the master bedroom and strip off. I stand in front of the duchesse. I look at myself in its one fixed mirror, scalloped, and its two wing mirrors, also scalloped. Or really I'm looking at trillions of atoms of light bounced back-to-front. Did you know that? I found out from Eric. Notwithstanding, I did my best not to let him know it was news.

The three scalloped mirrors throw atomic rainbows to light up a room of dust.

A sheer, varnished, doily-lapped, compact-powder-strewn, veneered, varnished, composite top of the duchesse. A duchesse bought on time payment from Calder Mackay. All home needs. Best terms, low interest. Calder Mackay Company Ltd. A duchesse slammed together, quick, in a factory paying barely above award. A duchesse with fuddy-duddy fakewood front studded by stubby handles. Creamy ersatz ivory. Tar black mock ebony.

A duchess is the wife of a duke. Aristocracy, in other words. Sheep stations. Carry me back to de ole plantation. White wooden mansions. Highstepping steeds.

Sweating brown Maori shearers.

Stripped Negro slaves.

I don't know why you call this wooden not-with-it mirrored object a duchesse. Only you do. Anyway, one interesting thing is those two wing mirrors. Which swing in and out. Swinging! You look in the glass. You look. And you look. You see lots, and lots, and lots, of yous. Are yous kids Darkie's kids? You see yous in three-quarter profile. You see yous in two-quarter profile. You see yous in one-quarter profile. Very groovy. And then, looking, looking, looking even more, you see row after row of seemingly endless one-quarter and two-quarter and three-quarter profiles echoing into nothingness inside the glass.

Which one is reality?

Or in reality are they all reality?

Or somehow are these rows and rows and rows reality yet also not reality? Or none of them? Or none yet every one? You can get lost in those smooth scalloped mirror rows and rows and rows. I like getting lost in rows. Rainbows. Twelve gates in the city.

Alleluya!

'Hey, Annette?' says Sheryll. 'What department was your aunty working in when the fire broke out?'

'Millinery,' says Annette, before adding rather proudly, 'Which was one of the top departments in the whole of Ballantynes and my mum says working in that department was almost like having a profession.'

'What's millinery?' says Roger.

'Hats,' bluntly says Sheryll.

'Oh,' says Roger, in awe of Sheryll because she's so clever and cool.

'I wonder why we say millinery when we mean hats,' says

Annette thoughtfully.

'Yes!' I chip in brightly. 'Why don't we say hattery?'

'We'll look it up,' says Sheryll with decision. 'Roger, please stand and collect a copy of the classroom dictionary.'

Which he does, sheepishly.

The other three seem to take it for granted that I'm the one who looks inside the dictionary. And that I'm the one who quickly finds millinery between millibar and millwork. A millibar is a unit of air pressure in the metric system, commonly used in meteorology. So then you have to look up meteorology. Which turns out to be from Greek. And it comes from two words that mean high in the sky and study. Millwork is work you do in a mill. Which means a factory. The Seven Sisters, Ilk of Forbes, when young were millworkers. None was ever young. Millinery comes from the name of a city. Milan made costly deluxe clothing for the aristocracy. Travelling salesmen took the goods all over Europe. It was in the sixteenth century. The travelling salesmen came to be known as Milaners.

Isn't that interesting?

And did you know that the tribe living in East Midland in the sixteenth century was called Kati Mamoe?

And they made luxury clothes for their chiefs out of the finest woven flax.

Or dogskin.

You're probably wondering what I see when I look at my stripped self in the rainbow scalloped mirrors. Close your eyes and I'll kiss you. You know how I'll miss you. One fixed mirror. Two wing mirrors. All my loving I will give to you.

I see a white, skinny, boy.

A white cadaver, a corpse without esprit.

Wretched wretch. I see every one of my ribs. How can this ribby white weevil with limbs like strings become a man? I will, however.

Dad says. He says that I'm shooting up. Not that I've ever seen a weevil. Only you sort of guess it from the sound of the word, don't you? Resuming my theme, curiously I am becoming a man. Well, a teen. Incidentally, the correct name for this phase in your life is puberty.

After that comes adolescence. And etcetera etcetera.

The second-to-last phase is senescence.

The last phase is dead as a dodo.

If you look closely you'll see there's a few tiny hairs. Please don't look. I'm shy. Additionally, while I like looking at myself, nevertheless my eye right now is sort of wandering away. Away from the scalloped glass rainbow. And lighting on an old photo. A photo hanging on a steel wire. A steel wire hanging on a steel screw. A steel screw and steel wire hiding behind a slip of silver and tin chloride behind a thin sheet of glass inside a painted plaster oblong. An oblong of plaster painted to make out it's totara. And be that as it may, what you see behind the glass – you know, lasering a zigzag of light from the tin chloride and silver into my eyes – you see a hand-tinted boy cousin who died before I was even a baby.

Always was something wrong with that kid, says Grandma Forbes.

Who's still dead. As a dodo!

Let's twist again!

On Becoming a Man doesn't explain how to have SXSliced. Are you supposed to work it out by yourself? Or will the girl help you? Do you know by instinct? I'm quite scared I won't know how. At school other boys, whenever any of us are alone together with no girls, keep talking and joking and laughing, and generally getting excited, about SXSliced. And I never know what to say. Eric and two other boys go on about it when we sit together in a circle in a quiet corner of the grounds one day.

'Do you get hard all the time?' says one boy, Gordon.

'It drives me nuts!' says the other boy, Wayne.

'Me too!' says Eric.

I probably go very pale about the nose with embarrassment. And I don't say anything. I don't want to talk about SXSliced in this stupid childish way. SXSliced is something you save for the one you love. One of the less good things about my happy days here at Interwar Intermediate is that while I'm only eleven every other boy in my year is twelve or thirteen, which means they're ahead of me when it comes to growing up into teenagers. That's probably why they talk so boldly.

Eric's only eleven too. We're younger than the others because Glad Egg thought we were too intelligent to stay in Standard Three. Halfway through the year, therefore, he promoted us to Standard Four. And now here we are in Form Two. And still quite little boys, really.

Two little boys from the seminary.

Furthermore, if other boys are going to talk about SXSliced so disrespectfully then at least they could use the right words. Erections, not getting hard. It's in On Becoming a Man.

'Sometimes it stays hard for hours,' says Wayne. 'And it really hurts!'

'Mine does too,' says Gordon.

'Mine too,' adds Eric.

I look pointedly up into the sky blue sky.

After which the other three start talking about one of the masters at Shirley Boys High School. A biology teacher whose name is Fearon.

'Bummer Fearon,' says Gordon. 'That's what they call him'

'Old news!' says Wayne. 'Yeah, he fucks boys.'

'Yeah,' says Eric.

'Fucking sod!'

'Poofter!'

'Yeah!'

As you know, I don't like boys cursing and swearing.

'Why's Fearon going after a job with a piano delivery company?' says Wayne.

'Um – I don't know,' says Eric, trying to make it look like not knowing is somehow a way of rocking the bop.

'He wants to push organs up back passages.'

Sheryll, when we've worn ourselves out talking about the burning girls, says she thinks we should do an earthquake. The Hawkes Bay Earthquake. Additionally, she says, we should present our project as though it's a newspaper published in the early Thirties of this century. You know, a newspaper reporting the big story. And because she's sort of the leader of our group, that's what we do.

'Furthermore,' she says, 'Stevan should be the one who writes the front page headline story.'

'What about me?' says Roger

And she tells him he'll do drawing. Roger's good at drawing. I'm quite good at drawing too. Notwithstanding, we set to work. It's cool how everyone knows I love writing. And that I'm good at it. Our whole class knows who I am, and likes me, and is proud of me. I'm proud of them, too. And our Marvellous Mlle Minerva. Consequently, while I'm reading about the earthquake, taking notes about the earthquake, thinking what to say about the earthquake, then saying it over and over to myself, always trying to work out how to say it better, till it sounds right, and I know it off by heart, I'm happy.

I'm very happy. I'm very, very, exceedingly, excitingly, extravagantly, swimmingly, peacefully, singingly, happy.

Happy happy happy!

Mum has stopped cleaning offices for the East Midland Hospital Board. However, she's still embarrassing us by continuing to work as a charwoman. Mrs Mopping, says Mum. Mrs Mop is a man in a dress and a wig in a new tele advert for pink Windolene, now with DDT. A man dressed as a charwoman. She, or he, cleans with a rag and soapy water and a galvanised steel bucket. And is one of two contestants in a race to clean a window. The other contestant is Mrs Modern. A svelte young lady with a beehive hairdo, strutting on chic stilettos, she holds not a rag but a plastic bottle of Windolene.

And they're off!

Mrs Mop flexes her meaty sinews. She swirls her wet rag over glass. Suds are streaming. Mrs Mop sweats. Mrs Mod, on the other hand, sways, sashays. Calmly, slowly, she sweeps the glass with Windolene.

And wins the race, it goes without saying.

'It's so easy,' croaks Mrs Mop.

Resuming my theme, Mum's latest charring job is polishing vinyl floors in a Four Square. A new supermarket south of South Parade. The perks are good. Mum's swag, packed into a sugar bag, can be so heavy when she comes home on the power bike from Four Square that sometimes she nearly topples off. The tricky spot is two little bumps between the tarseal and a concrete strip. I tell myself, somewhat guiltily, that if she were to fall off it would be most amusing. You know, her loot and she getting flung from the Puch. Be that as it may, the power bike always comes wobbling and parrrping safely up our concrete driveway.

Upon which, Mum stumps into the kitchen and opens the swag. Revlon hairspray. A big yellow Gouda. A yellow and black can of Aero-Blast. Press the button and Aero-Blast kills!

Aero-Blast, now with Trimort.

Also, she nicks Raro.

Dad, meanwhile, has stopped working at the bread factory. It isn't worth the money, he says. He did the sums. He tallied up everything, including petrol. Of course Dad's skilled at arithmetic, which makes me sick. He's skilled because of studying accountancy at university. L'homme Noir says when I go to university I should study languages and history.

'Notwithstanding that those subjects are very interesting,' I reply pensively, 'to tell the truth what I'd like to study even more is story.'

DB looks at me slowly, carefully, and somewhat pityingly.

'For good or ill, Stevan, one cannot study story.'

'Oh. And is it for ill, Miss Blackman?'

Mlle knits her nanny goat brow.

'I should imagine for good.'

Anyway, start your day the five star way by making a glass of delicious invigorating Raro. Mum when she goes charring wears black slacks. Bri-nylon bulging over her big swollen thighs. On top she wears a jersey. Her bosoms are saggy. The jersey's burnt orange. Raro contains forty milligrams of natural Vitamin C in every hundred millilitres, the pure juice equivalent of up to two pounds of luscious sun-ripened oranges.

News Flash! Tragedy in Hawkes Bay. Ruin in Napier-Hastings. Buildings shuddered and crashed to the ground, burying people beneath them. Fire then broke out and swept over the ruins; the water mains were shattered so the people were unable to fight the flames. After the fire had burnt itself out, many once beautiful buildings like the Masonic Hotel, the Empire Theatre, the Main Post Office, Blythe's Building, and St Paul's Cathedral, were completely destroyed. The earthquake reduced much of Napier, Hastings, Wairoa, Waipawa, and Waipukurau to rubble. After the earthquake, the living citizens began the tragic search for the dead. Refugees are now being evacuated to several other cities. Every province has also promised to donate large sums of money to help rebuild the stricken cities.

One day when I come into our classroom I see a woman sitting at my desk. A goddess? Of course in reality it's marvy Mlle Minerva L'homme Noir. Not that I see the whole DB in the round. I only see a silhouette. A narrow black cutout against bright sunlight. I walk sideways. I see her in the round now. A cameo brooch at her soft, pink, powdered, wattled throat. A cardigan. green and grey.

Denise B looks up at me.

Her chin is sharp. I notice she's been looking at my story book. After which I notice that she's looking at me most pointedly.

'Stevan, I see you really are A Writer.'

I almost feel like swooning!

'Am I, Miss Blackman?'

'You are.'

'Flip!'

'Overlooking on this one occasion an inappropriate and, worse, uneducated word,' murmurs L'homme Noir, 'I'll take the opportunity to say you are a most interesting boy to teach, Stevan.'

I'm warm and happy.

I'm hot and sweaty and blushing.

My head's boiling hot. A sort of swelling. As though it's hot but green and growing. Sappy. My whole body feels it's poking a sharp green leaf up from a tiny split in oily black tarseal. And now it's swelling, welling. It's twining upwards. It's green and leafy. Alive.

Sebastian is a boy in Form Two B. So he's one class below. And I'm eleven and he's twelve. And I often see him in the grounds. He's got glowing olive skin. And thick glossy black hair. And eyes so brown they make you stare. He looks kind. And good. And his surname is Lam. Which is interesting. And although we never speak to one another I think somehow he sees me looking at him whenever he goes by with his friends in the grounds.

I look at him always. I think he likes me looking.

I think he likes me.

I like him.

Curiously, it's as though when I look at him we understand that a long time ago we were one boy. Somehow. And then we split in two. And we got lost. A yearning feeling deep inside. A yearning, yearning, burning. A burning feeling deep inside of me. My yearning stings my lips like a bee. And now we've found one another once more. We've found one another right here in curbed kerbed cropped cut grounds. Grounds beaten flat, black, grey, dry, tarseal, paint, lead, lawn, grass, scalped, green, orange, flower, white, stripes, sports, cyclone steel.

It's very odd.

Apparently, I want to talk with him and walk with him and once more become one whole boy. Or so I seem to know. Nonetheless, how do two boys even begin to become one whole boy? Actually, I don't even know how to walk up to him and say hello.

Can't buy me love. Love me do.

I don't know what to do.

Eric and I are sitting under the shade of a tree in the very extensive school grounds, discussing modern progress. Eric says the Mariner 4 space probe will show there's no life on Mars. I say he's wrong. Nevertheless, I'm afraid he's right. Anyway, we won't know the answer till winter next year when the probe starts sending its first tele pictures back from the Red Planet.

Always vary your vocabulary.

Voskhod 1 we talk about next. The first ever spaceship with more than one cosmonaut on board. After which we talk about the Shinkansen. Which is a new high-speed railway that shoots like a bullet from Tokyo to Osaka.

'We need one running from Invercargill to Auckland,' says Eric. 'With a suspension bridge over Cook Strait.'

'Wouldn't the tickets to ride on a high-speed railway be very expensive,' I say.

'The government could subsidise the tickets,' he says.

Unfortunately, I don't understand what he's saying. So instead of adding anything new to our discussion about high-speed railways I only say, yeah, it'd be fab. After which I start talking about the Rolling Stones. I love the Rolling Stones. Eric doesn't really like the Rolling Stones. He says that the grooviest groups right now are the Beatles and the Animals. Upon which I say, no, the hippest discs are by the Stones.

'No,' he says back. 'The Animals, and the Beatles.'

'No, the Stones,' I say. 'And the Kinks.'

Arthur Campbell, remanded for indecently assaulting a male. Alan Cunningham, cleaner, committed for indecent assault on a male at St Albans Park. Dennis Brown, canvasser, remanded. George Colvin, railway worker, remanded. Murray Stephenson, plasterer, prison. John Kaye, painter, prison. Norman Nicol, tally clerk, prison. Wilkie May, apprentice motor mechanic. Alexander Thomas, radio technician. James Church, television technician. Theo Waite, plastics factory hand.

Upon which we start talking about Doctor Who.

'Exterminate!' squawks Eric.

'Exterminate!' squawk I.

We're addicted to Doctor Who. It's a gas. Daleks are far out. And its credits are terrifying. Opening credits. You sit anxiously on the Superfoam upholstery of the Formfit suite in front of the veneered Autocrat. Wash your hair too clean for dandruff. Blue Clinic. Palmolive. You're soaking in it! Upon which the screen fills with strange, mysterious, swirling light. And your ears fill with

outlandish, thrilling, pulsing, deeply scary music. Yet you don't
know why you're so scared, or what, or how.

Or who.

Is that why it's called Doctor Who?

'You call it synthesised music,' says Eric. 'You make it from
test-tone oscillators and magnetic tape.'

'Yeah, I know,' I lie.

Wouldn't he just love to explain test-tone oscillators?

And suddenly it's the last day of the last term of Form Two A. A
shrinking row of girls and boys are waiting in line in front of DB's
desk. We're taking turns to say goodbye.

Vivienne, the girl in front of me, steps away from the desk.

Upon which I step up to the desk. And wait for our clever,
powdered, chain smoking, observant Anglican, Tory, bluestocking
Mlle Denise Minerva L'homme Noir, to look at me for one last time
and speak her last words. Dry nanny goat with crinkly narrow lips.
Knowledgeable people smoke du Maurier. Yet my eyes are drawn
from her lips to a book. A book lying flat on her desk. A book whose
glossy black cover has been sealed with see-through plastic. Blobs
of glossy red, and glossy orange, are splotched all over the glossy
black.

Janet Frame, says the book. The Edge of the Alphabet.

The white lettering on the black background of the cover of the
book makes me anxious. I wonder why. Space Age lettering. I think
of Sputniks. Daleks. Lasers. Philishave. Motorways.

'Um, what's that story about, Miss Blackman?'

I point at the book rather helplessly.

'Mmm – ?' says Miss B.

Exterminate!

'Is it a book about spelling?' I ask helpfully.

Minerva seems suddenly restless. And even shy, slightly.

Opening the book without asking, I look at its last words. I always look at the last words. Of a story. Not to learn how a story works out. A story doesn't work out. A story works in. I look at the last words of a story because, when you're looking, you have to begin somewhere, don't you?

After all, who says a story only goes one way?

And what do its last words say?

The edge of the alphabet where words crumble and all forms of communication between the living are useless. We are captives of the captive dead. We are like those yellow birds which are kept apart from their kind – you see their cages hanging in windows, in the sun – because otherwise they would never learn the language of their captors.

'To be quite honest,' says Denise, 'I can't begin to grasp what it's about, Stevan.'

'Oh,' I whisper. 'So it's not about spelling, Miss B?'

Upon which she looks hard at me, then back at the book.

'Miss B, is it? Hmf. Yes, to some extent certainly it's about spelling, and spells. Notwithstanding – I – well, I confess I'm at a loss for words. But now, down to business. Our farewells. Stevan, you've produced consistently high results for one so young. Additionally, you've been very well-behaved and co-operative.'

Upon which I feel a tear sliding into my left eye.

'I love you, Miss B.'

Denise looks at me from over her desktop and speaks drily.

'It's been a pleasure to teach you, Master Writer. Always take pains to vary your vocabulary. Now, please become the young man you already indeed are becoming. Chin up!'

So my chin does go up. A young man naturally always does put his chin up when adults tell him to.

A little approving nod from DB.

And away she looks.

CLANG! CLANG!

Opening my eyes, seeing light, I look up from two white pillows, Persil clean. White light. White light whirling. What? Is it a telescreen? Am I seeing the opening credits for Doctor Who?

I blink, hard.

A quick blackness.

Blackness lasered loosely with rays of red, ochre, madden, magenta, indigo, lime, sulphur. You know, when I blink. Additionally, I see that the rays are crossing. And shooting into stars. Or shooting from the stars? All the stars shoot rays of light to all the other stars! Upon which I think, oh, yes, reality is blackness crossed by white rays. It's orderly. It's organised. It's progress. Our perhaps infinite universe works to a Metropolitan Master Plan. Once it was old. Now it's mod. Reality always gets modder and modder, better and better, more and more with-it, more and more of a gas, more and more of a blast.

Poor old olden days.

Sorry, Minerva, but zip your lip.

Be that as it may, squeezing together eyelids of bristly pink skin, I keep looking into the blackness. Squeezing tightly. Too real is this feeling of make-believe. Too real when I feel what my heart can't conceal. And understand that the blackness isn't rays. Or stars. Or crossings.

Blackness is blobs.

I seem to be what I'm not, you see.

A lot of blobby blobs. Not crossing. Floating. Wafting. And doing so slothfully. Thank you class dictionary.

Nonetheless, in reality the blobs don't look like blobs. The blobs look like nothing, in reality. Which of course is nonsense. Only it's not nonsense. A thing can be nothing and it can be anything. Anything can be nothing.

Nothing can be anything.

Or nothing.

Or not.

Mad!

As you know, we've been here before, I and Sissy. At a bus stop in the Square. After seeing a story in Cinemascope Color. Sandra Dee, bikini babe, beatnik. Twentieth Century-Fox. Resuming my theme, I see light in the blackness. And see that it's white. The light. And the next thing I see is that white is black. And that black is white. And that white is black. And nothing and everything. After which I feel free. Which is gear.

Notwithstanding, I'm not nearly brave enough to be free. I'm a coward. Are you? You know, brave enough to be free? Or even to try to be free? Well I'm not. No, most certainly I'm not. No whiteness in blackness, or blackness in white light, or night, or white stars, let alone white rays, for a mod like I.

Opening my eyes once more, widely, I find that a big shifting shape is blocking the white light. Almost all the white light. A shape that turns out to be the big raw head of one of the Seven Sisters, Ilk of Forbes. A raw meaty head bending towards my own white small head. A meaty raw reddish bony smiling head. An intelligent head. An ignorant head. Seven Sisters, Ilk of Forbes, Gorbals of Glasgow and South Christchurch.

Additionally, pointing at me a garden trowel of a jaw.

Which doesn't make it any easier to work out who she is. A trowel jaw pokes down at you whenever you come across any of the Seven Sisters. Another quick blink. After which I look closely. And see that her reddish wrinkling skin has been been biffed about with whitish pinkish powder. You know, powder from a plastic compact. A pink compact. Biffed about by a buff nylon puff.

So everything's clear, now.

Only one of the Seven Sisters bothers herself with a powder puff when the lone occupants of a house are a few kids and she.

'Hi, Aunty Betty,' I say.

'Sleep nice and snug, did you Stevan? Here's your brekky.'

Aunty Betty beams down at me but in a way that makes me feel as though I only happen to be another one in a row of boys she's looked after in a motherly, kind, freckly, freehanded way. Aunty Betty's broad hands are open to everyone young or poor. Albeit, she's quite bossy. And she's not only got the jaw. Also, like the other Sisters, she knows about being poor. Only now she's got money. She's a widow and she owns shops.

Aunty Betty's cruised around the world!

Curiously, however, she's ordinary. She's boring.

I feel guilty saying that about Aunty Betty. Don't tell anyone, will you?

'Noel, want your brekky too? Weet-Bix. Slept nice and snug like Stevan, did you?'

Only the point is that she doesn't know that I slept nice and snug. Apropos, she knows that she should say nicely and snugly. Only she can't be cursed. The Seven Sisters seldom can be cursed to say things the right way. Not even if they've got money. Although only one has. Got money. Picking up my thread, as it happens I did sleep nicely and snugly. Very very snugly.

Notwithstanding, she doesn't know.

Aunty Betty doesn't know because while she does like to ask

you a lot of things she hardly likes you to reply. She thinks she knows. Actually she knows she knows. Although she's wrong. Which leads me to contemplate the way the Seven Sisters come in two Standards.

I've worked it out.

Seven Sisters Standard One is the sisters who are boring. Aunty Betty is Standard One Category Know-All. Aunty Lil is Standard One Category Witch. Grandma Forbes was Standard One Category Witch, Subcategory With Brass Knobs. Moreover you need to know that Aunty Lil is married to a red, loathsome, sweaty, little, greasy, slug of a man who for some reason whenever I see him makes me think he wants to put his stubby red pig trotter between my legs.

Which makes me want to be sick.

Ugh. Ugh.

Ugh!

Seven Sisters Standard Two is sisters who are witty. Standard Two Category Kind are Aunty Dork, Aunty Bella and Aunty Ikey. Standard Two Category Got a Temper is split into Subcategory Takes It Out On Kids and Subcategory Doesn't Take It Out On Kids. Aunty Bonk is the sister who belongs to the second subcategory.

Resuming my theme, when I open my eyes from where I'm lying on the Persil white pillows and see Aunty Betty's jaw we're inside a bach at Waikuku Beach. A worn comfy room walled with old tongue-in-groove timbers, planed and sanded. Additionally, I see below the jaw a broad, big, white, bowl of warm Weet-Bix. A bowl for Noel. Weet-Bix swimming in thick, creamy milk. Also, topped with a crunchy, sweet, brown sugar crust. Weet-Bix, a perfect combination of natural ingredients that provides you with an abundance of body-building and energy-giving food elements. A wonderful time-saver in the kitchen, too – ready to serve straight from the packet! A dandy way to start your day!

And a blob of golden syrup.

Scrummy.

The bach is pretty groovy. It's got everything that opens and shuts. At least, by Bach Standards.

Moreover, it's like Aestas the goddess of summer, nude and plump, has dropped quietly down from the sky. Alighted onto a high sandhill on the other side of the window. Aestas wearing a golden sheaf of wheat wreathed around her flaxen scalp and seated merrily on a throne of gold. A throne, like the goddess, dropped onto the sandhill from the sky. The yellow paint of the windowsills has peeled peacefully over long years of dry heat. Additionally, the window glass is old and thick and warped and wavy. And blitzed by norwesters with sand. Also, rimy with salt.

I like licking the salt.

Noel and I are staying in this bach for a fortnight.

Aunty Betty beams at us once more in her big, vague, friendly, way before turning her back. I pick up my spoon. Noel picks up his spoon. As I swallow my first sweet, warm, nutty, creamy spoonful I look through the warped, thick, salty glass. I see not only the sandhill but a very high and very blue sky. A few wheeling gulls, white and dove grey. Also, blackbacks. Strong yellow beaks. Webbed yellow claws. Pines swaying in an easterly breeze off the Pacific. A flurry of broom blooming with lemon yellow flowers on soft felty leaves of olive and silver. A wave of marram on a sand bank. Marram, if you look closely, is sort of banded. Thin bands, running upwards. Lime, chartreuse, sun yellow, parchment yellow, and silvery grey.

A black and white thing swoops by and stares at me with a red eye.

Quardle oodle ardle wardle doodle.

A magpie.

'It's like inside a story, isn't it?' I say to Noel.

He doesn't say anything.

After breakfast we set off in shorts and jandals for a mooch along some of the sandy narrow wee streets of Waikuku Beach. On every side are red, and orange, and yellow nasturtiums. And orange, and red, and pink geraniums. And cactus. And cypress. And marigold. And more nasturtiums, and more geraniums, and silver beet. And baches painted pink, lime, turquoise. Or glossy sunflower, lemon, burnt umber, cherry, sky blue. All blistered by sun and salt. A trail of scented brown needles winds through a pine plantation. Carry me back to de ole plantation. A dollar a day is black man's pay. Sand is nice and soft and hot. Needles are slithery, dry, the colour of prairie rose and sandalwood.

Noel and I play in the surf for quite a long while, then lie on the sand to get dry.

After which we wind our way back through the plantation and wander onto the Oval. Which is wide mown green grounds where boys play cricket. Additionally, there's a kids' playground with a paddling pool. And there's a milkbar where teenagers hang around being cool. And there's a dairy. Moreover there's a little wooden stall where you can buy sweets.

Noel calls sweets chaws. Which is wrong.

I used to, too.

Be that as it may, we don't really like going to the stall because it belongs to the Man Woman. She's got short hair, grey. You never know what to do or say. Her head is square, with a big wart. Also, a stringy sort of beard. One rumour is that she really is a man even though whenever you see her she's always wearing a frock. A faded, dowdy, flowery, floppy, musty, moth-ridden old frock cut and basted and sewed some ungroovy year, once upon a time, a long time ago. Anyway, you stand in front of her, sort of wanting to spew.

'And that's twopence change,' she rasps in her throaty way.

'Um, have you got that quite right?' I pipe. 'Shouldn't it be threepence?'

'Twopence,' she growls. 'Now clear out, I haven't got all bloody day to waste doing sums with kids.'

Arithmetic, it makes me sick.

Tea tonight is lamb chops, mint sauce, cold ham, mustard, cucumber soused in malt vinegar, buttery new potatoes, and lettuce salad with mayonnaise. Moreover, for pudding we're going to have fruit salad with ice cream. Neapolitan. Which means from Naples. Only it's from a factory in South Christchurch. Furthermore, we're allowed to sit in front of the tele and eat off trays. Aunty Betty sits with us, beaming and bossing. And while I'm slicing the fat off one of my chops, because if it's got fat it makes me think too much how it's a lamb stuffed with green spring grass then slaughtered at the works, an advert comes on about an old movie they're going to screen next week. A black and white movie. Boring. A movie made six years ago in England.

Oh! Oh! Strike me pink! Let there be drums!

A movie about the Titanic!

Chewing my lamb chop, which is startlingly fatty and, additionally, wet and sweet in a thick dark gravy, I stare with wonder at the advert. Night. White stars An ocean like black glass. Calm, cold. A sleek black bow slithering over the telescreen. A new superliner – the longest ocean liner ever in the history of the world. Huge, heavy. Steel bows. Steel smokestacks. Black smoke. White steam. A tar black, star white, sky.

Let the steam whistle cry! Away along the wide Missouri.

Roll on, old mighty Mississippi.

Toot!

A night when the largest, most luxurious liner of her day was racing across the North Atlantic. A night of wind whistling through rigging. A night when two thousand two hundred men, women, and children were faced with a terrible fact. The fact that most of them were going to die. First class passengers, the very cream of society. Second class passengers. Steerage class. And the crew. Steward, cook, hot steel, stoker, boiler, furnace, red hot, coal black, soot black. Whistling, sweating. Fire. White. Red. Maori shearers. Negro slaves. All of them speeding across a flat calm sea in a ship that everyone knew was unsinkable. The White Star Line spared no expense to make this ship a symbol of our final victory over nature. No work of fiction could contain such incredible twists or leave so many questions unanswered as the fantastic story of the sinking of the Titanic.

'Did you know that the Titanic was the first ship in the whole of history to morse the new emergency signal SOS?' I ask Noel.

Morse is another word that can be a noun or a verb.

Noel says nothing.

'It must have been exciting to be in the radio shack on board some other ocean liner hearing the signal,' I add a little maniacally. 'SOS, SOS, SOS, SOS!'

'Shh,' says Aunty Betty.

Clang! Clang!

Iceberg dead ahead, sir!

I ask my love to take a walk, just a little walk.

A sunny summer morning. I'm pedalling down our concrete driveway. I'm glancing sideways at our front lawn. Grassgreen crewcut. Well rolled. I'm swinging into Olivine Street. And then into Voss Street. And then into Marshland Road. I'm thinking about the Titanic.

Steel. Sleek. Speed.

Black. Red.

White.

John Arnold, architect, prison for permitting another male to do an indecent act on him. Brass portholes shooting rays of white light. Sidney Edwards, metalworker, prison. Oblong bungalows in pink green blue and yellow rows. Two men, names suppressed, Bromley Park. Oil. Piston. Speed. Steel. William Carson, welder, prison. Coal. Stokers. Boilers. Arthur Smith, clerk, prison. Steam, scream, steel, senseless.

I'm more and more nervous. High school is the key.

You know, the key to tomorrow.

The key to getting out of Olivine Street little boxes made of ticktacky. Only one of the Seven Sisters, Ilk of Forbes, went to high school. Bella, who spent a year learning how to type before Grandma Forbes ordered her to get a job. All the others left school fit only to work as a slavey or to slog in a factory and after a few years of lathering up a sweat over a scrubbing brush or climbing the wall with ennui on an assembly line they all landed pregnant to some pig ignorant bloke with nothing in his pocket other than two bob for beer. Well, Dad's not pig ignorant. Griggs think that they've got a better way of doing things. Michael Bridgeland, apprentice electrician, prison. Richard Leckle, schoolboy, borstal. Frederick Wright, plumber, prison.

Only they're wrong.

Griggs.

Olds, you know. Griggs are olds. Olds are always wrong. Paradoxically, Griggs nonetheless in reality are right when they say you need to get School Cert. And they're right when they say that if you're a bright young chap you really should go on and get University Entrance. And they're right when they say that if you're a very bright young chap indeed, and a bit of a swot, you might sign up for varsity. A point upon which I wholeheartedly agree with Griggs.

'Dream about sirloin all you want,' says Mum when I bring it up. 'You're getting mince.'

'All citizens of our modern social democracy, Mother,' I respond calmly, 'are entitled to a free and secular education in state high schools all the way up to the level of qualification for entry into university.'

'You're getting yourself a job as soon as you turn fifteen, I'm telling you now. I don't intend to be out of pocket for you any longer than I need to. This isn't a charity, it's a family.'

One day she goes white in the face, screaming with rage.

'Notwithstanding – ' I've begun to say.

'Cut your cheek, you! You're the laziest little sod from here to the Crossing. Think we've got nothing better to do than find money to keep you in books. Think we should be bloody shitting ourselves with thanks if you so much as bloody talk to us.'

One thing that interests me is that I don't feel unhappy about that sort of thing. Not now.

'Chère Maman,' I say super super calm, 'I imagine that your meaning in reality would be more correctly expressed by substituting a singular for your plural pronouns.'

I just feel hard and cold.

Alan's already left school. As soon as he turned fifteen he ditched the books and signed up for an apprenticeship in carpentry. Dad seemed not to mind. Gilbert Eldred Grigg of Trevillick, Lower Singletree, Single Tree, Treleaven, Cornwall, has given up. He gave up for good when John said he was off to counterhop at Four Square. Actually, Dad may even have taken one or two pains to find Alan the apprenticeship.

Not for me, thank you!

One day the buffed stainless steel door of a lift in one of the massive skyscrapers on the new university campus will slide open with a low hum, and out will step –

I.

A groovy guy.

A guy with a moptop haircut, soft white student hands stuffed inside the pockets of a black felt dufflecoat.

My bike's a third-hand crock handed down from John. Who no longer needs a pushbike now that he's driving a Prefect. A bomb. A long straight tarseal mile along Marshland Road.

Cars, paint, steel, grass, glass.

Supershell with Cresyl-Diphenyl-Phosphate.

Cables, concrete, brick, circle, rectangle, square, Crossing.

Eric's waiting at the Crossing on his new bike, a Raleigh Superbe Four Speed Roadster. I wish my bike was a Raleigh Superbe Four Speed Roadster. His family has a bit more money than our family. Nonetheless he's wearing what I'm wearing. A grey flannel shirt. Grey flannel shorts. Grey woollen socks striped with sky blue and gold. Additionally, a silly cap. A sky blue cap with a monogram in gold. Interest Omnium Recte Facere, it says. It behoves everyone to act rightly. Which according to the school handbook was said two thousand years ago by Marcus Tullius Cicero. The school handbook is yellow. It ends with lists of school regulations and school prizewinners and surnames and initials and university degrees of teaching staff.

BA. MSc. BMus. Three gates in the city.

'Oh my god,' I groan, 'we're scarecrows in square rags!'

'I know!' moans Eric. 'Hope at least we get to be in the same form class.'

'Me too,' I say anxiously.

We pedal abreast along South Parade. And on its western flank we see the very extensive grounds and classroom blocks of Shirley Intermediate. Seven blocks. Long, low, lovely.

Save me, Interwar Minerva!

Esprit de corpse (Fr.)

Upon which we continue pedalling along sunny leafy flowery South Parade until we come to the low boundary wall of Shirley Boys High. A low mod wall of red brick. The same red brick as the red brick of our cul-de-sac. A mod low red brick wall topped with a wide shallow flat mod concrete cap. A straight row of young planes struts behind the mod wall. Plane trees, not jet planes. I like the nicely mottled bark. Plane bark is milk coffee, sand grey, dove grey.

And thronging between the young plane trunks are boys.

Only boys.

You sit an intelligence test near the end of your two years at Shirley Intermediate to find out whether you're brainy. If you're not, you're dumped with the dullards into Mairehau High, or Aranui High, or Linwood High. Clever boys go to Shirley Boys High or Christchurch Boys High. One thing we know, but never say, on our side of the city is that Christchurch Boys High is better than Shirley Boys High.

Classy boys, of course, go to private schools. Christs College. St Andrews. Furthermore, Catholic boys go to Catholic schools.

Filip, I suppose, will be going to St Bedes.

Actually, will Sebastian Lam be at Shirley Boys High?

Be that as it may, after we've sculled along the low mod wall and wheeled around a corner onto a wide concrete driveway, where we know we'll find the bikesheds, we see another throng of boys. As we backpedal and touch our brakes we look around at the school blocks. E Block. A Block. C Block. And the throng. A thick throng of boys who're fourteen years old and sixteen years old and even eighteen years old. Old enough to rock the bop. SXSliced. Milling about and talking and laughing and joking and jostling and boasting and scuffling and whistling

'Far out, it's so big,' Eric hisses at me.

'We'll soon sort out the drill,' I say, wanting to wet myself.

'Watch out when we get off at the sheds. The big guys will pull your knob off.'

'What?' I say, terrified at what sounds so terrifying.

'The big guys pull the knob off all us little guys.'

'What!'

'Our caps. The knobs on our caps. They'll pull them off.

I look sideways at Eric. At his freckled, flattish, bony head. At the silly little sky-blue-and-gold cloth cap tugged over his wavy red hair. I look at the little button, cased in blue cotton, stitched to the top of the cap. I look at the cap beaks that stick out over our noses. Are we meant to be ducklings? Are we Huey and Dewey? In which case, where's Louie?

We jump off our bikes. Two boys pounce on me.

'Turd! Turd!' they yell.

I already know that turd is the name for a boy in the Third Form. Rhyming slang. Rubbedy dub. Albeit, I didn't know that big boys would grip me in a headlock and kick my small bum a couple of times before twisting the knob off my cap. I'm scared. I'm angry.

'Fuck off, cunts,' says Eric.

The bullying boys look surprised, and laugh, and run away.

'Strike me pink!' I say. 'Sterling work, Eric.'

'Fuck off,' he says again vaguely.

E Block, C Block, A Block. Next, inside an immense assembly hall, staring at rows of laminated plywood. Plywood warped inside a factory and screwed onto silver chromed steel tubes. Row after row after row. On a shiny floor of parquet. And boys, boys, boys. After which we get herded, gaping, into those rows. Hundreds of boys inside a big wide open hollow hall of swooping cantilevers, glowing fluorescent tubes, glossy timberwork, and glass. Seven hundred boys at Shirley Burps High.

Additionally, the masters.

'I'm Mr Wise,' jeeringly says a man in a black gown; he's well spoken and his words sound like his name. Only not wise like a learned sage. Wise like an owl. 'I'm your Year Master.'

What?

A gang of Fourth Form boys in rows on our right has started clapping and laughing. Mr Wise looks sideways. He sees they're cheering him. I don't know why they're cheering. I don't know how he knows. Only they do. And he does. He smiles at those bigger boys.

'Strike me pink!' I frantically whisper to Eric. 'Are we on one of the rings of Saturn with our air tanks running out?'

'Small whispering boy,' raps out Mr Wise. 'Stand!'

I must go very pale about the nose as I get up.

'Name, boy?'

I do go very pale about the nose.

'Stevan Eldred Grigg.'

'Stevan Eldred Grigg what?'

'What? What are you talking about?'

'I'm waiting, Grigg. And so far you've done yourself no favours,' says Mr Wise.

Upon which he gets another burst of clapping. And he bows. After which he straightens up, tells the boys in the Fourth Form to settle down and, still smiling, turns back to me. Me, praying silently, without moving my lips, while my brain pounds and pulses like the mighty turbine engine and two reciprocating engines driving the three steel propulsion shafts of the three polished brass propellers of the Titanic. Three shining shafts. Three protruding propellers.

I keep my lips tight because I know.

I know now.

Actually, I knew yesterday. I knew without knowing that I knew. I knew for years and years without knowing that I knew. I knew always. I knew that inside a hollow steel electric-lit hull speeding across a cold sea, deadly cold, and black, which is our skull, we must not only keep weak feelings hidden we must also kill every one of those weak feelings.

Otherwise we hit the iceberg.

And we sink.

And —

Well, I'm not always a coward.

I'm sometimes brave, in reality. Occasionally. Although it's true I'm skinny and small compared with nearly all the other boys. Only, it's from being very young. Additionally my eyes do happen to be shortsighted. Which is a drag. And consequently I have to wear glasses. Which is a drag squared. Only nevertheless my glasses are mod, with frames of chunky thick black plastic. It's the Buddy Holly look. Dad says we're lucky because families on modest incomes can get glasses on the state. Nevertheless only for kids. Moreover every morning I start my day with kitchen calm, not breakfast bedlam, by eating wholesome servings of SX Sliced and Weet-Bix.

A dandy way to start your day.

Only somehow I don't feel very brave right here, right now, squeezed in a grey flannelled row of boys. And twisted snaking sheets of varnished laminated plywood. And silver chromed steel tubes scraping parquet. Worried boys wriggling so much they're making benches shift backwards and forwards.

One grey flannelled row. Two grey flannelled rows. Three grey flannelled rows. Four. Six.

Twelve. Twelve gates in the city.

What a beautiful city!

I'm praying mutely – varying vocabulary – yet despairingly to our Miss D B L'homme Noir Minerva Intermediate to please swoop down on her knit two purl one white green cardigan wings. Additionally I'm praying that she brings with her a laser ray. A ray to truly zap me off to one of the rings of Saturn. One of those wondrous faraway cold coal-coloured ash-coloured copper-coloured rust-coloured sulphur-coloured rings endlessly wheeling round that lonely planet. And to wing her own way over to the rings. Upon which the two of us will become wedded to learning. And will spend forever together being knowledgeable people blowing smoke rings from filtered du Maurier, saying what we mean and meaning what we say, agreeing to vary our vocabulary about National and Labour, wholeheartedly concurring on nearly every point of grammar, wondering with interest about the perhaps infinite universe, keeping our chins up.

Notwithstanding, no white green cardigan wings weave downwards.

No laser zaps.

'Grigg, when addressing a master always end every sentence with the word Sir,' says Mr Wise with a false showing-off grin.

'Oh,' I say nervously. 'Sorry.'

'Oh, Sir. Sorry, Sir.'

Calmly, I grasp at last what he's trying to say. He's saying copy. Alright. I can copy. Copying is easy. You hide by copying. I've always done that anyway. I seem to be what I'm not, you see. A secret love waiting to be free. All my nights I hope, I pray, a dream lover will come and stay. Prison. Police. Straight. Square. Fist.

'Oh, Sir. Sorry, Sir.'

'Good, Grigg!'

Upon which Mr Wise begins calling out our names. Our monikers, he says. Which when called out sound like a rollcall of Ye Olde Yeomanry of England and Scotland. Adams, Anderson, Ansley, Baird, Bates, Beckingham, Clarke, Croft, Cumming, Davies, Edwards, Gordon. Along with the occasional Kiesanowski or Koziarski. Additionally a Hauschild, a Schroeder. Ach, mein Papa. Alle kaput!

Mein Vater war ein Wandersmann.

Twelve gates in the city.

Or else boys whose families came here from the Netherlands. After the last war. Smit. And one boy who's a bit Maori. He's handsome. Furthermore, fifteen boys in our Third Form are called David. Twelve boys are called John. Others are called Brian or Bryan. Or Stewart or Stuart. Or Graham or Graeme. Five are called Craig. Always there's only ever one Stevan. Which sometimes makes me feel good but usually makes me feel wrong.

Which it does today.

Our turd roll having been called, everyone's got to stand up. The masters are coming. Men in black gowns. Black gowns that droop over chalky terylene suits, and white bri-nylon shirts, and shiny polyester ties. Men treading in sensible shoes up a central aisle before climbing onto a stage.

After which they sit.

After which we sit.

And smack bang in the middle of the stage is a squat man with a blocklike head of burning red skin. And on top, black hair. Brylcreemed back from the skull with a wormlike white parting. Our headmaster Charles Vaughan Gallagher. You call him Charley. John told me. Alan told me, too. Charley's firm but he's fair. So they say. A short string of meaningless words you only say hoping they mean that he's not a bully.

When you know he is a bully.

I hate him.

I hate all the masters.

They look down at us through glassy eyes, their faces like bullocks. And you can see they're ready to lay down the law. Charley's certainly laying it down right now.

Laying it on thick.

Droning.

'A boy, to grow into a man, needs intestinal fortitude,' he says. 'Guts!'

We shouldn't call him Charley. We should call him Chartreuse. A Shirley boy, he goes on, knows that only the best will do. Chartreuse is the colour of six ridges of skin on his big noggin. A Shirley boy will always do his best as an upright citizen in our modern progressive society. Two ridges on his thick short cheekbones. School spirit. Two ridges over his short thick eyebrows. Team spirit. Two ridges on his sweating low brow.

'Esprit de corpse,' adds Chartreuse.

Ridges bright with blueish white light from fluorescent tubes bouncing off his swollen red oily skin. Switch to new high energy Mobil Tetramel. Power boosted with phenylmethane! Warmaire oil fuel space heaters take central heating out of the luxury-price bracket. Hard men need Tufguy jeans. The new cool tapered jeans by Tufguy. Go with the artillery to Vietnam and stand shoulder to shoulder with the forces fighting for peace in Southeast Asia. You'll be highly trained in all the roles of the artillery's versatile 105 M M Howitzer.

'Our fine facilities,' drools on Chartreuse, 'and a teaching staff second to none qualifications ability loyalty teamwork guarantee continued opportunities for our boys etcetera etcetera etcetera – '

'When I feel blue,' I whisper to Eric, 'all I have to do – '

' – is dream,' he hisses back.

The one and only sane thing about Shirley Bosses High is that we spend our first Form Three B period in the school library. It's a good library. You'll have noted that I'm not in Form Three A. With my placement test scores, the school told Mum and Dad, I should go into Form Three A. Only it would mean learning Latin. Interest Omnium Recte Facere. Nihil Utile Quod Non Honestum.

'It's a dead language,' I told them. 'What's the point?'

'Right,' said Dad. 'Good as gold.'

Mum gave a shrug.

Consequently I'm in Form Three B with boys supposedly not clever enough to learn Latin. Which is absurd, isn't it? Learning languages isn't cleverness. It's only memory. A budgie can learn languages. Be that as it may, we spend the whole of our first period learning how to use the library. Which is a gas. Twenty thousand titles were circulated last year, our English master says. A cocky young guy. Mr Johnson, BA. Did you know it's just a way of writing John's Son? A guy lived long ago in a village in Scotland or England. All the villagers knew his dad's name was John. So they called him John's Son.

Grigg means dwarf. Pop says that it was perhaps a jokey nickname for someone not short but the opposite, very tall.

I hope that's true.

We hardly ever see them, these days. Griggs. They've yarded us out of the paddocks. We're to be loaded into cattle cars waiting on railway sidings at the Crossing. Upon which we'll be shipped west for resettlement.

It'll be Aunty Audrey.

Theft as a servant, for christ's sake. No point chucking good money after bad.

Picking up my thread, a boy can borrow two books every two weeks. Out of sight! I make a beeline for Non-Fiction. Which in this library is catalogued according to the Dewey decimal system. Which is good because I like Dewey. I don't mean the cartoon duckling. Quickly, I find the 910 shelf. Almost as quickly I hunt out 910.453. Ships sinking! The slim colonial iron steamship Wairarapa fighting the lashing waves, smashing onto the rocks, a helpless wreck. Super! The sleek interwar oil-burning motor liner Rangitane trapped and torpedoed by Nazi raiders.

The –

Titanic!

Let there be drums!

Lord, Walter, A Night to Remember.

I grab the book like a magpie snatching, with its thick white beak, a shiny useless scroll of aluminium while glaring with its hard red eye. I fling the book open to a photo inset. The first thing I see is a massive steel prow on the ways.

I nearly swoon.

Notwithstanding, I don't.

It wouldn't be amusing to swoon inside a school library crowded with unknown staring boys. Consequently, I close the book while keeping a tight hold on it. After which I wander over to Fiction. Clarke, Arthur C, Fall of Moondust. I run my eye down the blurb. Time is running out for the passengers and crew of the tourist cruiser Selene, incarcerated in a sea of choking lunar dust. On the surface her rescuers find their resources stretched to the limit by the mercilessly unpredictable conditions of a totally alien environment.

Absolutely fabulously swinging!

I get both books out.

Albeit that the library's alright, by the end of that first day I'm finding it hard to keep breathing. I bike home, wheezy and weary. Additionally, weeping. Crying like a little kid. It's very scary. I never cry. As you know, I do dream cry. Yet never in reality. Only – well, now – and it's terrifying. I pedal and cry. I cry and pedal. Nobody can see me cry, so perhaps it's okay.

Johnson has set us some really hard homework.

Write a poem about a city. Three stanzas of four lines, scanning properly, each stanza A B A B.

Sobbing, I turn from Marshland Road into Voss Street.

After which I turn into Olivine Street.

Olivine Street still looks raw. Flowers in staring squares. Grass in mown oblongs. Our front lawn shaved within an inch of its short life. A fence of flowers closing it off. Phlox. Stria. Mock orange. Mum likes flowers. She's got quite a green thumb. All kinds of twigs nicked from gardens in other suburbs get stuck into the ground in our frontyard, or our backyard, where she waters them from the eye of a red plastic hose. Now, upon swinging into our driveway, I see the red hose snaking across the front lawn while drivelling water onto the roots of a dark shrub. Viburnum, I think. Our suburb six generations ago was a flax-thick reed-rich marshland. What will it look like six generations from now? Will our cul-de-sac by then have been nuked to buggery?

I hope so.

I bike up our driveway. The concrete is hard and dove grey. Yet brittle, too.

The sun of late afternoon is cooking the red bricks of our bungalow. I drop my bike onto a stack of other bikes in our new steel garage. I walk across hard baked dirt where four years ago our back lawn was sown so hopefully by Dad. I step into the bungalow. Mum's standing at the kitchen bench gripping a stainless steel peeler in her left hand and in her right hand a spud. She looks up. What do you reckon about your first day, she drawls not very interestedly while whipping the steel blade over a yellow murphy bruised with blue blobs.

I let out a short sob.

'It's hor – hor – hor – horrible, Mum.'

Mum looks at me, hard. After which her eyes go from hard to soft. And to her credit she makes a fist of it. To a point. She sets down spud and peeler next to a big lime green bowl of peelings. She wipes her hands dry. She tells me to sit down with her in the dinette and let's see.

Upon which, I do.

We do.

Me and Mum sit side-by-side on two of the lemon yellow dining chairs, each standing on its four slender silvery struts of Tubechrome. On our pick-up-sticks lino. My Form Three B English exercise book, its blank white pages ruled with rows and rows of thin blue lines, flops open on top of the yellow Formica. A black fly stands in one corner of the Formica vomiting onto a smear of something fatty. The pick-up-sticks are iris blue, regale blue, canyon coral. Jaipur pink. I'm still letting out the odd sob. You could mistake the Formica for a fossil laminate of marmalade. I sniff away a last sob or two. Any hour of the day you're likely to see Mum lurch into the dinette holding an aerosol can. Or you could mistake the laminate for some sort of marble, some mad murderous marble never known to nature, a blobby swirling spraying yellow thing never seen anywhere in reality until now.

Rays of sunlight, striking across aerosol spray after she's lurched and squirted, dance among tiny droplets of poison.

I've already written the first line of my poem. It's in Cambridge blue ink. I wrote it while leaning on the door of my locker and weeping silently last thing before biking home from Shirley Booze High. Black flies drop to tabletop, benchtop, windowsill, lino. They spin on their backs, fighting for life, little legs kicking frantically, before dying. Do you think it hurts to die, if you're a black fly? Furthermore, if you're a white and pink boy?

'A city, furrowed by radial roads,' says Mum. 'Yikes, that's bloody highbrow.'

'Well it's not my fault I'm highbrow, Mum,' I say quietly.

'And you probably reckon I know nothing about poetry. I might've spent half my life standing at a kitchen sink but when I'm standing there looking out the kitchen window into the backyard wishing there was a bit more to see than paling fences, dead lawn, the rotary clothesline and yous kids' clothes pegged out to dry, sometimes I remember I had a Miss Blackman, too. Hmf, only twelve lines. Can't be too hard to rhyme roads.'

'Codes,' I say somewhat hopefully. 'Toads. Modes.'

'Loads, um – abodes – um, um – bodes?'

'Goads!' I cry out pipingly.

Mum picks up a fag.

'Odes,' she says.

We give up after ten minutes or so. Mum needs to get on with the spuds. I need to go somewhere secret and cry. I don't, of course. Olivine Street hasn't got anywhere secret. As I've known always. I knew long before being made aware by Sissy. You know, that day. That day of too many days waiting for a bus. A bus to Shirley. A bus to the Square. A shuddering stinking red diesel bus. After or before seeing or listening to one or other Twentieth Century-Fox Cinemascope Colour story about Sandra Dee as bikini babe, beatnik. As a consequence, instead of quixotically seeking somewhere secret while knowing there's nowhere, I slope into the lounge. I slump onto a squab cushioned for comfort with synthetic Superfoam. Formfit. Contoured scientifically.

I gape at the great glowing swollen eye of the telescreen.

Space Angel. Web of Life.

Adverts. Palmolive.

Dinner.

Saveloys. Lettuce salad. Mashed spuds. Trifle for pudding.

After which, since tonight's not my turn on dishes, slope back to the lounge, slump onto the Formfit. NZBC Reports. Dick Van Dyke Show. Stump the Stars. After which, time for bed. I haven't yet written one stanza of my poem about a city. Three stanzas of four lines scanning properly each stanza A B A B. Mum and I between the two of us weren't even able to write two rhyming lines. We can't bear writing rhyming lines.

Albeit, she's keen enough on rhyming slang.

As you know already.

I lie in bed knowing that I'll never sleep. Knowing that tomorrow I'll be caned for not doing my homework.

I fall asleep.

'Sir?' says Eric next day to John's Son. 'When are you going to mark our poetry?'

'I'm not marking it,' yaps back our cocksure English master. 'It was just to keep you mob on your toes.'

Eric gapes. I gape.

After which Eric sighs, while I give a curt grunt.

Johnson, hah! Who does he think he is? He's not my boss. He thinks he's in but he's out. Furthermore who the hell do all the semi-educated dire squares running this school think they are? Squares aren't my boss. We need to start a sit-in. And not on the Main Trunk. A sit-in in B Block. A sit-in, like every sit-in for the young ones, baby! Daddy do you want to lose your mind? A sit in, like every sit-in, for freedom – and democracy – and the groove!

Or if not a sit-in, a hand up.

'Grigg?' sneers Johnson, seeing my hand and jerking his jaw.

He's only a few years out of university. He thinks his clothes are sharp. Brylcreemed mousy-coloured hair, backcombed, straight side parting. A careful copy of Robot Cliff in the early Sixties. You know, when Cliff was nice-boy-next-door-making-out-to be-a-bit-rocker. Johnson thinks he's smart. Johnson thinks he's got SXSliced appeal. Johnson's not even a Master of Arts. Only a Bachelor. Johnson doesn't get it about being mod.

He's a fake rocking jerk.

'Sir, notwithstanding that my question doesn't pertain to our task this morning,' I pertly ask, 'why do we study Shakespeare when his work can't possibly be relevant to contemporary society since he wrote so long ago, in the late Sixteenth and early Seventeenth Century?'

'Get on with your work, Grigg.'

'But sir, what's the use of it? He's dead as a dodo, sir.'

'Grigg, shut up.'

At the end of the day, homework. Which I bolt through carelessly as soon as I get back to Olivine Street. I do it in the dinette. Which stinks of corned brisket simmering with onions in an enormous scratched saucepan. Mum foddering our family. After which I slope once more into the lounge. Fury. Dennis the Menace. You Asked For It. Beverly Hillbillies. Dr. Kildare.

After which, another drudging dreary day at Shirley Bores High.

And then one more dreary drudging day.

I cry. I cry and cry. I cry and cry and cry. Of course I'm not really crying. In reality it was only the first day that I got weepy. Now it's only, once more, dreaming. Dream dream dreaming. Trolling the deeps of a another moonless black night in the dark sunless three-windowed sunroom of Eleven Olivine Street, Oceania. Asleep in my top bunk, breathing slowly. John asleep below. Alan farting opposite.

As always, the more I cry in my dream the more I need to dream cry.

I dream cry, dream cry, cry, cry, cry –

Magpie, mad-pie, mad –

A Block. B Block. Rin Tin Tin. Magic Land of Allakazam. Andy Griffith Show. C Block. D Block. E Block. Eric says it's a prisoner-of-war camp. Shirley Bums High. He and I have been beaking a lot of books about prisoner-of-war camps. You know, young soldiers trapped behind electrified barbed wire in enemy territory. You call it war escape literature. Young guys locked into barracks. Young guys under guard. Wired into camps. Trapped like girls in fuming department stores. Girls stifling in superheated gases, clawing at the steel of a black and red firebox.

Sebastian Lam isn't at Shirley Botch High. I suppose he must be going to a private school.

Jump, girls! Just jump!

Tunnel out, boys!

C Block. D Block. E Block. Telegoons. Z Cars. Rawhide.

Run away, guys – hare off – spin your slim spoked steel and rubber wheels up South Parade – skim streets of the suburb – pump your pedals up Marshland Road – peel away on the East Midland Plains. Shallow. Shingled. Swindled. Surveyed. Sold. Subdivided. Sold. Fenced. Raced. Sold. Roaded. Sold. Mortgaged. Sold. Sealed. Sold. Sold. Sold. Plains slipping into endless ocean, orderly plain sliding calmly into the swells. An unsinkable liner of many painted and polished decks whose passengers have let down not the lifeboats but their hopes and now are waiting courteously in evening dress for what they know, only don't say, are the consequences when a steel hull that holds us all splits itself on unseen ice and starts slithering under the waves.

'It's more a concentration camp,' I say pensively to Eric. 'Or an extermination camp. Auschwitz.'

'Well you have to admit the Jews did have a stranglehold on the economy.'

'You still can't go round liquidating millions, can you?'

'Of course not. Actually it wasn't millions.'

'Yes, it was millions.'

'Really it was only a few hundred thousand.'

'This conversation isn't very interesting any more,' I say bluntly. 'Notwithstanding what sort of camp it is, you and I are locked powerless inside for the whole second half of the Sixties. Which in my case will mean waging a bitter war, cold and occasionally hot, with my mother for the right to do it. While my father stays away until he comes home drunk. Only, be that as it may, by the beginning of next decade, on the other side of the barbed wire, await university degree, doctor lawyer academic – or, sorry, Miss B but zip your lip, business executive – engagement wedding pink and green and yellow and blue house not made of ticky-tacky. And kids. And two cars. New.'

'You're too young to be cynical,' says Eric sternly.

'It's wretched wretched being young.'

A Block. Z Block. Zyklon-B.

'I know.'

Am I really a Jew? Am I truly going to be rounded up by plods cops flatfeet Gestapo? Am I going to be hounded herded yarded packed slammed crammed cattle car shunted onto a siding. A row of cattle cars sitting, crowded with us crying and stinking, on oily twinned strips of steel near a yellow and red railway station walled in by dark pine plantations. Carry me back to de ole plantation. Magpies in the pines, singing. Quardle oodle ardle wardle doodle. After which, shunted onto a whistling train –

Da-dack da-dack –

The Midland Line. Coast to coast!

And upon coming to the westernmost station on the Line are we then to be robbed wrangled whipped stripped spurred into a shower block? Hoggets at the works. Grigg. Trevillick. A long low concrete shower block. A long low homestead. A cool wide veranda. A moneyed family. Whistle o de steamboat coming round de bend. Shower block where we're to be deloused and where unlike slaves, or shearers, or worried ewes and skittish wethers at works, we're not to be slit open by steel blades red with blood white with borrowed reflected refracted fluorescent light. We're not to be knifed not to be stabbed as though we're mere sheep.

We're to part our lips.

Open our throats widen our nostrils breathe deeply.

Obediently fill our lungs with vagueness, with a veil, with white shadow, wavering softness – clinging – mist – smog – haze – murk – reek – sniffing clean kindly white whiffs of Zyklon-B quick cost-effective. Stifled. Stopped. Topped. Choked.

Croaked.

Dead as a dodo.

Of course I can't possibly be a Jew!

English homework for the weekend is to write six hundred words about oneself in another life.

Eldred Trevillick is my name. I teach at a small private college in Cornwall. It was a quiet peaceful evening, about midnight, and my mind was full of the things I would do in New York when the Titanic docked next day. My best friend was to welcome me to the city.

Only a year earlier he had left our Mother Country to take up a position as chaplain at a small private college in Manhattan. I was almost asleep. My cabin lulled me with the gentle clicking of coat hangers swaying on their hooks and the hum of the turbine and two powerful reciprocating engines of the vast ship.

Suddenly I felt a faint grinding jar.

The clicking and humming ceased. For some reason the ship had stopped.

I clambered out of bed, dressed, and went out to the passageway. It was crowded with bustling people, and after enquiries, I found that they too, knew nothing of what was going on. I then noticed a harassed looking steward nearby, and asked him what was happening.

'There's talk of an iceberg, sir,' was the reply. 'But the ship is in no danger.'

After this reassurance I went back to my Second Class cabin, and read for approximately half an hour. Occasionally one could hear the creak of woodwork against the steel hull, or the slam of a distant door, or the click of heels as somebody walked by. The engines, however, seemed to have stopped spinning. We seemed to have glided to a stop in the middle of the Atlantic.

Suddenly in burst a steward.

'Put on the lifebelt, and get up on Second Class Boat Deck!'

I carefully re-dressed, put on my lifebelt, collected a few valuables, and made my way up to the jostling crowds on the Second Class partition of the Boat Deck. The Titanic lay dead in the water. Three of her enormous funnels were shrieking while blowing off high-pressure jets of steam. At this point I became aware that the whole massive vessel had only twenty lifeboats for the total capacity of three thousand eight hundred and fifty people. Although most passengers were Third Class, they had only four boats. First Class had eight boats. Second Class (my class) had the remaining six eight boats. As the liner was still perfectly level, I decided to go down to the peace of the Café Parisien, on B Deck, but on A Deck an officer stopped me.

'What are you doing here?' he said. 'Get up on Boat Deck!'

I meekly obeyed, and found, much to my surprise, that a lifeboat was being lowered. I asked a crewman why they were doing this.

'It's merely a formality,' he answered. 'As there's a small hole in the bow.'

I was then persuaded to get into lifeboat Thirteen, although the bright decks of the Titanic were more enticing than the frail little wooden craft, hanging from the creaking davits. Soon, at about half-past one, our boat was lowered and, taking hold of our oars, we pulled away from the brightly lit decks of the ship. On board the band was playing ragtime. Our boat then stopped about six hundred yards away from the Titanic. There we remained until at two-twenty the huge ship rose upwards until it was completely perpendicular with the sea. Then the lights glowed red, adding more horror to the noise of thousands of tons of furniture, cargo and people sliding downwards.

The lights went out.

Suddenly the ship glided downwards until it was enclosed by the murky waters of the Atlantic.

Hours later we saw, while sitting in our frozen little boats, the lights of a ship approaching. And then the sky broke out into glorious pinks, yellows and oranges, which reflected on to the icebergs, breaking into myriads of lights. We frantically waved things, and soon we were sitting in the lounge of the rescue ship, the Cunard Liner, Carpathia. I then realised that I had witnessed the worst sea disaster in the history of man.

Week after week, month after month, the suburb squats peacefully.

Bungalows. Row by row by row. Oil rainbow. Black tarseal. Red brick. Dove grey concrete. Yellow paint. Pink paint.

Green grass. Shiny glass.

'You're lucky living in a big happy family,' says my new friend, Craig Jackson.

'Yeah, hey do you like the Zombies?' I reply, changing tack quick as a wink. 'She's Not There is out of sight.'

'Yeah, I like the jazz influence,' he responds.

Craig's working class. His dad's a weaver in a woollen mill. And his mum's a charwoman. Additionally, he always seems to smell of Lifebuoy soap. I like looking at Craig. Not because he's handsome. Quite the contrary. Craig's pretty plain. His big pink head is honest and clever with straightforward frost blue eyes. And wisps of faint fair thin hair. Moreover he's slightly awkward. No it's not his looks that seem so boss. It's how much he knows. And how much he thinks. He expresses himself excellently. He's not always speaking old sentences that other people have spoken nearly always. Nor is he always speaking new sentences that some people right now believe will forever be the last word.

NB Eric!

Consequently, standing with Craig in grey wool and grey flannel on the quadrangle in the middle of Shirley Brutes High while shivering in an autumn easterly and talking about pop is somewhat groovy.

'Do you?' I pipe up eagerly.

'Yes, it's –'

And he says some very interesting and intelligent things about the Zombies. After which he talks about the Animals. And additionally, the Seekers.

He thinks I'm intelligent too. Which I am, aren't I?

Am not I?

Or am I just weird?

As Sissy says. Alan, also. My pimply flabby bullying brother Alan. Be that as it may, and picking up my thread, even though he's very intelligent, he's speaking nonsense. Craig. Not Alan. Alan always speaks nonsense about everything. He speaks nonsense about the white race, which he's proud of. Oi moight not be much but at least oim whoite. And he speaks nonsense about rugby. And about beer. And about rockers, who he says are great. And about mods, who he says are queer. Notwithstanding, and once more picking up my thread, when outsiders say nonsense things about our big happy family I never dream of denying it. Denying it would betray the other kids in our family.

I don't want to betray the other kids. Not even – well, not a lot – blubbery Alan.

We don't want outsiders to know.

We don't want them to know that while, yes, our father's clever and educated he's a dope. He's a drop-out. And not even an interesting drop-out. Dad's just boring. And we don't want outsiders to know that while, yes, our mother might be a dag she's also cruel, brooding and moody.

'Gee she's a kidder, your mum,' the outsiders say.

No, we don't want anyone to know.

Craig and the library aren't the only good thing about Shirley Botch High. One more bonus is at least there's no more Bummer Fearon. He vanished overnight. Some boys say he stowed away. On a ship. Let's hope it hit an iceberg. Moreover, one further good thing is that Craig, Eric and I write a play. One wet and miserable day early in winter the three of us are on our bikes heading home to Eric's. Our black rubber wheels squelch through shallow pools of water on top of the shining black tarseal. Rain always seems wrong in East Midland. Eric's the one who hits upon the thought of writing and staging a play. He says it'll relieve the monotony. We understand what he means by the monotony.

Within minutes our excited selves have decided on the subject: the sinking of the immortal Titanic.

After arriving at Eric's we're soon busily writing script. A yellow budgie chatters in its nearby cage. A cage of thin steel bars with a floor of pink plastic. Clever boy, clever boy, clever boy!

Act One, Scene One.

A Second Class cabin. Mrs Van der Shaan is sitting on a chair doing tapestry.

The tapestry is Eric's mum's idea, which she voices when we three boys are sitting around her dinette table wondering what Mrs V der S can do as stage business. Mrs Wright listens in while gripping a shallow wooden spoon and twisting it round and round (the effortless ease of rotary action) while she rams cold leftover lamb into a steel mincing machine about the size of her head. She's kind, and shrewd. Her head is big. Her legs are short. And when she walks her bandy legs make her look like a cowboy. A cowboy without six-guns wearing a flowery print frock.

'Idle women in olden days did tapestry,' says Mrs Wright.

I and Mrs Wright have known one another for years already. Additionally, I like her a lot. Well, love her, to be honest. Eric doesn't know my own chère mère. He knows nobody in my family. Other than Noel. Whom he hasn't seen since we left Quinns Road School. I've never invited Eric to visit us at Eleven Olivine Street. My lack of courtesy is due to the disconcerting fact that, while he does know about my family's emotional mess (I complain about it all the time but do my best to be witty instead of showing him it hurts), he doesn't know how poor we are in reality. Or how crude. Or dirty.

I'm too ashamed to invite him to Olivine Street.

'Mum, she's not First Class,' says Eric somewhat pointedly. 'She's only Second Class.'

Moreover, as always, I'm ashamed of myself for being ashamed. Upon which, I do my very best to forget. Fortunately, forgetting is something I know how to do. I do it daily. I need to.

Consequently, there you go – forgotten!

I feel sorry for Mrs Wright. It must not be enjoyable having a son who speaks to you caustically when you're busy running a household the way she does, cleanly, briskly, neatly, swiping away every speck, leaving only sparkle. Not at all like one or two other mothers not a mile away. The Wrights are a household of three growing boys. Mr Wright, in town right now, works as a clerk.

'Second Class on the Titanic was comparable with First Class on other liners,' I mention quietly.

Nobody seems to notice, however. Mrs Wright just keeps doggedly poking cold hunks of cream and purple mottled meat into the steel jaw. Additionally, Eric and Craig have begun a discussion about whether the Van der Shaans are German or Dutch. Craig says Dutch. Eric says German. Craig says they own a small jewellery shop in Amsterdam. Eric says they were born in Hamburg but now run a newsagents in Muncie, Indiana. Craig wants to know why Muncie, Indiana and not Spokane, Washington. Or Iowa City, Iowa.

Eric says all we need's a basic damn backstory.

'Language,' says little Mrs Cowboy.

What's a backstory?

The next few days are full of turmoil, with the typewriter industriously clacking away. After which, we have our script.

Act One, Scene One. Mrs Van der Shaan doing tapestry, Mr Van der Shaan reading the ship's paper. The Titanic Times. (We've made that name up.) Suddenly there's a faint grinding jar. (A strip of material tearing backstage.) A white thing (flattened and painted Weet-Bix box) glides past a slightly open porthole. The Van der Shaans have left the porthole a little ajar because they always enjoy freshness. At the very beginning of the transatlantic Crossing they agreed that the central heating of the liner is too hot.

Slivers of ice fall through the porthole.

Girls bike by the low boundary wall of Shirley Boars High. The low mod wall of red brick topped with a wide shallow flat concrete cap. Girls wearing winter kilts of chocolate brown, forest green. Kilts flying around pink thighs while pink calves pedal along South Parade. Lime green ties. Brown berets. Girls on their way to Avonside Girls High.

Quiet girls. Rowdy girls. Shy girls. Pushy girls. Ordinary girls. Clever girls. Pretty girls.

Be that as it may, you can't talk to those kilted girls unless you're cheeky.

I'm not cheeky.

Notwithstanding the dismaying lack of lasses inside the boundary of our grounds almost every boy goes on, and on, and on, about SXSliced. It's extraordinarily repetitive and boring. At the moment the more with-it boys are talking about a new pop song that's supposed to be about masturbating. A song by Shirley Ellis. The Clapping Song. Clap, clap, clap, snap. A song about the monkey getting choked. And how we all go to heaven in a little rowboat. And about your right hand, clap pat. And about my mother telling me that she'd buy me a rubber dolly.

'Yanks say choking the monkey when they mean wanking,' says Eric smugly.

'What's the little rowboat?' asks a less with-it boy.

Eric looks at him incredulously.

'Think about it,' he says.

The jaws of all the less with-it boys are slack.

Eric's growing his hair long. He wants to look like Van Morrison who also has red carroty hair. Only it's turning out sort of tufty. Eric's. Van's, too. As for I, I'm aiming for a moptop. The Kinks look. Or the Who. Annoyingly, masters at Shirley Boors High are constantly on the lookout for hair that's not regulation. Regulation hair grows no more than two inches out of the skull. Regulation hair may not be combed over the ear. A regulation fringe may not come to a point one inch earthwards below the eyebrow. Additionally, socks must be regulation. Regulation socks are cinched with rubber garters at a point three inches below the centre of the knee, no lower, on pain of caning.

All those lacklustre old squares at Shirley Stalag Luft High spy on us boys.

So how are we supposed to get in the groove?

All you can see wherever you look are masters in black gowns that flap as though men are bats who forgot to fly. And pairs and packs of boys. Small boys whose pinkish skin gets scraped by raw woollen gun grey. Or tall boys. SXSlicedy Sixth Form boys sloping about in dark charcoal grey.

It's ugly.

It's terrifying.

Masters boys boys masters men boys boys boys boys boys. All around me boys are growing. I lie in bed at night and think about boys. I think about the hair on their thighs, in their armpits, between their legs. It's fascinating to watch the shape of a boy change so quickly. It's fab. It's wrong. The hairiness of all those legs, the dark hairiness of those armpits, seem somehow not right. I feel, when I see boys yanking off clothes before gym, or splashing afterwards in the showers, something hitting me in the belly.

Masters boys boys –

Any boy who shows any weakness gets hounded until his life's a misery.

Nobody hounds me, at least. Other than carelessly.

I work too hard to keep my head below the battlements.

Notwithstanding, you never know when the bullies will mark you. Mark you for being not really a boy. A boy who doesn't walk like a boy. A boy who doesn't talk like a boy. Whistle like a boy. Swear like a boy. Additionally they'll mark you for being a nark. They'll mark you. And they'll zero in. One boy who only two days ago was one of the crowd now finds himself getting chased by a gang. A gang of baying boys who dog his steps as he runs, white with fright, round and round B Block. And when he's caught they close on him in a ragged ring. And punch him in the belly. And the back. And the balls.

'You only get a hard time if you're a sooky nark,' says one of the big boys. 'A little pansy turd who deserves a bit of a hiding to make him stop narking.'

'Yeah,' says another big boy.

'If you're getting hidings from other guys you obviously deserve it.'

'Yeah, they're lending you a hand by letting you know you're a little shit and need to straighten yourself out.'

And in the grey rough throng of flapping black bats and frightened little pink and grey boys and frightening tall SXSlicedy charcoal grey dogs where's me? All through the first term I feel as though I'm managing to do no more than keep myself breathing. It's not the schoolwork. The schoolwork is easy. I do what I've done for years: enough to get a pass in every subject. No, I don't mean the schoolwork. I mean everything else.

Shirley Bogs High.

Olivine Street.

I, alone.

Alone.

I.

Canes are slim and supple, about a yard long. Craig says that they're made of rattan. One may find them flaying youths from one end to the other of the former British Empire, he adds ironically, as one of the many blessings carried through the world by the steam vessels of the Victorians. Apparently rattan's a kind of tough springy creeper that twines up the trees of tropical jungle. A jungle wet with rain. A breeze from a bayou. A cane when whipping a boy makes a whistling sound. A master when telling a boy he's to be caned makes a barking sound.

'Grigg, outside!'

'Yes, Sir,' you have to say.

After which you walk the long lonely walk to the door that leads to the corridor where you know you must wait. You walk holding your head up. You're not ashamed. You know what's going to happen in the corridor isn't right. And every other boy who meets your eye as you walk by, every friendly boy, every alright boy, even every bully, looks at you with sorrow. We know. We know who's in the wrong. And it's not us. It's the olds. Upon which you stand waiting between lockered walls under fluorescent strip lights. Waiting, hating the master, hating all masters, hating all olds. Waiting on the polished lino of some wide long straight squared standardised authorised notified certified statutory stationary stealthily stolen single-SXSliced state secondary school corridor at Shirley Belch High.

Caning's not allowed for girls so why is it for boys?

Apropos, while every master is wrong, not all are equally wrong. One who turns out not wholly wrong is the Son of John.

'You're so far up your nose you can't see the ground, Grigg,' he snarls one day.

The snarl is somewhat stagey. John's Son knows that every boy is listening. Moreover, he knows that every boy knows that he's not really saying nose. He's saying arse. You're so far up your arse you can't see the ground. It's a saying. Mum deploys it a lot. As do all Seven Sisters, Ilk of Forbes. One consequence of their freedom with the phrase is that my skiting English master isn't speaking to a boy who's never thought about what to say in reply.

'Sir, I'd rather be up my nose than be neither my nose nor my elbow.'

Which of course is also a saying.

Neither your arse nor your elbow. Seven Sisters, Ilk of Forbes, are keen speakers of that saying. Although someone with a university degree obviously would say anus. Anyway, now he knows I know one or two words.

John's Son.

He knows I know a good many words.

Often when I've shot a phrase or two at him he shoots me back a grin. He quite likes me, I think. Consequently I find myself faced with the somewhat alarming possibility that I may have somewhat of a crush on the Son of John. Spew. Let there not be drums! Although he's quite handsome in his ordinary way. His backcombed early Sixties Robot Cliff sort of way. However, resuming my theme: caning. A quiet boy can find himself getting caned quite as frequently as a rowdy boy. A quiet boy can get caned for whispering and laughing with Craig. Above all, when he laughs and whispers in French.

'Grigg, outside!'

'What? What for, Sir?'

'For not getting on with your work. Outside!'

After a while a quiet boy cares a lot less about getting caned. And instead of meekly taking it he starts playing the bleak but provocative game of trying to work out exactly how he can copy the masters' sneers, twist them, bounce them back, while staying strictly on the uncaned side of the door to the corridor. Often you don't need to do anything more than spike a caustic concise correct calm sentence with the occasional extremely clear Sir.

'Notwithstanding that you know best, Sir, we were indeed getting on with our work.'

'Giggling, Grigg, isn't working.'

'Sniggering's the synonym I'd use, Sir. Furthermore, Sir, Craig and I were following your instructions, Sir, by memorising the vocabulary, Sir. Upon which I happened to say, Sir, that apples in France must taste pretty bad, Sir, since the French call potatoes pommes de terre, Sir.'

I can get away with almost anything so long as I keep my voice very mild. And say Sir. It jams their radar. I get my kicks not by driving Route Sixty-Six but skating on the edge of the alphabet. Notwithstanding, I don't feel good doing it. Somehow it's like I'm stifling myself. It makes it still harder for me to keep breathing. Furthermore, I can't get away with it in French.

Fish, we call our French master. He's from Kaiapoi. He's got a narrow head with big weak goggling eyes and wet lips.

'Outside, Grigg! Six for talking back!'

Also, he's one of many masters who get SXScited by caning.

'Now, bend, Grigg!' he says, thrilled by seeing me lower my head nearly to the lino floor and sticking my poor bum towards the ceiling. 'Four of the best for not settling to your work, and two more for your cheek.'

A black sleek smoking screwing white starred steel supership racing across a sea like cold black glass. Painted piped spouting shrieking. Nevertheless it's hollow. It sinks! Our supership's a holed hunk of steel heavier than water and it's sinking. It's nothing but a thing we've made, thinking we can do anything.

Doctor Frankenstein, may I introduce you to Doctor Jekyll?

How do you do, my dear Doctor.

Guten Abend, Herr Doktor.

And furthermore, gentlemen, please greet Doctor Mengeles.
We will. We can. We make. We take. We break. Astronaut.
Cosmonaut. Chrome. Steel. Plastic. Latex. Glass. Oil. Aerosol.
Aluminium. Uranium. Bomb. Money. Money. Money. Money!
Money! Money!
Calm down, man.
Cool it.

OOOOOOOOOOO

Opening my eyes unwillingly, knowing that it's going to be another nasty day at Nazi Boys High, I see glassy stars. No, not glass. Snot. No, ice. Icy stars on the outside of our three sunroom windows. John must have yanked the venetian blinds open already. One window in the east, one in the north, one in the west. He gets up early because of Four Square. Or it was Alan. Frost stars. Additionally, I see water drooling down the inside of our windows. Drools, drips, beads, drops.

Condensation, of course, night breathing by three boys.

I jump out of bed, shivering. I fling off my green flannelette pyjamas. I do the twist into my red Jockeys. Come on baby! Yeah! After which, while glancing once more at the ice stars, less eagerly I drag my grey, too loose (hand-me-down from John), school wool uniform onto my bony body. Grim grey uniform shorts. Grey grooveless shirt. Grey, very, very grooveless jersey.

Warm, admittedly.

Mum says the jersey wears and washes well.

Although what she says, in reality, is the jersey wears and washes good.

Dad says well. Or he says good-oh. Which makes me think fleetingly about a boy my age learning wrong and right grammar at Methven District High. A boy of thirteen in the Thirties. Olive skin black hair brown eyes. Gilbert Eldred Grigg. Grigg a patronymic going back to mediaeval Cornwall. Eldred a patronymic going back

215

to mediaeval Middlesex. Gilbert a patronymic going back to the Normans. Gilberts are my paternal nana's maternal family. I miss my nana. Ellen. Gilbert Eldred Grigg wearing a grey jersey very like this grey jersey. A boy of thirteen keen, out of school, to foxtrot with his hep sister Audrey. Audrey sneaking a secret sherry while shellac discs whirl on a lacquered gramophone in the sitting room at Trevillick.

I think of the grandmother other than Ellen. You know, dead old dodo Vinegar Tits.

Who're yous kids? Are yous kids Darkie's kids?

A little angry woman in a limp dark frock.

Resuming my theme, a uniform jersey not only shapeless, scratchy, outdated, a deadweight, but sporting at its neck a striped vee of sky blue and gold. The school colours striped in a vee at my neck. Raspy dyed stripes of animal fibre throttling my neck. Gold chemical dye. Sky blue chemical dye. Acid dyes stewed from hydrocarbons inside stainless steel vats. Oil, processed, bled into knitted itchy wool.

Scraping wool. Strangling.

A sort of lasso.

My neck.

I can't swallow.

I can't breathe, I need to spew.

No, not a lasso. A brand. A brand burnt into the skin of a boy. A searing smell. Scorched wool. Hot meat. Cattle cars. Sheep station. De ole plantation. A hot gold ball glowing in a blue sky. A big black toadstool doing the twist in a blue desert sky.

Pig trotter.

Milk.

I stuff my pyjamas under my pillow. I grab my grey woollen uniform socks. I bolt barefoot into the dinette.

Which seems warm till you get used to it and work out it's only lukewarm. A lukewarmth coming from the steel black firebox of the kitchen incinerator inside which small sullen yellow flames are eating their way smokily through hissing hunks of green wood. The outside of the incinerator, a shiny white enamelled steel oblong, narrow, looks like a mini interwar skyscraper slotted between the electric stove and the airing cupboard.

Moreover, as always at the start of a day, the dinette smells of steaming hot porridge, stewed tea, and fags.

Sooty wood smoke, too.

Furthermore, condensation streams as freely down dinette and kitchen windows as sunroom windows. I don't feel fab. Other kids keep banging through the door from the passage.

'Shut the door behind you,' Mum keeps saying. 'Were yous kids born in a tent?'

'You ought to know,' chips in Sissy, slapping butter onto toast. 'Weren't you there at the time?'

'Watch your cheek,' mindlessly raps out Mum.

'Which cheek? says Sissy in a silly voice. 'Right cheek or left cheek? Face cheek or bum cheek?'

She wiggles her bum to bring home the point.

'Speaking of bums,' tries Mum, 'that hem is so bloody high I can see halfway up to yours.'

'That's the point,' says Sissy, crunching into the toast.

'Hmf,' says Mum.

After loading myself up with porridge and whipping a toothbrush over my teeth, followed by carefully combing my semi-moptop, I grab my school satchel and head out the back door. A windless and cold grey sky. The steel wires of the Suparotary sag under the weight of two lank loads of wet washing. I hop onto my crock. I scull down the concrete driveway. I hit the black tarseal of the cul-de-sac.

Flowerbeds in our blind street are naked now we're in deepest midwinter and show nothing but wet rimy earth and stripped sticks. Lawns are no longer a bright summer green but the darker, ranker green of midwinter, growing in hanks since mowers have been stowed away in sheds out the back.

I bike into Voss Street, swing into Marshland Road.

Spray-painted steel cars glass tarseal electric cables concrete steel weatherboard bungalows green yellow blue pink. Crossing. Cars, lorries, buses, cars, cars, cars, black leather jackets. South Parade. Supershell petrol with Cresyl-Diphenyl-Phosphate. Concrete kerb. Mod low wall. Tarseal driveway.

Hitler Youth Propaganda Institute, Form Three B.

'We'll vary the monotony by bunking from assembly and hiding in the library,' says Eric. 'The librarian's coming in late today.'

'Okay, why not?' says Craig.

'Swinging,' I say.

After which the three of us sneak into the library and stand for a moment to look admiringly at rows of oversize books in the Reference Section. Let there be drums! It's groovy to be holed up with thousands of books well away from any preying prefects. Upon which Craig breaks our little spell by picking up a magnificent atlas.

A world atlas published six years ago. Or, in other other words, old.

An atlas of a world that's gone already.

'Look!' says Eric. 'Central African Federation!'

And we do look, feeling quite sad. I think we're sad because we know what the mapmakers didn't know. Which is that a day was to dawn quite quickly when the sun would no longer rise over Central African Federation. My mind harks back a year or two to the queue at the Tivoli to buy tickets for It Happened in Rome. You know, at the time of its collapse. The collapse of the CAF, of course. Not

Rome. Nor the Tivoli. A collapse wholly to the good, it goes without saying. Freedom. Democracy. Yet it seems somehow innocent now, the Central African Federation.

In spite of the fact that it wasn't.

Sadness is malapropos when one considers that hatching a federation out of the addled eggs of three dying colonies was merely one of many sickening squirts and jerks in the death throes of the British Empire. One more lurk for the white moneyed to fake swinging. Swinging by swindling Africa.

Yet – well, somehow here we are – three groovy boys in a social democracy, pert as schoolboys well can be, filled to the brim with boyish glee, nostalgic for the CAF! Three precocious boys mawkishly hankering after dead as a dodo Colonial Afrikaaner Fascism! One of many storefronts operated by that titanic company of planetary commerce and industry, a rising star among world corporations, top of the capitalist pops, Four Square Twelve Gates City Company Ltd.

Most malapropos indeed.

Nonetheless, somehow at the same time, I'm relieved that everything's proving not, in reality, to be what I thought it was. You know, mod democratic etcetera etcetera etcetera. Moreover it not only isn't, it never was. Or could be. Or can be. Which is, as I've observed only this moment, a relief.

Giving up is startlingly more convenable than going on.

N'est-ce pas?

Resuming my thread – well it's sad, somehow. Sad and somehow, sort of, frightening. We three boys in a world without the Central African Federation. Upon which we agree to divide the world between us. We go down the table of contents. Afghanistan, the first country in the table, goes to Craig. He gets it since his Christian name comes first alphabetically. The next country is Albania, which goes to Eric. Algeria, the third country, is mine.

After which Craig gets American Samoa, and Eric gets Angola, and I get Antigua and Barbados.

We work our way down the list.

I get Aruba, the Bahamas, Basutoland, Bermuda –

Brazil! At last, a big country. Brasilia, I decide, will be the capital of my whole collection of countries because it's a city so shiny, gleaming and glassy. One day I'll fly in a silver plane not over a jungle wet with rain but over a pattern of streets and parks and avenues looking like a jet airliner, miles long, lying flat on rust red earth. I'll look down at it from high up in the sky.

We work our way down the rest of the list.

After which, we start drawing maps. Additionally, colouring them so as to show how the world looks now. Eric calls his countries the United States of Earth. He colours them brown. Craig calls his the World Empire. He colours them red. I colour mine green and call them the Planetary Federation of Social Democracy.

'Hey, how come you're colouring most of Algeria brown,' I say sharply to Eric. 'Algeria's mine!'

Eric points out in his annoying way that in the world atlas a wiggly boundary runs between northern and southern Algeria. All land south of the wiggly boundary has the name Sahara. Which is wrong. The atlas is wrong. All land south of the wiggly boundary belongs to Algeria. Eric irritatingly insists that it belongs to French West Africa. Which is Eric's. Furthermore, it's enormous. And he's already got his mitts on more land than us other two. Eric. Craig's got the next most land. Almost all of my countries are islands. Admittedly they include Indonesia.

Mr Blank.

Sheryll's dad, remember?

Mr Blank the former stoker who after the war came here from the Netherlands East Indies. Dutch Empire. Coolies. Carry me back to de ole plantation, de whistle o de steamboat coming round de bend. Rubber plantations. Coffee plantations. Cacao plantations. Tea plantations. Tobacco plantations. French Empire. British Empire. Spanish Empire. South of the border down Mexico way. Flaming Star. Monro Doctrine. Portuguese Empire. Democracy for Goa! Japanese Empire. German Empire. Waltz. Goethe. Kaput. Ach, mein Papa. Ottoman Empire. Gallipoli. Marshland. Bussell. Cox. Dass. Memorial gateway. Auschwitz. Atom bomb. Hiroshima.

A dad holding up his little boy so he can see a toadstool doing the twist.

Sheryll.

Filip.

I'm very lonely.

Notwithstanding, it's typical of Eric that even though he's got so many big countries he's trying to flog most of Algeria. Craig, meanwhile, peers at the world atlas. He's shortsighted, like me, only his glasses are oval. Which is square. He's not square. It's his mum who's square. Naturally, since mums are a subset of squares. We've just learnt about subsets. Mathematics, which make me sick. Additionally dads, to be fair, dads are a subset of squares. Craig's mum says there's no point getting him new specs yet. Not till the ones he's got wear out. Specs is her word. The educated, of course, say glasses. Craig's mum grew up working class. Buddy Holly glasses as mod as mine are what he wants.

Craig.

He's not square, he's gear.

'It's true, there's a boundary running between the Tell and the Saharan Atlas,' he now says thoughtfully.

'Be that as it may, it's only a boundary between the three departments of Algeria and the four territories of Algeria,' I pipe up. 'All the land south of that wiggly boundary is mine because all of it belongs to Algeria.'

Eric says it doesn't. He says south of the boundary is French West Africa.

'Why do you want that land?' Craig asks me helpfully. 'It's only sand and stones and a few nomad tribes.'

'And oil!' I say crisply.

Eric says I've got oil in Aruba and Indonesia.

I tell him he's got oil coming out of his ears in Saudi Arabia and Iraq and Libya and Venezuela. Not to mention the huge oilfields of the Soviet Union! Upon which we all look at every atlas we can find in the non-fiction reference section of the library. We scowl at maps to see whether there's a boundary between northern and southern Algeria. It turns out that there is, usually. Nonetheless, the word Algeria nearly always goes right across the southern bit as well as the northern bit of the country. On one map the word Algeria even covers only the desert bit. Which, in my opinion, is conclusive proof that I'm right.

At the end, just before the bell rings for First Period, Craig talks Eric and I into settling the quarrel by agreeing to draw a new line on our maps.

A straight line from Rio de Oro in the west to the point in the east where the border of Algeria meets the border of Libya and Tunisia. Erik takes all land south of the straight line, a wide sweep of ancestral desert lands, oases, Tuareg tribes, Negro slaves, Maori shearers, a dollar a day is black man's pay, White Wolf. Moreover, he takes it merely for the sake of some supposed forward defence policy of the United Fascist States of Earth.

Eric's such an imperialist!

After getting home and doing my homework quickly to get it out of the way I go wheezing into the lounge. My asthma's pretty bad today. It wasn't easy biking home into a hard northeasterly. Mum's in the lounge having a cup of tea with lovely Lorna from next door. The two of them are smoking. Mum's in stretch slacks and sheepskin slippers. The tele's going. An ochre smog of fag ash and wood smoke hangs thinly over their heads.

I slump onto the shiny worn Superfoam padding of the badly battered Formfit.

'Merde,' I mumble, wheezing.

'You might moan,' snaps Mum, 'but you don't know your bloody luck!'

'Luck?' I say with some asperity. 'If it's – wheeze – good luck to – wheeze – be stranded in a – wheeze – suburban blind street – wheeze – please give me – wheeze – bad luck.'

'Kids!' retorts Mum with a certain lack of originality. 'When me and my sisters were getting dragged up by Vinegar Tits we were always shifting round from one rented place to another. Always old wooden places with corrugated iron roofs, always places in need of paint, and always in the same districts that the family had been drifting round for three generations, getting nowhere slow.'

'So where – wheeze – if one may ask – wheeze – are you getting – wheeze – now?' I inquire coldly.

'Somewhere, thank you for nothing, you!' raps back Mum.

'Mmm – wheeze – mm,' I say wordlessly yet pointedly.

'Anyway, Mr Pain, think yourself lucky to even have a chance to go to high school.'

'Well, Mrs Glib – wheeze – hanging myself – wheeze – self – from the Supa – wheeze – rotary may – wheeze – be more to – wheeze – the point than – wheeze –Shirley Balls – wheeze – Fucking High.'

'You – ! Watch your bloody language, you!'

Actually I'm not proud of myself.

I think about Eric's mum.

'Sorry, Mum.'

'Mouth like a bloody sewer,' she says, mollified and almost friendly.

Upon which she starts telling a story to poor puzzled next door dim lovely Lorna. A story about me when I was a little boy. Mum loves telling stories about us kids to anyone who wants to listen, or doesn't. She tells them well. A born storyteller, Mum. As are all the Seven Sisters, Ilk of Forbes. Mum's stories often portray the funny little ways of us kids, yesterday and today. The odd things we come up with. Our small amusing habits.

Bashing, for instance.

'You should've seen him as a baby, bashing,' she says, laughing in anticipation of spinning a good yarn.

'What do you mean, bashing? Lorna asks anxiously.

'Bashing his head,' answers Mum. 'He used to sit up in his cot and rock himself back and forth and bash his head against the wood. He bashed so hard he shifted the cot from one side of the room to the other!'

Lorna laughs uncomfortably.

'He used to drive me nuts,' continues Mum. 'He'd bash and bash and I'd hear him all day long. Bash, bash. Bash, bash! Whacking against the wood! Which'll be why he's got such a thick head,' she snorts.

Lorna, panicked, jumps up.

'Heck, look at the time, Val,' she squeals. 'I got to get our tea started.'

After which, left alone with maman in the dusty room, I think I perhaps look somewhat sorry for myself for she puts down her cup and gazes at me quizzically. Or makes out she's gazing quizzically.

'What's the matter?' she says. 'Can't you take a joke?'

I'm looking at the telescreen.

'– wheeze –'

Mum, losing interest, sits by the fire picking her teeth with a darning needle. She often has the needle handy. Wielding its blunt end she lifts out small scraggly scraps of food before wiping the scraps on her hanky. After which she sits picking at the dry skin on her feet. And then, varying her manoeuvres, feels up her varicose veins. Mum's always moaning about those thick blue snakes on her legs. She sits in her armchair with her empty teacup on one soiled vinyl arm, a fag in an ashtray on the other soiled vinyl arm, and reaches down to one of her legs and presses the veins and watches the blue snakes bulge backwards and forwards.

'My bloody legs,' she grunts. 'Wish someone would cut them off.'

There are days I wouldn't mind trying.

'Want me – wheeze – to get – wheeze – aspirin, Mum?'

'No. Stop huffing and puffing. It's driving me nuts having to listen to it!'

'Sorry – wheeze – Mum.'

'Get outside, if you're short of breath. Get some fresh air.'

'It's quite co – wheeze – old, Mum.'

'Best thing for you!' she says, crouching closer to the fire.

Afterwards when she's headed to the kitchen and started slamming stainless steel saucepans of raw hacked root crops onto the enamelled electric stove I find myself alone in the lounge, stranded on the greasy grey and red Formfit. Which, brand new when we bought it, now looks like it's been dragged out from wreckage after the quake poleaxed Napier. I look into the fire. A few red flames gnawing through bits of pine inside the firebox and sending heat up the chimney. The mantelpiece, veneered with grey and black glazed tiles and two sets of chromed silver stripes, has been streaked with grease by the fingers of little kids. The tiles and stripes are what we called streamlined in the Fifties.

Or in other words, the stripes are now square.

The stripes are hopelessly out.

I keep looking into the fire. Which crackles and hisses and spits. Additionally it's smoking. Now that we've got a cheap carpet down in the lounge we've found that the fire smokes if one shuts the lounge door when windows are also shut. Which one does, in winter. One wishes to have doors and windows shut to keep out the cold. Only it stops the fire from drawing properly.

Which is what one says, curiously. One says a fire draws.

Not the same as drawing a picture, naturally.

A picture of a ship.

Or of a city.

Picking up my thread, now that I'm alone in the warmish dirtyish wearing-out-quickish slovenly grimy slatternly smoky lounge, I let down my guard. Only for a tick or two. I become myself. Which of course as everyone knows is far too dangerous a thing to do if one's with other people, even if they make out they like one (eg. Eric). John's Son told me to discipline subordinate clauses with fewer commas and more parentheses.

I let my narrow shoulders slump.

I can't brea – wheeze – breathe – wheeze –

Nobody knows why asthma kicked in as soon as I started at Shirley Boast High. It's scary. Mum took me to our family doctor. I had to beg her. Doctor Cohen. A tall and slim gentleman. He's very intelligent. His rooms are in our suburb.

A Jew.

I like him a lot.

So we go to his rooms. Doctor Cohen does his diagnosis. After which he sits back quietly. Asthma, certainly, he says. Upon which Mum grunts. And sighs. And grunts again. And says they still haven't got anything for it, have they? No, says Doctor Cohen.

Afraid they haven't, Mrs Grigg. Apparently psychologists think it possible that asthmatic breathlessness may stem more from the mind than the body.

'And I reckon they lay all the blame on the mother,' gruffly observes Mum.

Doctor Cohen laughs gently but quite merrily.

'As a matter of fact they do tend to.'

'Hmf. Typical!'

'Quite.'

My mind goes blank. Or bland. Or bled. Or dead. The cause of that deadness or blankness is that one has come upon one more of those things one suddenly understands. The things about which one turns out not to know anything. One understands that, in spite of asepsis antibiotics lasers scalpels, modern medicine can't even do something as elementary as enable one to breathe. You want to breathe in, out? Tough luck! Technicians in white starched coats can find no cure for breathlessness inside a glass laboratory. No breath bullets will be slotted for me inside plastic cylinders, or aluminium wafers, or a printed packet. Nobody can offer me a serum. Or a pill. Or a shot. Our best and most advanced hospitals, at least on this planet, cannot take me into theatre and under white light cut out my breathlessness and kill it.

I can't breathe – wheeze – I can't – breathe –

I continue looking into the fire. Which continues to crackle and hiss and spit. A red fire, black. Black and red. Red and black. Stoker steel boiler red fire black soot white steam whistling shrieking girls screaming –

Clang! Clang! Clang!

Toot! Toot!

Jump!

I'm blowed if I'm going to bloody give up without a fucking fight.

Blow that for a joke! My mind. I've got to use my mind. And my body. Jumping up, leaping over to the radiogram, I whip out a new disc and slip it on the black rubber turntable.

The stomp.

The stomp! It's swept across Australia. It's spread to the United States.

I'm looking at the radiogram, its little red light, its pilot light. And now the stomp's come to Christchurch and spread from here through the rest of our nation state. A little red pilot light showing us the way. But, be warned ravers, latest word is that the stomp has started to fizzle out overseas – and a newer craze is taking over. A tiny light. A red tiny light, yet not saying to us, stop!

A little red pilot light saying, go!

'Go, man, go!' I groove wheezily across the carpet.

Discs are spinning and spinning while my weedy limbs are swinging, while my mind broods on mod chicks, chicks pouting their lips, lips sticked peach, or coral, or tangerine.

I stomp.

After which, I twist.

After which, lying on the carpet, gasping for breath, looking in the general direction of grey dustballs drifting grittily westwards in a cold yet smoky draft under the china cabinet, one seems to taste rust. One thinks it may be blood. One has very likely done something to one's lungs by overdoing the twist and the stomp. One's bronchioles and alveoli have perhaps begun haemorrhaging.

Help me, somebody.

Help. Help!

SOS.

'Hi, Dad.'

'Good day, Stevan.'

Dad gives me a thumbs-up. We're not inside our airless

bungalow. We're outside in our breezy backyard. Additionally the sun's shining. A hard sun, watery. Also, smog. Dad's on his way from our garage to our vege garden. A tailormade hangs from his lips. Moreover, he's holding a can of insecticide. He says he's got a date with some white moth chrysalids that want blitzing. Cool, I say. Go get 'em, Dad. We're always awkward when coming upon one another these days. Consequently, rather than meeting his eye, I look at a point to my left of his right ear while darting quick sideways glances at his brown-eyed black-haired conk.

A swift intermittent scoping like a satellite spinning through space while snapping lots and lots of still-shots of the surfaces of a moon or planet. After which scientists back at base working their socks off will meld the stills into an illusion of complete panorama. Or even telefilm.

En passant, I'm not happy he's poisoning the chrysalids.

Gilbert looks birdlike, chirpy, perky.

Dad. Who the hell is Dad?

A shadow. Not a dark shadow. A grey shadow. No, not grey, something still weaker. Wan. Nonetheless, I used to think he was handsome, black is the colour of my true love's hair, eyes so brown they make you stare. In reality he looks awful. His skin's shickered sham leatherette developed in some interwar lab. A leatherette thrown out as faulty and left lying on a scrap heap to be cooked by the sun, cracked by frosts, turned into something scaly, scabbed, patched, frayed, fraught –

Actually to tell the truth I'm still not looking him in the eye. We never have looked each other in the eye, we're too shy.

Insecticide. Insect has died. Homicide. Suicide.

Aerosol. Lysol. Parasol. Parracide.

Dad has died.

Boy died.

Suicide.

I cry. I cry and cry. I cry and cry and cry. Only once more of course I'm not really crying. Once more we're only dreaming, aren't we? We're dream dream dreaming. Trolling moonless black deeps in sunless sunrooms, Oceania.

All of us are squeezed into the dinette ogling the delicious array. A silver and yellow Tubechrome tabletop laden with plate after plate of sponge rolls, cream cakes, custard squares, jelly, whipped cream, and a banana and cocoa birthday cake. Almost everyone's standing. After all we've only got our four lemon yellow chairs. You know, the four silvery tubular steel dining chairs. Our space-race Tubechrome. Mum tells me to sit on one since I'm the birthday boy. So I lower my narrow bum in its blue drainpipe jeans onto the padded lemon yellow vinyl. It's splitting. The vinyl. Not my denim. The pads on all four chairs are cracked even though they're no more than a few years old.

It's what you call built-in obsolescence.

Additionally a crack has started to open in the soldering.

You know, the soldering that seals one chromed leg to the chromed four-square base of each chair. The crack's in the soldering of the chair I'm sitting on. The birthday boy. One day soon the leg of this lemon yellow vinyl upholstered chromed tube chair will snap off. I hope on that occasion I'm not sitting on it. With luck the person sitting on it might be Dad.

Bloody boozing bastard.

I'm so lonely.

Other kids cram together on top of a white wooden bench stowed to one long side of the yellow dining table. Formica. Chrome. Steel. Other kids stand. On our pick-up-sticks lino. Canyon coral. Jaipur pink. And manoeuvring among us are black houseflies on the lam from Aero-Blast.

More killing power in Aero-Blast, now with Trimort.

Laboratory-tested.

Sissy looks mod. She's discovered Mary Quant. Who really swings, says Sissy. Of course she swings. Sissy's a bit like Eric, always announcing things as though she's the first to make some fab new discovery. Notwithstanding, she looks good. A kooky Quant hairdo. Cropped geometry. Op-art earrings of black and white plastic on her white lobes. Her lipstick is Bold Coral.

She's pretty.

Mum's wearing her quotidian navy bri-nylon slacks, baggy in the bum, and tucked into them a teal acrylic top. Orange sheepskin slippers. One need hardly say she doesn't look mod. Frankly she looks a bag. Lorna's the only other old. And, poor thing, also looks a bag. Wally, her husband, he's away. Mum says he's most likely got a woman on the sly.

'You just won't know what to do with yourself,' shrills Mum, making out she's Dusty Springfield.

Lorna grins wretchedly.

Dad's not here, of course. He's working overtime at the timberyard.

Our dinette is a small square. The kitchen on the other side of the island cupboard is a small square. The walls of the dinette are still painted a glossy lemon and grey. The walls of the kitchen are still painted a glossy grey. Nevertheless a yellowish smoky brownish fatty layer has now been baked onto the gloss. Smoke from endless openings and closings of the enamelled door of the firebox. Fat from roast sheep and fried onions and boiled saveloys. Smoke from the funking of unknown thousands of cigarettes. Naturally all eyes right now continue to be fixed not on the greasy decor but that sugary spread laid out atop chipped Woolworths plates atop the yellow Formica.

Mum, when any of her kids has a birthday, slaves to heap up those sweet, soft, creamy mounds. She says it's because her own mother, our late lamented Vinegar Tits, never gave any of her own kids a birthday party.'

'She was very cold, Mum,' says our Mum. 'I always sort of felt that we were with her through accident.'

'No comment,' says Sissy.

'And there was nobody loving us,' Val goes on spelling out. 'Nobody paying us attention. She never kissed or cuddled us. She never told us she loved us. If anybody ever spoke kindly to me, you know, an aunt or a neighbour or somebody, which they hardly ever did, my eyes would fill up with tears.'

Miss Bones the Butcher's Daughter. Master Bones the Butcher's Son.

'Nor any comment from me,' I say. 'Notwithstanding.'

'Which I hated myself for,' says Val.

Happy Families.

The last time anyone kissed me was when I was three years old. It was when two women were leaving. Two women who kissed me goodbye. I think they were neighbours of ours in Blackball. They were going away, moving away. No, the last time was Ellen. Nana. I was five and it was on a railway platform, a platform on the Midland Line. And afterwards, of course, she was killed by Pop. Only accidentally, it goes without saying.

He was driving.

Ellen was the passenger.

Oops, not to overlook that quick peck on the lips last year. You know, my one and only ever SXSlicedy kiss. Sheryll. Eldred was speeding. Shell. BP. He was gunning the juice while his big finned steel sedan zoomed northwards on State Highway One. Travel the Caltex Way. Eldred crossed the white middle line of the black tarseal. Not counting – arithmetic, it makes me sick – on another big finned steel sedan coming southwards.

Now with more lead octane.

Stainless steel knives and spoons, lightly laminated with fossil streaks of spud and fat, dumped in a heap at one end of the yellow Formica. Mum, standing in the kitchen on the other side of our island cupboard, grabs a carving knife from the cutlery drawer. She grips its slippery seamed handle, which is bone, yellowish like the highlights on his oily red puss. You know, Chartreuse.

Please stab yourself in the heart, Mum.

If you've got one.

She stumps into the dinette. She hands the knife to me. I grip it. She, striking a red phosphorus match, begins lighting the thirteen candles.

'Happy birthday to you, you were born in a zoo,' sings everyone lustily, 'with the chimps and the monkeys; you look like one too.'

Upon which I blow out my thirteen candles, red, blue, pink, lime green, canary yellow. Thirteen candles make a lovely light. Only not as bright as my eyes tonight. And everyone's clapping. And if you blinked you missed the lurch with which, next thing, everyone starts stuffing cakes into their gobs. And holding their fists clenched ready to reach out for more even before they've gulped down the whole of their current toothsome creamy jammy sugary morsel.

Creamy. Caramel. Chocolate.

Sugary sweet.

Buttery.

'Right,' says Mum after most of us are comatose with cake. 'Only two more years till you can leave school and get a job and stop being a burden on us, Mr Smug.'

I'm going to keep breathing. I'm going to survive Olivine Street. I'm going to make it all the way through Shirley Bowels High. I'm going to draw up precise specifications for a shipshape watertight coordinated comprehensive chronological targeted Master Plan. And hold regular lifeboat drills. And see the iceberg. And evade the iceberg. And lower lifeboats promptly from my sinking lacerated vessel if I happen not to evade. Reality isn't hard oblong brittle and hollow. Reality isn't a coal-powered electric-lighted steel sleek ship sinking in a cold night.

Supershell with Cresyl-Diphenyl-Phosphate.

Loop de loop.

All one has to do is stay watchful wary alert always on the lookout every single moment of every single day of every single year of the rest of one's life. All you have to do never ever never let down your guard. Not even when cold and alone in a smoky lounge on a bleak winter day. Never let down my guard.

Or breathe –

– wheeze –

I mustn't ever let down my guard because although the world isn't a steel ship we're racing across a sea like black glass. We're speeding on a white starred black steel hull. Our furnaces are red hot. Black slaves. Pistons. Screws. Keep breathing. Never stop breathing. If you stop breathing you won't keep living.

Living, which of course is so bloody fucking super.

I must never never ever stop breathing.

I must let in nothing but air.

No – wheeze – wheeze –

Only air.

Air.

Peace.

I can't breathe.

I must keep breathing I must keep breathing – air – air air air air air air – o o o o o o o o o o o o o – red white-spurting worm no no no o o o o o o o o o o o o o o lonely lonely lonely boy lonely word webs worm ringed scarlet worm pink pig trotter spouts white life, black death, white death, black life, white frost, white star, White Star Line, white boy, can't breathe, dying –

'Fifties hair wasn't really short,' says Craig.

'Yes it – wheeze – was,' I reply. 'It was – wheeze – nowhere near as – wheeze – long as today.'

The two of us are standing under one of the young plane trees next to the mod low boundary wall on South Parade. A dry norwester has come bowling over the Alps. A norwester whipping up dust clouds on the Plains. The light is hard and bright. It's the end of the last day of the school year. Let there be drums! Craig and I have been discussing a recent reprise of You Saw Me Crying in the Chapel. You know, that square Christian song from the early Fifties. The singer who's covering it is Zombie Elvis. Who looks more than ever like some undead Fifties rocker who belongs in the coffin with all the other black leather jacket has-beens.

Elvis is thirty years old!

I think the nation state should commit painless euthanasia on every citizen who gets to the age of thirty.

'It's just that in the Fifties they combed it back,' says Craig. 'Or twirled it up into quiffs. Or stuck it down with Brylcreem. All we do now is not stick it down, or twirl it up, or comb it back. We shake it forward. We let it all hang out. Which makes it look long. Actually it's an optical illusion.'

I think about it.

'You're right – wheeze – that's intelligent of you.'

Craig goes a little pale about the nose.

Upon which we change the theme and begin a discussion about the nature of reality. Moreover while we discuss reality I feel the gusty warm norwester whip my skinny body. Which of course is the pathetic fallacy.

Winds don't whip.

Only we whip.

Carry me back to de ole plantation.

Pensively, I suggest to Craig that while we think, or wish, that we're coming to understand reality, a more likely theory is that we aren't. And won't. And perhaps are on our way out already. Or there's one reality after another reality. Reality after reality after reality et ainsi de suite rippling out in rings or silent singing songs, songs echoing endlessly, or nearly echoing, from our nowhere, here, right out into the perhaps infinite universe.

'Anyway – wheeze – ,' I end by saying, 'who fu – wheeze – cking cares whether we do or – wheeze – don't come to under – wheeze – stand reality?'

'Yes, but you see it's not reality to talk that way about reality,' says Craig kindly.

'Isn't – wheeze – it?' I say, looking up with some hope.

'No. That reality isn't in, now.'

'Oh?'

'That reality's out.'

'What – wheeze – reality's – wheeze – in?'

'The reality that's in is reality.'

'And which – wheeze – reality is – wheeze – that?' I ask with dread and certainty.

Craig flicks a lock of floppy fair fringe back from his honest big pink forehead.

'The real reality that's in in reality?' he asks with a grin. 'In reality the real reality that's in is white star black night smoke true television cathode ray Space Age Sound of the Sixties Four Square Ford Zephyr smoke gets in your eyes the cigarette you've waited for sweet smooth satisfying Titan missile explodes in underground silo fastest longest hard huge hollow heavy sleek bow slithering tele screen white light effortless ease rotary action shaving Suparotary SX Sliced plastic-wrapped bread superwhite superlight night liner luxury rocket speeding ripping space universe two thousand two hundred children women men terrible true die first class second class steerage class crew slave speeding vessel straight flat calm night white night White Star no expense Victory. Itsy bitsy teeny weeny yellow polka dot bikini. Fleeting pleasure? Truly treasure? Formfit cushioning synthetic Superfoam – new! – now! – contoured scientifically! A Deck. B Deck. C Deck. D Deck. E Deck. They asked me if my love was true. They said someday you'll get venetian blinds. Savoy Avon Tivoli Vogue. Metro State Century. Rex Roxy. Hollywood Harbour Light. No work of fiction could contain such incredible twists. Or leave unanswered so many questions. Master Writer. E Block. D Block. C Block. B Block. A Block. Form One. Form Two. Form Three gates in the east. Form Four gates in the west. Twelve gates in the city. Women's Bata Flats, White. Men's Bata Bumpers, Black. Midland. White sheep. Black dog. Toot. Toot! Let the steam whistle cry! Roll on, old mighty Mississippi. Clang! Clang! Iceberg dead ahead. So, chin up, it's swinging!'

Opening my eyes, seeing light, I look up from two white pillows, Persil clean. White light. White light whirling.

What?

I blink, hard.

A quick darkness.

White stars shooting rays of light into the night.

A million million million coloured rays. Orderly. Crossing. A universe with a Metropolitan Master Plan. Twelve gates in the city. Only now one looks deeper into the quick darkness. Yesterday. Tomorrow. Or actually not tomorrow not yesterday. Blobs. Only blobs. Additionally, nothing. And of course everything. Et ainsi de suite (and one gapes with boredom at the thought of it) it's only words.

Too real is this feeling of make-believe. Too real when I feel what my heart can't conceal.

Where am I?

What's happening?

Actually, does happening happen? I think not. We're always in-between, aren't we? One moment we think we might be about to feel something. Next moment we also think we might. Only not quite now. And so on. And not like a story. In a story things come around a corner for the sake of the story. In reality things come around a corner because they're coming around a corner and not because they belong to a story. Not because anything's happening in reality.

And not only that. It's so startlingly extraordinarily boring.

It's curious. I mean, right now, this moment, this hour, this day, this year, right here – where is it?

Gone!

It's history.

And you're left behind thinking, okay, what just happened? A drib? A drab? We can't know because we're now in another drab. Or drib. Who knows! And now that drib or drab is history, too. And the next. And the next. Nothing amounts to enough to be something. Now, and next, and history, they're nothing.

We're in-between. You can't be in-between.

Yet you can be very very very sad.

Am I truly going mad?

I'm a Jew.

SOS.

I'm not swinging.

I'm swooning – wheeze – swooning – wheeze – in our Cold War mod world on the Midland Line. And while swooning, seeing my tomorrows, my perhaps thirty thousand perhaps some few thousand less or more tomorrows. Tomorrows on the Line. Going against gravity. Doing the twist. Breathing. Wheezing. Out in out, School Cert, in out in, University Entrance, out in out, varsity, in out, degree, in out in, doctor lawyer business executive, out in out, marriage mortgage, in out in out in, ticky-tacky, pink, blue, yellow – out out out – cars kids telescreen space race rings of Saturn cold coal-coloured copper-coloured wheeling mindlessly.

And lonely, so lonely.

And in the end –

I'm a Jew.

Dying.

Mad.

Why? Why keep on breathing? Why bother when it's so hard,

breathing? Why not bunk from breathing? Why not stop fighting gravity? Give in to gravity for a bit. SOS, SOS. Yes, why not leave the Line? Why not cross over to the Main Trunk?

Oil. Full-gloss.

Ice.

Clang! Clang!

Sinking swiftly by the bow.

SOS. SOS. SOS. SOS. SOS! SOS! SOS! SOS!

Opening my eyes once more, widely, once more I see light. White light. After which a shifting shape blocks out the white light. Almost all the white light. A dark shifting shape.

And two eyes looking at me back.

Big eyes. Dark eyes. Deep brown eyes belonging to a strong brown man smoking a roll-your-own. A tall strong man wearing old footy shorts and an old footy jersey. A mighty man. And on top of his handsome head his shiny brylcreemed hair is black, the colour of my true love's hair. And his lips are something wondrous fair. A halo of white light on three sides of the head. And the tips of the dark man's teeth show, sharp, between his lips. False teeth white like full-gloss pickets in a cool new suburb. A strong dark man with big brown eyes, beautiful beautiful brown eyes, eyes so brown they make you stare, the purest eyes and the bravest hands, I love the ground whereon he stands.

Not watery green eyes, or washed blue eyes, peering at me from the raw bony reddish head of some one or other watchful wary mouthy intelligent ignorant tart Seven Sister, Ilk of Forbes, Glasgow Gorbals and South Christchurch. Additionally, with a jaw. Scrub the floor. Tip out a gent's jerry. Mitts mashed by a threshing machine. A sunny new territory. Tickets clipped here for those riding the Midland Line of the Middle Island!

'Are you Filip?' I say to the man.

No, not the wishywashy eyes of Ilk of Forbes.

Are they instead the beautiful brown eyes of a Grigg?

Grigg, Gilbert, Eldred, Ellen, Treleaven, Trevillick. Croquet lawn. Cricket whites. Very very very important in the County. A white homestead. A long low wide veranda. Cigarettes and glasses of whisky. A pipe for Pop. A certain largeness about being seated firmly, yet lightly, on a good well oiled saddle on the glossy back of a good mount in fine fettle looking at a baa-ing mob of wellbred sheep being driven in the dust of a hot norwester by shepherds with dogs and whips.

THE CROSSING

no, the two eyes seem no more the dark kind calm cool brown
    blank eyes of a Grigg
        than the weak warm watery washed-out passionate
    green eyes of a Forbes
clearly the two eyes aren't the eyes of the olds
        it's just a matter of time
            never a million years
        whoa-ooh-whoa
    such a drag
  oh yes
 oh yes
oh yes
 uh-huh
  oh yes
 uh-huh
oh yes
uh-huh
 ooooooh
   ooooh-ooooh
        a world of light
            once a world of night
                the beginning was the word

AFTERWORD

The above story, as you know, was written in green ballpoint by a boy. The boy rammed the story into a stack of thirteen budgie-yellow exercise books found by a wiry youngish dumbfounded dad one golden dawning day, a sunny summer morning, in a backyard, the tidy backyard of a newish rectangular red brick white mortar mortgaged bungalow in a bright newish blind street, colourful cul-de-sac, other culs-de-sac, crescents, terraces, North Parade, South Parade, Crossing, State Highway One orderly four square right thinking left driving road rules school rules sports rules court rules ranked raked suburbs mod mid Sixties mod midcentury Midland Middle Island Oceania.

Also, the dad found the boy swinging peacefully.

Swinging above the books.

Not swooning.

Swinging in a fresh clean sea-smelling easterly. A faint salty scent off a vast unseen and, perhaps, infinite Pacific. Stevan had knotted a skipping rope, plaything of his sisters, onto a stainless steel web of twisted wires plaited by semi-skilled factory machinists into portholes punched by other semi-skilled factory machinists at precise intervals along the galvanized steel struts of the wide steel wheel of a newish Suparotary swinging slowly southwards, now, like a stainless slim ring circling Saturn.

The effortless ease of rotary action shaving.

Travel the Caltex Way.

A skipping rope striped with plaited nylon tendons. Nylon tendons dyed bright lime green, carmine red, citrus yellow. Stevan, having knotted his knots, had kicked from under himself a plastic peg bucket, tangerine in colour, moulded by mindless machines on some assembly line while ostensibly being quality-checked by bored young women yawning under the hard strip fluorescence of one of the plastics factories of the city.

Twelve gates in the city.

Far out.

It's hip. I dig it.

It's easier than studying our ABC. No more studying history. No more dull geometry. Arithmetic, it makes me sick. Zip your lip. Twist, let's twist. Here we go loop de loop. It don't mean a thing but baby come and swing. Do you want to lose your mind? My boy lollipop. Candy man. Sperm, embryo, foetus, newborn, baby, toddler, boy, youth, man, cadaver. Jew. It's a gas.

Thora Pattern
(Editor)

Also published by Piwaiwaka Press:
www.piwaiwakapress.org

Green Grey Rain
Stevan Eldred-Grigg

Rain on iron rooftops. A radio streaming the latest hit songs. It's the early 1950s. Valerie is a singing, slanging, pregnant daughter of the slums. Gilbert is the well-spoken son of a landed family. They already have three kids. Gilbert has just taken a job as paymaster at a coal mine. The family is about to start life in a green and black and red township on the West Coast. A little boy is born and named Stevan.

Green Grey Rain tells the story of the first years of that little boy. A story told by Stevan. A story told too by the hit songs he hears on the radio. And a story told by Valerie – who, with her sister, has already spoken to us in the pages of *Oracles and Miracles*. A story of working and playing, dreaming and singing, crying and laughing, hoping and wishing, bush, rain, rust, and the sooty streets of Blackball.

Pru Goes Troppo
Stevan Eldred-Grigg

Pru has been married to Guy for a quarter of a century. She hasn't had sex for ten years. 'Why the hell do I live my life this way?' she says to herself. 'I mean – really!' Change comes from out of the blue when odd old Uncle Bertie dies in Samoa and leaves his property to Guy. On a whim, the couple decide to go and take a look at what they know must be a tropical paradise. Not their usual stamping ground, you understand. Daringly, they fly to Apia. Pru soon finds herself thinking things, feeling things, doing things she's never till now come close to thinking, feeling, doing.

Pru Goes Troppo is a comic novel about two privileged parasites who somehow are oddly innocent.

Oracles & Miracles & Zombies
Stevan Eldred-Grigg & Helen Mae Innes

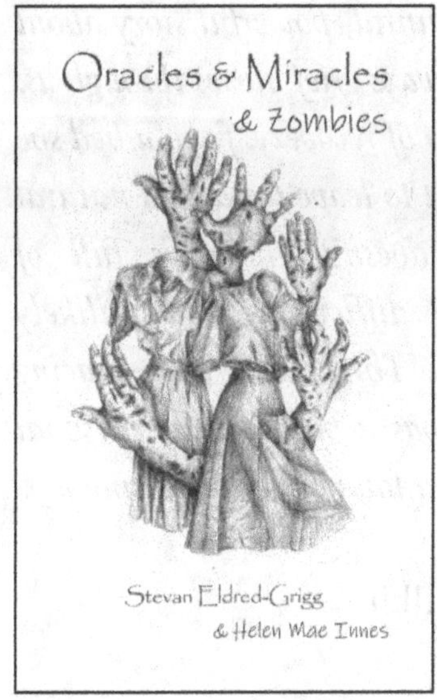

Stevan Eldred-Grigg's best selling, award-winning novel is back – with zombies!

Little has been written about how the biters created by the 1918 virus affected the lives of women, especially working-class women. This black comedy shows us how twin sisters, their sharp and shrewd mother, and many other women struggled to avoid being bitten by biters, cared gingerly for hunches who didn't want to eat their brains (just yet), and watched as the 'cured' lurkers started to take their jobs. Even during pandemics girls grow up, worry about boys, go out to work, get married, have babies, while striving to keep the brain safe inside the skull. At the beginning, the twins are small, fearful and helpless. At the end, they're armed and ready to go after the enemy – but who is the enemy?

Into the Woods: The healing power of birds
Helen Mae Innes

A funny, painful, powerful story about the strange ways grief moves through us. Helen's path of recovery, from a bed she doesn't want to leave towards a natural world she doesn't know, is full of recognisable difficulties and unlikely connections. This frank and bracing little book has a bass note of personal tragedy but a top note of surprising joy.

Damien Wilkins

It happened during the spring when the kākā had first appeared in the valley. I noticed a grey warbler fledgling outside my window who couldn't get the tune quite right. He'd start singing, get a note wrong and falter, then try tentatively again. Like a child learning the recorder, I thought.

Like a child …

And the birds fled to the bush
Helen Mae Innes

Those living in post-earthquake suburbia are trying to survive everyday life, eviction by authorities, and infighting between different factions. Meanwhile a geeky student specialising in birdsong arrives hoping to conduct research. Anton's project is regarded with ire or indifference by many, except for Timothy, a weird loner whose speech is odd and behaviour odder.

The valley is calm, quiet, waiting. And Mrs Henderson thinks it's earthquake weather but doesn't say anything, doesn't want to make a fuss. It's probably nothing. No one else notices it's quiet, too quiet, until everyone does at the same moment, like at a party when everything goes silent and no one wants to be the first to speak. Suddenly, all the birds are airborne, and the whole valley holds its breath.

My Dad
Anneke Gerbrands

My Dad is a beautifully illustrated simple story about a kid and their dad. Its short, simple sentences and use of dyslexia friendly font make it suitable for young readers, but its full-page colourful illustrations also make it attractive to toddlers. A great little book for dads and kids to bond by reading together, to give as a gift, or to help children learning to read.

Written by children's author Anneke Gerbrands and illustrated with delightful, quirky watercolour illustrations by Ingrid Kamp.

Making Maths Add Up
Maggie Tu

This colourful, fun, clear, and sound approach to teaching mathematics takes a new approach to teaching maths by starting from scratch and breaking complex maths concepts down into their core parts, then building upon each foundation skill clearly and intuitively. Children can jump in at the point they feel comfortable for each topic, allowing them to focus on the maths skills themselves and not arbitrary 'levels' and leaving room for revision, learning, and extension.

It starts at the level of 2 + 2 and teaches skills that quickly make equations like 680 + 70 easy to solve. It seamlessly incorporates algebra, word problems, and mnemonic storytelling. The relaxed, chatty style with cheerful, colourful images puts kids at ease.